No Sanctuary

by

BJ Creighton

No Sanctuary

This book is a work of fiction and all of its characters are figments of the author's imagination.

ISBN: 978-0-69251-960-8
Also available as an ebook with ISBN 978-1-63348-000-1

Nebraska detective Bobby Lee searches for the murderer of a wealthy New Yorker while chasing the demons of her past and evading the demons of her present.

Acknowledgments

The cover was designed by Lee Higbie using a photograph taken by him in Nebraska near Rowe Sanctuary.

The author received help from several of the employees and volunteers at Rowe Sanctuary and from Nebraska State Trooper Leonard, Buffalo County Sheriff Neil A. Miller as well as critiquers and editors, especially Betsy James and Chris Eboch, who helped improve the manuscript. Thank you all.

Other BJ Creighton Novels

Agenda Ebola	A bio-terrorism thriller set in Atlanta and the Mideast ebook: 978-1-63348-005-6 paper: 978-0-69252-291-2
Stringship Vandenberg	Describes Horse Cooke's 25th Century World (at Scribl.com)
Return to Groomby	Horse Cooke returns to Groombridge to save a colony from attack (in late 2018)

Table of Contents

No Sanctuary

by

BJ Creighton

Chapter 1

Blood and Cuts

Wednesday, 1:10 P.M.

Detective Bobbie Lee looked at the bloodiest corpse she'd seen in Nebraska. Head smashed. Arm nearly severed. "Those al Qa'ida bastards would do a better job," she muttered to Odran O'Dell, the 911 first-responder cop. "But nothing like this around here."

She felt sweat trickle down her back, surprising for this cold day. Why did O'Dell stare at her so intently? Why does he remind her of kids in Iraq, where any of them could be a suicide bomber? No danger here. She shook her shoulders. Tried to calm down.

She wrote, "First impression: Vic half-prone, left shoulder and face to side, wearing black outdoor gear. A bit of lumber-jack plaid shirttail showing. Jacket's colors match red in shirt. Gray beard stubble." She stayed about ten feet away from the body for her first walk-around of the scene. Looked like a compound fracture at the back of the skull. "What the hell are those patches of snow on the body? Sure looks weird." It hadn't snowed in more than a week.

"Think he was run down by a bloodmobile?" O'Dell spoke only to be heard over the faint sound of the Platte, the only other sound.

She didn't turn to address him. "Yeah. Maybe that's it. Gives Gore-Tex a whole new meaning, doesn't it?"

The corpse was about twenty feet from a tiny shack and about fifty from the little-used access lane. Woods surrounded the area, except to the north where the "mile-wide, inch-deep" Platte River flowed. Everything was gray or muted. Even the blood was almost black. The usual nauseating smell from the body was mostly suppressed by the cool weather and overpowered by the soft mold odors of decaying forest plants. She turned and studied the shack.

Following her gaze, O'Dell pointed at the plywood shack. "That's the photo-blind where the vic was supposed to be for the night. They told me it's typical for two photographers to work in the blind. To shoot from inside."

"Looks like the perp really wanted to make sure he was dead." Bobbie spoke more to the body on the ground than to O'Dell. She turned to look at the young deputy and walked to the blind. She added to her notes, "Open windows facing river are shuttered--couldn't be seen in from bank even if open. Door has lock on outside. Blind is tiny. Looks to be one sheet of plywood for front, back and top." She returned to the corpse.

Bobbie took the camera from her shoulder bag and photographed the area around the body. She had to get close to the victim's head to get detailed photos of the injuries. At this proximity the cloying aroma of death assaulted her. She stood to run to the woods. O'Dell would see her heave her McDonald's burger and fries. She clenched her stomach muscles, stooped down as she had been, but kept further from the body so its cold-inhibited odor was not so intense.

This was ridiculous. She shouldn't feel nauseous. "Seeing guys blown apart by IEDs should've prepared me for this," she mumbled to the body. She recalled dragging two marines from their Humvees in Iraq. Dismembered by improvised explosive devices. They hadn't nauseated her. Maybe overall as bloody, but less from the head, more from the torso. Why were brains worse than guts?

O'Dell laughed. "I've got some syrup of ipecac in my car." He stood upwind and did not look at the corpse.

Bobbie looked at him. "You're all heart, O'." How'd he know she was about to upchuck? She shouldn't have gotten permission to touch bodies and wished she had some water to rinse her mouth. She put on surgical gloves from her shoulder bag.

"How's your stomach for this?" She looked at him. "Still think you want to be a detective?"

"You're the expert. You can check the vic as closely as you like." He looked north, like he was searching for someone across the Platte, which put the victim out of his field of view.

At least looking north kept him from staring at her. "Never have been able to push messes like this out of my mind. It'll be my nightmare for days." She spit. "Well, Jeez. Here goes." She gingerly touched the face—it was stiff. She poked at his legs, still flaccid, biceps, stiff. So he'd been dead for hours. The cold weather would slow rigor mortis. The stiffening of the victim's body parts would be slow. So, maybe something like ten to twenty hours since death.

She concentrated on the marks in the ground around the vic and on the blood-soaked clothes so she could avoid looking at his head. Possible drag marks ended at the corpse. His Jack Wolfskin jacket and shirt were nicely detailed but he wore relatively plain black jeans. The clothes were carefully hand-tailored, or maybe they had been gone over by a tailor after manufacture. None of the tell-tale threads from seams, pockets or belt loops that marked all clothes on the racks at the stores where she could afford to shop.

She carefully extracted a supple black leather wallet from the hip pocket of his pants. The wallet was in good condition. A New York driver's license identified its owner as Paul Georgio Capodicasa, born in 1945. The listed size and age looked to match their vic. He had American Express and Visa cards, same name, and a bunch of hundred dollar and smaller bills, in no particular order. Several were dog-eared. She returned the wallet and rebuttoned the hip pocket.

She looked back at his face, not really wanting to see but she needed to verify if he had drooled blood. Yup. His black hair showed gray at the roots and he had the characteristic dark Italian complexion. Why would someone have hurt this old geezer? This rich old geezer? Couldn't be money. Too much still in his wallet.

She scraped some samples from his clothes and noticed the jeans were made from a stretchy fabric and the blood, mud and paint came off the slick fabric easily. Some expensive, treated denim.

Bobbie looked up at the deputy. "Any idea how many people have been out here today?"

O'Dell consulted his notebook. "William Martinez, he's the guy who found the bod, told me he was the only person out here this morning. His job included picking up the vic from the blind and taking him back to the Visitor Center." O'Dell nodded toward the shack. "Martinez said no one was allowed out here until he came out. No one was even supposed to come out of the blind."

Bobbie looked up from her work. "Why not? Any idea?"

"Don't know. Didn't ask him."

Bobbie grimaced and shook her head. She went back to photographing and collecting samples of the dirt from the ruts and footprints.

As she finished, Deputy Scotty Leslie arrived with Buffalo County Assistant Coroner Herb Smithson. The coroner, a trim African-American, wore a three-piece suit with a tie and paisley vest that gave him a dated but definitely dapper look, especially at a murder scene.

"By the time you get your hearse back here, I'll have all the pics I need." She labeled another evidence bag, scraped more material from the drag mark and put it into the bag. "By the way, Herb, please revoke my permission to touch any bodies." She shuddered.

Scotty and Coroner Smithson looked at the body briefly then Smithson headed back for his hearse.

"Any idea about the second vehicle?" Bobbie pointed to a tire mark crossing the drag mark. She looked at O'Dell to see if he had an answer. The tire track barely showed and had no visible tread marks. The bald-tire rut was close to the deeper one with the distinctive tread marks of a deeply lugged, all-terrain vehicle tire. "Was the ATV pulling a trailer?"

"Don't know." O'Dell nodded and squinted at the marks. "I left all the questions like that for you."

"Okay, O'. Look here." Bobbie pointed to the various tire and drag marks. "You won't learn anything staring at me or the trees. You gotta look at the body parts if you want to learn to puke like a real detective."

Bobbie traced the tread mark and the crossing mark from a smooth tire. "If the ATV pulled a trailer to haul out the gear and photographers, it would have been empty when he got here this morning." Bobbie forgot about her lesson for the young deputy and mumbled to herself. "Big trailer. No load. Barely left a trace. Fits." Bobbie made notes in her pad. She walked to the blind, making notes, taking pictures, and collecting samples.

She walked around the blind to check the north side. A short jump to a cottonwood snag in the river gave her access to the front of the shack. She could barely reach the shutter over the closest window. As she slid the shutter open, she saw there was no glass, just an hole. She lost her balance and stepped into the Platte. "Damn." Muddy water, halfway to her knees. Some chunks of ice and a mouse nest with drowned mother and babies floated by. "Yuck. Damn it's cold. Where's the inch-deep Platte when I fall in?"

Bobbie could no longer see in the openings. She reached up, poked the camera through the window, and blindly pushed the button for photographs in all directions. Her review showed blood-covered camping gear. She slid the other shutter open and took five more pictures through the second opening.

Bobbie climbed up on the bank and stamped off most of the mud and water. "Sure is nice to have some dry, sunny weather." She spoke so O'Dell could hear her over the burbling of the river. "Finally getting warm." Wet and muddy boots were definitely more pleasant in this week's mild weather than the sub-freezing a week ago.

O'Dell watched Bobbie. "Yep. River even looks higher than an hour ago when I got here."

Bobbie nodded. "Heard this morning they're releasing water from McConaughy ahead of the spring runoff." One hundred fifty miles up the Platte was the North Platte's 20-mile-long McConaughy reservoir, Nebraska's largest lake, being shrunk now to make room for its share of the melting snows of Colorado and Wyoming.

At the back of the blind Bobbie opened the door with her gloved hand. The door, like the window shutters, were made of the same camo plywood as the whole blind. She photographed everything.

The mess resembled a tent after a week of teen-age boys camping. Actually, more like after their food fight with a bloody carcass. And in a snow storm. Blood splattered on everything. The down scattered on the blood gave an alien appearance. Goose down both on top of and under the blood.

"We're lucky for the cool weather. Any warmer and this place would really be a mass of flies and maggots. Too many as it is." She shuddered and scrunched her stomach muscles to stop a heave caused by the memory of how quickly flies attacked injuries in Iraq.

From the doorway of the blind she looked at thousands of dollars worth of gear scattered around the hut. Two of the bulky image-stabilized binoculars, three telephoto lenses, including one of the super-expensive white Canon telephotos, and two tripods and a monopod, all sturdy and heavy looking. Each telephoto lens had its own Canon EOS body. And none were the little, relatively inexpensive Rebel EOSs. Nice Marmot Plasma sleeping pads and bags, one torn, lending its down for the appearance of a snowfall during the bloody murder.

She noticed blood on nearly all the equipment. The legs on one tripod were bowed like a cowboy's. The biggest telephoto lens, the white Canon, was over a foot long and close to six inches in diameter. The scratches on its body looked consistent with having been hit, perhaps by something like a heavy tripod falling on it.

Jesus H Christ. God, this is a lot worse than I saw from the first pics. Who the hell would beat the living shit out of rich old Mr. Capodicasa? Had to be strong. Very strong and psychotic. Or totally enraged. That morning she had filled out an application for a police job in Minneapolis. Now her notion to move away from Nebraska were pushed completely aside by her determination to find at least a little justice for Mr. Capodicasa.

She stood outside the blind and turned. "Hey, O'. Tell Scotty to bring Iris and Tom in as soon as the hearse is out of their way. Have them drive the trailer in. They *will* need it here. There's a ton of crap to process." She reached back inside to snap more pictures.

"They probably won't finish processing everything until tomorrow. I can't say for sure but I think there were parts of the deceased on several of the lenses and a tripod." Bobbie retched again. She ripped off her left glove, covered her eyes, and squeezed her temples.

"Time for me to go talk to people. I hope Iris and Tom have strong stomachs. At least they won't have to look at the corpse." Bobbie closed the door and put a seal from her bag on it and waded into the Platte to repeat the process for each of the window shutters.

The coroner and deputy were loading the victim into the hearse. She turned to O'Dell. "How long will you be here? We'll have to cover this scene, at least for the next day or two."

"My shift ends at four." O'Dell's smirk spoke of resignation. "We'll have someone here all night and I hope it isn't me."

"You're a good man, O'," Bobbie repeated, trailing off and looking at her feet. She looked up, made eye contact and smiled at him and nodded. "Yeah. Hope you get relieved. I haven't pulled 32 hours straight duty since Desert Storm."

His smile and nod said he was glad she sympathized.

"Always like working with you," Bobbie said. They'd often need to cooperate in the future. Always better to work with a friend. A few white lies and an occasional doughnut would keep her fellow officers happy and friendly.

She took out her notebook and wrote a note on it, which she tore out and tendered to O'. "Can you give this note to Tom Shirk when he gets here? I want him to check all the vehicles in the parking lot. Tell him to look in all the car windows."

"Yes, ma'am. Will do."

Bobbie thanked him.

Her blood spatter specialist, Deputy Tom Shirk, was on the way and he'd bring a fingerprint specialist Sergeant Iris Goldman from Kearney PD.

Her biggest problem would be from the elected officials, especially the new County Attorney who seemed to think the Sheriff's Deputies worked for him. County Asshole was more like it. CA Mentes Petite, *Uncle Bastard*. Well, she had to remember that most of the voters preferred him, probably because of all the work he did for kids, especially supporting the Kearney Youth Home.

Bobbie ducked under the crime scene tape O'Dell had put around the area and walked back to the Visitor Center looking at the ground. "Now let's see who'll tell us what happened and who'll lie." She spoke to the ground. It never lied.

Slow down. She repeated her mentor's advice, "If you want people to be open, flirt and gossip, don't interrogate." She had to keep it amicable. She should be chatty and make it a friendly conversation, not an inquisition. Play the dumb blonde, not the cop, to get leads on this murderous madman.

Chapter 2

The Pick-up Driver's Story

Wednesday, 3:45 P.M.

Near the end of the quarter-mile walk back to the Nicolson Center, Bobbie met a gaunt man in Army fatigues whose blond hair was cut like a marine's. His green name tag said Duane. "Are you the detective investigating Mr. Capodicasa's death?" He offered his hand in a gesture that matched the friendly tone of his words. Words spoken with a non-American accent. British? Aussie?

"Yes. I'm Bobbie Lee and I'm leading the investigation." She shook his hand. His eyes were the hard-to-describe hazel color.

"I'm Duane Mulcahy, the Rowe Sanctuary Volunteer Coordinator. I assume you want to talk to everyone who had anything to do with Paul. I've put out a call to all the volunteers. I asked everyone who was here yesterday and had any contact with Paul to come talk to you." He turned and they walked toward the Visitor Center entrance.

"Paul?" Bobbie looked at her notes. "Paul Capodicasa?"

He nodded again. "Yes. He *was* one of our principal contributors." Duane looked down and seemed to say a prayer for the man.

Bobbie slowed to admire the seven-foot-tall ceramic crane in the vestibule. She realized that she was not well acquainted with this major

9

organization in her own backyard. "Do you view yourself as a bird sanctuary or a crane sanctuary?" The sculpture looked vaguely oriental.

Duane looked at the crane, as though he hadn't noticed it in years. "We're an Audubon *bird* sanctuary, no doubt about that. But it is certainly true that cranes are our biggest attraction, in several meanings of the word." He motioned toward the crane. "Our sandhill cranes stand about a yard tall."

Duane led her through the gift shop, which had a new and clean adobe look. He replied to her query on his accent. He was from Adelaide, South Australia. They went through the "Staff Only" door. He spoke quietly to a guy standing in the hallway. Bobbie couldn't hear. According to a hand-lettered sign on the door jamb, Bobbie stood next to Duane's office.

He motioned for her to enter and closed the office door for privacy. "I may have to interrupt, but this office is yours whenever you need it during your investigation. It should be more convenient than your facilities. I hope I have everything I'll need out of here. Shouldn't have to come in at all while you're using it. I'll use it when you're not around, but I can clear out fast." Duane motioned toward the chair behind his desk. "Please sit down." He waited next to the door.

Bobbie looked around at the cluttered nine-foot-square office. She couldn't imagine many people would be so generous with their offices. Was it generosity? Some sort of subtle bribe? She decided not to check the gift horse's mouth.

Piles of books or junk on every horizontal surface in the office. New looking books on birds or Rowe Sanctuary. The junk included used and mangled equipment. She saw birdhouses in need of repair, electrical gadgets with dangling wires or broken parts, and some reflectors that looked like they'd been swiped from a highway. She picked up one of the reflectors, with its weird clamp.

"That's a broken firefly," Duane said. "We have them on the high--tension wires to help the cranes see the power lines at night."

Bobbie nodded. "Thank you." A dangling computer cable led to the only open space in the office—just enough room for a laptop. The office had the musty smell of fungus that seemed to come from the birdhouses and feeders awaiting cleaning, restoration or maintenance of some sort.

"Thank you for making your space available. You're right, this is much nicer than the tiny interrogation closet in our trailer."

She turned from inspecting the office to look at Duane. "What's your position here? You said you're the Volunteer Coordinator?"

Duane smiled and nodded. "Yes. That's my title."

"What's that entail?"

Duane rubbed his chin. "I try, usually with modest success, to keep track of our dozens of volunteers. What they're doing and where they're staying."

"How many of the people here are volunteers?" Bobbie stared at the wall behind Duane as she worked on understanding Rowe.

"Practically everyone. Only four paid staff. Paul's death makes the Sanctuary's immediate financial future somewhat less secure. We'll be scrambling to find other sources for the funding he's been providing." Duane shook his head. His face said despair or personal loss, either that or he was trying to hide something.

Duane opened the door in response to a tentative knock. The man from the hall was at the door. "This is Bill Martinez." His emphasis was on the first syllable, MARtinez, like O'Dell's pronunciation, giving the name an Anglo-Saxon sound. Duane turned and pointed toward Bobbie and identified her to Bill.

"Bill was designated to pick up Paul from the photo-blind. Since I figured you want to talk to everyone, I thought you'd like to get started. The others should be coming in soon, as fast as any herd of cats. Shall I introduce each of them when you finish with the last?"

"Yes, that would be great. Please tell them not to discuss anything about the situation with anyone else before they talk to me." Bobbie scowled at Duane to be sure he got the message.

"Will do. I figured you'd want to privately interview everyone." Duane started to leave then turned toward Bobbie. "Want some coffee?"

"Thanks. That'd be great. Black, no sugar."

"Coming up." He left and shut the door.

"I'm the only one here right now." Martinez had an aura of guilt. "I was drinking coffee in our break room when you came in." At about six-foot-two and trim, Bill had a full head of neatly cut black hair and matching mustache. He wore mirrored dark glasses in his hair, but upside down so he'd have to take them off and put them back on to use them. Apparently a fashion statement, not sun protection. Or maybe he had no other place to carry them. His hands had many small cuts and some bruises, his cracked nails were filthy, but he smelled like soap, perhaps Irish Spring.

He wore a blue sweat-shirt with a Rowe crane logo with his green name tag aligned under it. His name tag was generic. BILL typed on a sticker on the tag, not at all like Mulcahy's engraved DUANE.

Bobbie started with the standard preliminaries. "This is an official murder investigation. I will record the interview." Bobbie studied the volunteer as she decided not to Mirandize him. She asked that he state his name and address for the record. "I understand you found the body. Please tell me about it including all details you can remember."

Bill accented the second syllable of his name, not the first as Duane and O' had, marTEENez. The earlier pronunciations had sounded wrong. "I went to pick up Paul Capodicasa about 10:30."

Bobbie interrupted. "Why were you so late going to get him, Bill?" She made sure her tone was friendly. "By then he'd been in that tiny shack for something like eighteen hours, right?" She watched his brown eyes. He refused to sit and looked at the junk in the office or out the window.

"We always wait until the birds are off the river, until the cranes have moved out into the fields. The photo-blinds are so close to the cranes, we can't get the visitors much earlier without the birds seeing us. We have to be sure to avoid disturbing them. Our sandhill cranes need to increase their weight by twenty per cent while they're here, and do it in only three to four weeks. Spooking them will slow the weight gain need-ed for their long migration north and breeding next summer."

Martinez continued to fidget and chewed a fingernail. What made him so tense? Was there some racial issue? Maybe he worried he was a suspect? She needed to calm him. "The cranes don't complain about look-ing fat?"

He laughed. "They're really pretty small birds; they just look big. Our cranes run about the same weight as chickens, five to eight pounds live weight. Did you know they eat their own weight in less than a month? They completely clean up the corn and weed seeds all around here. Hardly any Round-Up used near Rowe anymore."

Bobbie nodded. "Wow." Before the driver could continue, she asked, "You knew the victim?"

"Yeah. Everyone here knows Paul Capodicasa. He's donated millions to Rowe. We all do everything we can to make his stay as comfortable and pleasant as possible when he comes each spring. I'm new here, but I met him last night before he went out to the blind."

Duane tapped on the door, opened it and handed a mug to Bobbie.

"Thank you, Duane. Sure looks good." She smelled the steaming coffee as Duane left. The interruption should calm Martinez some. "Okay, continue. Put in all the details."

"Gotcha. At about 10:30 I went to pick him up.

Bill drove the old clunker four wheeler, that's what Alaskans call ATVs, on the lane between the corn fields and the woods and turned down the last path, the one into the west photo-blind. He enjoyed the beautiful day and the cool weather. Two of the birds he saw, a red-headed woodpecker and a turkey, were ones he especially liked because he never saw them at home.

The four wheeler pulled a large flatbed trailer so he could haul the people and their equipment. In this case, he only expected one person, but Paul was a serious photographer and would have a ton of equipment.

Often the birders walk back instead of enduring the seat-less trailer. Usually Bill only hauled their gear. Sitting in the trailer was like riding on a trotting horse, but with a palette in place of the saddle.

While he was still on the lane Bill saw Paul lying outside and drove over next to him. *Oh my God, he's fallen from a tree. Even has a cut on his head.* Bill called to him and got off the four-wheeler. He touched Paul on the shoulder.

From this angle Bill saw Paul's bloody clothes. He tried to roll him over. *Oh, damn. Damn. That might hurt Paul more. What if he has spinal damage? Don't move him. Might aggravate an injury.* Bill checked Paul's pulse. He didn't know why, he'd never have been able to find a pulse. Perhaps so many movies had shown a witness checking a victim's pulse. Anyway, Paul was stiff and his wrist was cold.

Bill ran back to the four-wheeler and called 911 as he drove to the visitor center without seeing the song birds, the trees with turkeys, the corn fields full of cranes and vultures, or anything else. He finished his 911 report and hit a rock in the path at such a high speed the trailer tried to break loose and the four wheeler nearly bucked him off. He was surprised he didn't lose the phone.

How had he missed all the blood when he first drove up? Had he looking in the trees or out into the fields for birds? Did some birds distract him? He had driven up by Paul's feet so the bloodiest part of the scene was hidden. He had not paid attention. Maybe some of Paul's injuries were hidden. Could he have messed up a crime scene? Was it a crime scene? Maybe his reaction to Paul's injuries pushed his imagination way off into some nether land.

He had to tell Frank. He jumped from the four wheeler and ran through the east door of the Nicolson Center down the hallway to Rowe Sanctuary Director Frank Armstrong's door. It was closed.

Funny, his door was never closed. Whatever it was, Frank would be free in a few seconds. Bill ran back to the volunteer break room and poured himself some coffee. He hurried back to Frank's office spilling coffee in the hall, still in a quandary about knocking. The door to his left opened. A cop pushed the door so it almost hit Bill.

Bill jumped out of the way. "Did 9-1-1 send you?"

"Yeah. I was just down the road when they told me to come in. An ambulance is on the way."

"God I hope it does some good. I hope we're not way past needing an ambulance." His cold and stiff hand indicated death, didn't it? "Want me to take you out there?"

"That's why I'm here."

During the five minute walk to the blind, Bill described what he'd seen and done. He apologized for touching the body and ran on about how he hoped he'd done nothing wrong. The cop asked some questions and wrote some notes.

About fifteen minutes after he left with the cop, Bill walked toward Frank's door, which was open. "I found Paul Capodicasa by his blind. I'm sure he's dead, but an ambulance just pulled in. I better be wrong. This is so awful...."

When he finished his story Bobbie added more notes to her pad. She already had "Martinez nervous. Avoids eye contact. Must be watching me closely—he explained himself every time I wondered what something meant." She looked up and nodded. "Okay, the cop would be Deputy O'Dell."

"Could be. I didn't ask his name but he did ask mine. I told him William Martinez." He scratched his chin as he had several other times during the explanation of what happened. "That's everything, I think." He looked down again.

"Do you mind if I access your phone logs? It will allow me to accurately fix the time when you left the body." He agreed and gave Bobbie his cell number. Maybe very nervous, but doesn't act guilty.

His 505 area code was not local, but one she saw from time to time. She nodded. "When you talked about the ATV, you called it a *four wheeler* and said you're Alaskan?" The twinge in her tummy told her she was not getting the whole, true story. "Is 505 Alaska?"

"No. It's Albuquerque. I was Alaskan. We moved back to New Mexico from Fairbanks. My wife got tired of freezing her butt off for eleven months every year." It seemed like Martinez would continue, but he said nothing.

Bobbie jotted a note and flashed a big smile at Martinez as she nodded. "You're Alaskan? 'Martinez' doesn't sound typically Alaskan." Bobbie put a laugh in her voice.

"I wasn't born there but we lived in Fairbanks for the last five winters."

"Winters? Where were you in the summers?"

"We were there five years. Summers don't really count, so we always say 'winters' for years. Actually, the summers are one of the greatest times in Fairbanks. The sun's up day and night. The economy's booming. And the cranes come through spring and fall."

"Twice a year? Hmm. Thank you. Go on." Bobbie never recalled seeing cranes in Nebraska except during the spring. The farmers don't mind when the cranes eat last year's corn. They're just gleaning the part left by the combines. In the fall, the cranes might suffer at the hands of farmers who would probably insist on protecting unharvested crops.

Bobbie waited, hoping the silence would elicit something. The silence grew awkward. Martinez broke it. "You ever been to Alaska? To interior Alaska?"

Bobbie waited a second before saying, "No." She consulted her notes. "You said you had only one person to pick up?" This place was so disorganized that he didn't even know how many people were in a blind. Or maybe they don't bother to tell the volunteers anything about what they're doing. Was it secrecy, incompetence or something else?

"Yes, just Paul Capodicasa, at least that's all anyone mentioned."

"You said you talked to him last night, right?"

He nodded. "He sat right out there." Martinez pointed out the window. "I said *Hi* and welcomed him to Nebraska."

"Thank you," Bobbie said. "As a matter of form I have to ask where you were last night."

"I was in my room in the old farmhouse."

"Can anyone verify that you were there?" His nervousness said one thing but his simple story was the sort an innocent bystander would provide. Maybe Bill's nervousness was primarily due to touching the body.

"My wife is the only person who can verify my story for most of the night," Martinez said. "We did talk to Dick and Mary for 15 minutes or so when we first went back after dinner."

Bobbie Lee asked about Dick and Mary and added Ms. Martinez to her list of people to interview. "Where is *the old farmhouse*, where you're staying?"

He waved eastward, away from the gift shop. "It's the middle building over there, between the classroom and the big machine shed." Bobbie recalled seeing several outbuildings, beyond the privacy fence along the north side of the parking lot.

"Hmm. Be sure you keep me informed of your whereabouts for the next few days. If I need to ask you more questions, I want to know where you are."

"Yes, ma'am. I have to return to Albuquerque on Sunday. Is that okay? I only have two weeks vacation."

Bobbie assured him it was and verified his cell number and got his work phone-contact info. Were many of the volunteers from out of state?

Martinez also gave her his email address. "That's usually the best way to reach me during business hours."

She repeated her demand that he be available for further questions and shut off her recorder and made her standard closing requests: don't talk to others about what had happened until she'd talked to everyone and give a fingerprint set to the Kearney fingerprint specialist, probably tomorrow. "She's still out at the photo-blind, but we'll need to eliminate your prints from the ones we find out there."

The door closed behind Bill Martinez and her phone vibrated. She glanced at the caller-ID. "Hey, Mommom. Thanks for calling. Does that mean you couldn't find your old recipe book?" Bobbie had asked how to make a dessert the evening before and expected an email from her grandmother with the family heirloom recipe.

"No. I've got it. Do you remember what shoofly pie is?"

Bobbie tried to recall. "It's a sort of molasses pie, isn't it?" She could not bring any definite recollections to mind. Did she really remember only the name? Did she recall the actual dessert? Her fading youth gnawed. She needed to reclaim the time before the nastiness had reached her.

"Grandma's recipe is authentic, but it's not a pie I like much. Too dry. Too strong a flavor. I'll email it to you but I wanted to warn you. Its name is better than it is."

Bobbie recalled the story about her Uncle. Family rumor said he tried to poison his father using shoofly pie. No official complaints were ever filed, the family kicked him out of the house. Forced him into home-lessness toward the end of law school. The Petites never talked about it, but the extended family was convinced he tried to get even for his old man's abuse or imagined abuse. Better not go there. "Ah yes," Bobbie said, "the fond childhood memory that bears no relation to reality, like my sock monkey doll."

"Mmm," her grandmother replied. "You tried so hard to hide your disappointment when I found Misty in the barn."

The brightly colored and animated chimpanzee in Bobbie's mind did not closely resemble the tattered puppet her grandmother found. "I know it was my faulty memory, not age or anything you let happen to her. I know you didn't hurt her. My accusatory look after she fell out of the hay was for the ravages of time, not anyone's neglect."

"And shoofly pie is kind of crumbly. Try it, but don't expect a moist cake like my Lazy Daisy Cake you like. Molasses pies are *not* to die for." They chatted until Bobbie heard people approaching the door to Mulcahy's office.

Chapter 3

Carole Sue's Story

Wednesday, 4:35 P.M.

Duane Mulcahy brought his fifth volunteer to see Bobbie. "This is Carole Sue Williams. She drove Paul to the photo-blind yesterday afternoon."

Bobbie studied Duane for a moment. She felt her eyes droop, tired from the nauseating afternoon investigation and the boring and probably useless interviews she'd been doing. At least the last three seemed to have been a waste of time. "Thank you for the introduction." She frowned and asked him, "Have you been talking to people about what they were doing yesterday?"

"No. Why?" Duane looked confused and bothered, as though he'd been accused of a crime. "I haven't discussed the events with anyone except to tell them not to discuss them with anyone until all present have talked to you."

"How do you know what they all did yesterday?" Bobbie tried to look stern. "You did say you don't schedule the volunteers, didn't you? That they are uncontrollable?"

"Schedule the volunteers? Herd cats?" Mulcahy seemed to relax. "No, they schedule themselves. I have a notebook that lists what everyone

19

has volunteered for. I've been selecting people who signed up for something where they would have had direct contact with Paul. I haven't even been checking to be sure they did what they signed up for. I have assumed they all did their jobs, though."

"Very good. Thank you for following procedures." Bobbie smiled. She hoped he felt her criticism was unintentional. Duane motioned to refill her coffee. She nodded. He took her cup and left.

Bobbie turned to the blonde woman who had come in. "So you drove Mr. Capodicasa to the blind last night?"

Carole Sue wore jeans and a tee shirt—a sort of Rowe Sanctuary volunteer uniform it seemed. The only scent Bobbie picked up was from Dove or a similar deodorant. She had an engraved name tag with a 4-year service pendant. From an earlier interview Bobbie knew that meant volunteering at Rowe over a 4 year period, not 4 years of year-round service. Sure was nice they all had name tags.

Bobbie went through the preliminaries to ensure the law would be satisfied with her procedures, if it came to that. "Please tell me about your contact with Mr. Capodicasa. Include all the details you can remember."

"Okay." Carole Sue clenched her jaw muscles and frowned for a few seconds. "Talked to him for a few minutes when he first arrived. You know, so he'd know who I am. Drove him and the kid, Mikey Something, out to the blind."

"Mikey?" Bobbie felt herself start at the idea. It was the first confirmation of another person with the victim. "So there were two guys?"

"Yeah, there were two." Carole Sue answered. She frowned momentarily, apparently recollecting her thoughts. "Didn't really say anything except about the cold weather. Actually, I drove their gear; they walked. Didn't give them the usual orders. Figured Paul knew it better than me. Left them and drove back. Had already taken the others to their blinds. That's all."

Bobbie invited in the person knocking at the door and smiled at Duane as he refilled her coffee. "Thank you, Duane. Love your strong coffee."

She turned back to Carole Sue as Duane closed the door. "Please tell me about the *kid* with Paul?" She wondered why no one else had mentioned a Capodicasa companion. Finding him should make the whole investigation much easier.

Carole Sue's warm blue eyes showed slight redness from years outside. "Big skinny guy, 'bout 20. Seemed lost and snuffly." She returned Bobbie's steady gaze. "Dark hair." She studied Bobbie Lee's face. "Fact he kinda looked like you. But darker. Maybe more tan."

"How big?" Bobbie felt uneasy about this interview, like she was losing control of it.

"Six-two, like my partner's son. Less than 200, I'd guess. Skinny. But big arms." Carole Sue flexed her arm as a kid might to show of his biceps. "Maybe he worked out or took steroids. Nice looking kid, as I said."

Bobbie looked at her notes for a moment. Why did she care if Carole Sue had a *partner?* She'd never had homophobic thoughts before. What's going on? "Can you tell me everything you did with them yesterday?"

Paul and Mikey were waiting by Paul's rented Town Car when Carole Sue came to pick them up. Paul pressed the button on the key fob so the trunk popped open to reveal two small foot lockers and two large backpacks. Mikey picked up one pack and easily tossed it on his back with his arms through the shoulder straps.

"You can put that on the trailer, if you like." Paul put the other pack on the trailer and walked back to the car.

Mikey put his pack on the trailer and stood by its side. Paul pulled one end of a foot locker up onto the lip of the trunk. Carole Sue dismounted from the ATV seat and walked over to the rear of the car. She grabbed the end handle of the footlocker that was still in the car and helped Paul lift it onto the trailer.

Paul and Carole Sue started for the second foot locker. "Come on, Mikey," Paul said. "This one's pretty heavy. Give me a hand, okay?"

Carole Sue backed off. Mikey rubbed his nose with his sleeve and repeated Carole Sue's grabbing the inboard end, but he lifted it clear of the car and grabbed the handle on the other end of their equipment case from Paul and carried it like it was a cafeteria tray. His jacket sleeve rode up as he carried the footlocker revealing a tattoo on his right wrist that looked vaguely like a Jolly Roger but was actually a Parrot with writing under it. He put the second case beside the first. Again he rubbed his nose.

"Hey, Mikey, We'll just walk to the blind." Paul led the way west from the parking lot to the trail south of the Visitor Center. Carole Sue followed them with the ATV and trailer.

At the blind, Mikey easily carried the heavier equipment footlocker, but only after being asked to help. Paul ducked into the blind. Carole Sue gave Paul the pee bottle and stood by to close the blind door.

"Hey, Mikey." Paul poked his head out of the blind. "Come help me unpack the cameras and binocs. We want to have everything set up before the cranes come."

Mikey went into the blind, but immediately came back out. "That place gives me the creeps."

"I'll open the shutters, it'll make it much lighter and airier." The sound of Paul sliding the wooden shutters open was almost drowned by the noise of thousands of cranes flying across the river a few hundred feet above them.

"You have to stay in the blind so you don't scare the birds." Carole Sue felt like a school teacher scolding a wayward pupil. Mikey went into the blind.

"I'll close the door when the birds come. Is that okay." Paul left the door ajar. "The cranes can't see the door at all."

Carole Sue nodded hesitantly. "See you tomorrow morning."

"What color was Mikey's hair?"

"Brunette, almost black. Little mustache and pointy beard. Haircut done by a stylist—tapered, lots of different lengths." She stared at the wall behind Bobbie.

Bobbie glanced at the wall behind her. Next to the window was a framed and autographed crane festival poster from Bosque del Apache, New Mexico.

"Looked like beard was an attempt to hide chin scar. Didn't cover it well."

"What did he wear?"

"Dark brown leather jacket. Black jeans. Bunch of earrings. Maybe jacket was black, too. Think it was. Can't remember anything else."

"Were the earrings hoops? Studs? What?" Bobbie realized she sat at attention mimicking Carole Sue.

"Little hoops. No studs? No studs. Silver hoops about so big." She held her fingers up about a quarter inch apart.

"Finally, I have to ask where you were last night."

"You mean after dropping 'em off? Except for a couple of hours in the breakroom, I was in my camper." Carole Sue frowned. "Slept in my camper, by myself. No way to prove I was there."

"What did you do in the breakroom? Who else was there?"

"Was there most of evening, except for wandering into the classroom." Carole Sue stared blankly at the wall above Bobbie.

"What? You said you were in the breakroom for a couple of hours." Bobbie made sure her voice was congenial. "Was it *a couple of hours* or *most of the evening*?"

Carole Sue's head swayed and she looked at her watch. "Meant most of the evening. Was probably here about five or six hours."

Bobbie nodded approval. "Thank you."

"Chatted with Ruth while she operated cranecam. Ate some of the bread and cake in breakroom. Snitched some wine. Actually, quite a bit of wine. Someone brought in several bottles of Crane Valley Merlot and Chardonnay. Figured it should be for us all. Might have been Paul brought it. He often brings gifts for we volunteers. Or, rather, brought gifts."

"So you were not in the breakroom the whole time?" Bobbie's voice sounded confrontational to herself. She couldn't help it.

"Wandered around the Nicolson Center, but stayed in or near breakroom most of the time. Left the building once to walk over to my camper and get some food. Rest of the time I was in this building. After the volunteers finished their evening guiding, we sat around. Drank some more wine and ate goodies. Eddie and I were the last ones to leave. About 10:30 or 11, I think."

"Who is Eddie?" Bobbie studied Carole Sue. No sign of duplicity.

"All I know is Eddie," Carole Sue said. "He's been volunteering for years. Longer than me. Nebraskan."

Bobbie nodded. Her stomach growled. She turned off the recorder and concluded the interview.

When Carole Sue left, Mulcahy asked who else she'd still like to see. "Don't know. Ms. Martinez" Bobbie coughed. *Talking like Carole Sue is not me. Why am I doing it?* "I guess I should talk to Bill's wife and Eddie. Is there only one Eddie?"

"Uh, yeah." Duane frowned. "The only Eddie I can think of is Eddie Stuart."

"Is he Nebraskan and been around for years?" Bobbie watched Duane's reactions.

Duane frowned and rubbed the bridge of his nose. "Yes. That's Eddie Stuart."

"My Cousin Eddie." Damn. Good old obnoxious Eddie. He'd do anything for Carole Sue's attention. Or probably even mine.

Chapter 4

The Kid

Wednesday, 5:00 P.M.

Eddie's clothes were rumpled. "Hey, Eddie. Haven't seen you in ages." Bobbie studied her cousin. His face had aged, more tanned and lined than she remembered, no doubt changes since she'd last seen him and probably the same things he thought about her. His eyes still had that beady look that had irritated her decades earlier.

"It seems I've seen you in your cruiser every few months or so," he said. "But, yeah, we haven't talked more than a couple of words since when? Julia's wedding? Fifteen years or more?"

"Yeah, sounds about right. Maybe even longer." They had been placed at the same table for the reception. Julia's wedding and the party had been a roaring bore, so bad she'd actually talked to Eddie, or at least tried and pretended to, for an hour until she could quietly sneak away.

Bobbie gave Cousin Eddie the usual preliminaries and looked at her notebook. Carole Sue said she and Eddie had talked, but he wouldn't know about that. She wrinkled her face. How might he have been involved? "So, what were you doing here last night?"

"I took a group of visitors to Jamalee, which put me back here a little after nine. Then I spent an hour or two here talking to Carole Sue and Ruth." His small green eyes said he related a simple story about himself, his favorite activity, with none of his usual self-aggrandizing embellishments.

"Jamalee? One of the blinds?" She waved west toward the blinds on the way out to the murder scene.

"Yep, it's the first one west of here."

"Thank you and thanks for coming forward to help me with the time-line." Bobbie smiled as warmly as she could. She hoped she didn't look as plastic as she felt. "Who is Ruth? I haven't met her yet."

"She's an artist, steers the cranecam whenever she's here. Very nice older lady."

Very nice meant Ruth gave Eddie the impression she liked to listen to him. "Do you recall when you went home?"

"About eleven." Eddie looked up at the ceiling. "I'm not sure beyond that, but it couldn't have been much later. Might have been a little earlier."

"Any idea when Carole Sue left?"

"She went to her camper about the same time I started home, close to eleven, I'm sure. Ruth had already left, probably at least thirty minutes before us."

After a few strained remarks updating each other on family news, Eddie said, "I came to see you because I talked to Mikey Ippolito, the boy Paul brought out this year."

Bobbie nodded. Pretty soon she would have gotten to him, anyway. "Thank you." She remembered Eddie Stuart had a sister and, like their cousin Mentes Petite, both were involved with kids for some city or county agencies. "This year? Did he often bring young people out with him?"

"Every year, as far as I can recall. Started with his own kids then others like Mikey."

"Oh. That's pretty neat."

Eddie nodded. "I think you know I work with troubled youths in Kearney so I know all about the Mikeys of the world."

"I just remembered. Only a glimmer of the thought. Thank you for confirming it."

Her fourth-generation Husker cousin was a huge man, big enough that he'd been an offensive lineman at the University of Nebraska. His clothes needed ironing, which reinforced Bobbie's recollection of the family rumors, that he was still single. She didn't notice any scent on him.

She tried to remember the organization he worked for. "So tell me what you know about Mikey."

A day earlier Eddie had come to Rowe right after his last class. Because he was a serious birder, he visited the sanctuary almost every day during crane season and made a little extra money by leading visitors to birding hot spots in Central Nebraska. When he arrived he walked up to the visitor center and saw a lost young man who looked in need of a friend, someone to talk to. "Hi. I'm Eddie Stuart. Is this your first visit to Rowe?" They shook hands.

"Hello, Mr. Stuart. I'm Mikey Ippolito. Mr. Capodicasa brought me out to see the cranes. It's my first time to Rowe, in fact it's my first time out west." He straightened and smiled.

"I'm Eddie. Not Mr. Stuart." Eddie pointed toward the field to the south. "If Paul brought you out, you must be a serious birder."

"Yes, sir. I will graduate in a few months. I'm going to Cornell in Ornithology this fall. This is like the best possible graduation present." His eyes lit up and his goatee accentuated his bright smile.

"Paul has been generous with Rowe Sanctuary, as he has been with you and the other young men he's brought." As far as Eddie could recall, every year Paul had brought someone with him to witness one of the greatest bird migrations in the world.

"We went on a number of birding trips together. All in and around New York. I saw lots of areas I couldn't have afforded by myself. Lots of new birds."

"Speaking of new birds, want to go see some whoopers? They're several within an hour or so." Eddie used the common slang for whooping cranes, one of the rarest and largest birds in North America.

"That would be wonderful. Thank you, Eddie. I'd love to." His face was like a child's on Christmas morning.

"Have you identified all of these?" Eddie pointed to several birds at the feeders outside the Visitor Center windows. "Some of them have to be new."

"I got the Harris's sparrow, but ..." Mikey looked out the window for many seconds without saying more. "I feel so weird here. Outside I can't hear anything and see practically nobody. It's so empty here. Aren't there any people in Nebraska?"

"Part of the reason the birding is so great here is the lack of people."

"Creepy." Mikey shuddered as though he was outside. "I need to concentrate on the new birds more."

"The cities east of here have pushed the cranes to this small stretch of the Platte so we have something like ten times as many as a couple of centuries ago." Many urbanites feel threatened by the sounds of animals and comforted by human noises like traffic. What else could Eddie say to soothe Mikey? "Even experienced birders from other parts of the country often make many additions to the life lists on their first visit here."

Mikey bit a fingernail then cleared his throat. He put his hands behind his back.

"I wish I could do something to show you how beautiful the quiet and openness are." Eddie planned a trip to the Sandhills in ten days. He would take a large group to see the mating displays of the greater prairie chickens, one of nature's truly magnificent dances. "Would you like to come see the prairie chickens and pelicans with me? And when we go down to see the whoopers this weekend, we'll go by some prairie dog villages and maybe we'll spot some burrowing owls."

"The cows, dogs, coyotes and even some of the bird calls are so strange." Mikey hunched his shoulders even though it was warm in the Nicolson Center. "I'd like to see them, but the whole area makes me jumpy."

"So you think Mikey was really frightened?" Bobbie studied her cousin.

"*Frightened* would be too strong a word. But he was ill at ease with the wide open spaces and the sounds of animals instead of the city nois-es." Eddie looked down as he spoke and rubbed his face.

"Do you think he could have hurt Mr. Capodicasa?"

"No!" Eddie spoke with authority. "Well, anything is possible. But this guy was so over his head being out in corn-country for the first time in his life that I am very worried about his welfare. He seemed gentle and interested in the cranes and other birds. Nothing surly or mean in his actions." Eddie shook his head. "No, my worry is that he might be injured and managed to escape the killer. He's probably in trouble out there." Eddie waved his hand upriver, in the direction of the murder scene.

"Did he have a cold or anything you noticed?"

"Hmm." Eddie knit his brows in thought. "Now that you mention it, I think he sneezed some and had a runny nose he kept blowing and rubbing. He acted like he was cold even in here. I thought he was, uh, apprehensive, but maybe he was really cold."

"Do you think he was on drugs?" She realized she speculated out loud instead of asking open-ended questions, but Eddie ought to know the signs of drug use, like almost any teacher.

"Hell no. No way." He stared at the ceiling. He must be visualizing Mikey, recalling details. "No other sign of drug use or being stoned. He was sober. Nice young man." Eddie frowned for a few seconds. "Well, anything is possible, but I saw no indication of drug problems. None."

He looked at Bobbie and bit his lip. "You know, most families are not as dysfunctional as ours. Seems we have the most secrets"

"You're right there. Hell, if they were, I'd be ten times as busy." Most people heard rumors about the Lee-Stuart-Petite fights, but some of the worst stories were true, or understatements.

"More secrets," he quietly repeated several times.

"I can't imagine anyone as bad as the Petites." Eddie referred to their cousins. "Mentes should have been locked up years ago. How the hell'd he ever get to be CA?"

Bobbie grimaced and rolled her eyes. A miracle of politics had put Mentes Petite in the County Attorney job.

After further discussion and small talk, Eddie left and Ruth Bingham came in, introduced by Mulcahy. She was probably at least 75, but erect with penetrating brown eyes and curly white hair. She wore a dress with a large floral print and was the first woman Bobbie had seen in a skirt since she got to Rowe. Typical old-lady dress. She wore black shoes with medium heels.

Ruth carried a large piece of paper. "I glimpsed the boy," she said in a soft voice. "I thought you might want a better sketch of him than the police artists can create so I drew his picture." She put the large piece of paper on the junk on Mulcahy's desk.

Bobbie stared at the picture. "Oh my God," she said in a barely audible tone. "I see what Carole Sue meant. That is a lot like me." Bobbie continued looking at the picture as Ruth turned it right-side-up for herself.

Ruth put her hands over the ears and earrings in the drawing. "I guess we all have memories of ourselves from some high-school or college yearbook. Did you look like that when you were twenty?" Ruth held the picture up and covered the forehead with her other hand and looked back and forth between Bobbie and the picture. "Yeah. Could be your brother or son."

"Eddie Stuart thinks he may be wandering around lost." Bobbie rubbed her holster, further burnishing its front and the strap that secured her pistol.

"That's why I thought you'd need a good picture. I assume you'd want to get everyone in the state helping to find him."

"Thank you." Bobbie turned the picture so she could look at it right-side-up again and shook her head. "Thank you very much. I'll get this out right away." She looked at her watch. "I wonder if we can still make the evening news. At least we can make the ten o'clocks."

Even before Ruth left, Bobbie started calling Sheriff Leon Grayson. He would call the County Attorney, Nebraska's term for their district attorney. Mentes Petite insisted on being the public face of any news that might contribute to his reelection. They would get the picture and description on the Kearney, Hastings and Grand Island TV Stations. She'd have to get Ruth's drawing to them and they'd have to contact the TV stations by 9:30 or so to stage their press conferences or interviews or whatever, even for the late news. CA Petite, who had only been in office about eighteen months, would revel in the publicity, the news shows should love the story, and they would find Mikey much faster. It should be a win for everyone involved.

"I'll send a deputy for the drawing," Grayson said. "Be sure to let me know when you're done there. I want a full briefing tonight. No matter how late."

"Yes, sir." Bobbie cringed. She would have to prepare as many demonstrable minutia of the investigation as she could. *On the other hand, if Sheriff Grayson is sending a deputy for the drawing, he is sure this is an extremely critical situation.* He was usually too tight with the county's money to spend it on an extra trip when Bobbie could deliver the drawing to him in time for this evening's broadcasts.

Chapter 5

Rowe Sanctuary

Wednesday, 5:45 P.M.

Bobbie requested a tour of Nicolson, the visitor center at Rowe Sanctuary. "I'll do the honors, detective," said Director Frank Armstrong, who stood next to Duane in the hallway. He led Bobbie to his office. "In case you ever need to talk to me, Detective, this is the best place to find me." It was a little bigger than Mulcahy's and uncluttered. The west wall had a number of pictures of cranes. The east wall was mostly book-shelves.

"Call me Bobbie, Frank. You don't need to be so formal." Frank's manner made Bobbie feel at ease, like everything in the office.

"Okay, Bobbie. One reason I wanted you to come here is so I could relay a personal message. Naturally I called Paul's wife as soon as I learned he was dead. At that time, all I could tell her was that he was all beat up, that it looked like he'd fallen from the roof of the blind or a tree."

"Did you go out to see him?" Bobbie had demanded to talk to everyone who'd seen Capodicasa and Frank had not come forward.

"No."

"Oh. How'd you know what he looked like?" Bobbie made sure her facial expression was non-confrontational, that it showed interest in the answer. She also made her voice friendly.

"Bill Martinez told me what he found. I worked completely on hearsay. In fact, I told Sophie Capodicasa that his condition was from the guide's description." Frank pronounced the guide's name in the Latino fashion with a long *E* sound in the accented second syllable.

"Oh. Okay. Thank you. Go on."

When Bill came into Frank's office to tell him about Paul Capodicasa, Frank's first thought and action was to notify Paul's wife, Sophie. "Oh my God. Oh Damn. Oh my God. Oh God, this is terrible. I have to let Sophie know. Thank you for telling me right away." In two clicks his phone book was on his screen. He picked up his phone and motioned for Bill to leave as he dialed.

"Hello, Sophie?" Frank bit his lip and clenched the phone so tightly it dug into his hand. "I have awful news. Paul is dead. He had a horrible accident." He breathed again. At least the worst part of the call was over.

"Oh, I better call you right back." She hung up before Frank could say anything more.

What should he do now? He couldn't leave. Crap. This was terrible. He couldn't even go see what was going on. Frank stewed and wished he'd used a cell phone or at least had a wireless phone. He went as far as the hall, but nobody was in sight. They must have all gone out to see Paul. Or to pay their last respects.

He paced and waited. Waited and chewed his neatly trimmed nails. More than a half hour passed. Finally the phone rang. His caller ID did not show Sophie, only a New York City number. He answered, found that it was Sophie as he suspected, and repeated the news.

"It was a mob hit." Her voice was flat. Like a newscaster describing a murder.

"What?" Frank jumped to attention and held the phone away and stared at it for a second. He heard Sophie's voice and put it back to his ear.

She repeated her assertion with the same flat voice. She was certain. Her voice was authoritative. "Paul was killed by one his *associates*. Be careful, Frank. No small town cop is prepared to deal with this, and you certainly are not. Don't pursue his murderer and don't let your local cops go after him."

"I'll tell them, but I can't stop the investigation."

"Tell them to be careful and watch their backs. I'll ask Chuck to come out and make all the arrangements for Paul." Her voice showed no emotion. When he'd met the Capodicasas together, it was clear they were still in love after decades of marriage. She must be terrified for her own safety. Why did she ask her son to come out? She was really frightened of someone or some group.

Wait a minute, could his death really have been murder? How'd she decide that?

"So, you think she didn't call from home?"

"No. The caller ID only gave me 212 area code. Nothing else. I assume it means she called from a pay phone."

"Pay phone? They still have them? I can't recall seeing one in years."

"Yeah. If you had to go find one, it would take hours around here." Frank had a blank stare.

"On the other hand, if she felt that insecure...." Bobbie frowned. "Don't you think she'd know where to go find one?"

"Yeah. I would anyway. But even that could take a long time. It could cause the delay." Frank nodded. Shook his head. "If you use a pay phone only once a year? Don't know."

"So, after talking to Sophie, did you go out to Mr. Capodicasa's photo-blind?" Bobbie asked.

"No. By that time the deputies were here and somebody or other told me the area had been closed off as a crime scene. I stood around talking to people. Like everyone, I was in shock. I never made it out there, not even to pay my last respects. I felt like the deputies forced me to abandon an old friend, but what could I do?"

"Yeah. Tough situation." She studied his desk and face. "So, what are your duties here?"

"My duty is to keep the place running and solvent, which means that raising money and courting potential donors is an important part of my job. Next is getting tourists to come in and keep them happy and coming back. Actually most of our operating income is from the gift shop and blind visits. People think we get money from Audubon, but we don't, we actually have to pay them. Our tithing to Audubon covers bookkeeping, stuff like tax preparation and payroll paperwork."

"Tax preparation?" Bobbie sat up straight. "I thought you were tax exempt."

"Yeah, we are." Frank had a crooked smile, apparently amused by Bobbie's misunderstanding or naiveté. "Tax Exempt doesn't mean exempt from filing a tax return. We still have to do the paperwork and show the IRS we aren't making money and stuff like that."

"Death and taxes." Bobbie muttered to herself.

"Uh huh. Audubon also gives us any legal support we need. Looks like we'll be using some of that now. And they were instrumental in the initial land acquisition for Rowe about a half century ago, but we pay for their services every year." He hit his left hand with his fist.

"So the National's charges hurt you?"

"Oh. No. We *are* the National Audubon Society here." He looked irritated at her misconception. We are one very important strand in Audubon *and* in the web of life."

"Thank you. Sorry I misread you. So, what else do you do?"

"Anything and everything that needs to be done from cleaning rest rooms to fixing trucks and tractors."

Bobbie knew her surprise at the breadth of his duties showed. "One other question, a formality, where were you last night?"

"I was home with my family." He put his finger to his lips in a contemplative gesture. "I attended an Ornithological Society meeting in Kearney in the evening and got home about ten or ten-thirty. I had a cup of tea with my wife and we went to bed."

"Ornithological? That means birds, right?" She knew her puzzlement was obvious. "Is it a local group? Was it Rowe's luck they met here so close to you?"

"Oh no." Frank shook his head vigorously. "They plan their meeting to be here this time of year. The meeting coordinators regularly schedule an extra-cost excursion so a gaggle come out to one of our blinds each year. It's good for us and gives many of these professional and super-serious birders a chance to see the cranes up close and personal."

"Do you spend most of your time on fund raising in one way or other?" The victim had not been robbed, but money might still be an important factor in the murder.

"Yeah, directly and indirectly. For example, Paul had indicated that he had named both Rowe and the Kearney Youth Home in his estate planning. In fact, he said he planned to give more to us and less to KYH."

After their brief chat, Frank started Bobbie's tour in the east end of the Nicolson Center, the "Staff Only" area. He showed her the nice breakroom, where she'd had the group meeting with the volunteers. It had a pleasant aroma of coffee and quick bread. He pointed to the offices for two of the employees that were no larger than her cube in Kearney, their library, a shared office, and storage space with multiple recycle bins.

"We are very conscientious about the environment." He motioned toward the bins. "Here we separate everything we can to make our waste stream as small as possible. We send most trash to recycling." The whole area was cramped with paraphernalia.

The Rowe gift shop filled the middle of the Nicolson Center. It displayed many types of crane-related bling, nick knacks, and must-have collectibles for the tourists. Bobbie looked at the Rowe logo shirts, like the ones most volunteers and employees wore. Bobbie turned a tag to look at the price, which seemed competitive.

Frank explained "The gift shop provides quite a bit of support for Rowe. The sales are respectable, especially during the crane season."

"Do you give shirts to the volunteers?" She still held the sleeve of a sweatshirt.

"We can't afford to give them much except coffee." Frank looked confused.

"Most of the volunteers had Rowe shirts. It seemed to be their uniform."

"They've all bought them. We give them a ten percent discount, but they support us with their help, their purchases, *and* their donations."

Quite a racket. She thanked him. The center had been carefully constructed and green-certified. He proudly described the eco-architecture: stucco covered hay bales with ground-up blue jeans for insulation in the ceilings where the bales would be too heavy. "Oh, look here. You can see some of the green construction techniques." He pointed to a glass panel in the rough stucco interior wall of the gift shop, where the hay bales inside the wall were visible, and handed her a box of shredded denim. "This is the stuff used in the ceilings."

Bobbie took the box and poked it around with her finger. Nothing special. Looked and felt like the ordinary jeans cloth. Like blue jeans run through a paper shredder. She handed the box back to Frank and followed his gaze to the reception desk.

Bobbie watched a volunteer behind the desk greet a visitor with a white cane. She marveled at a blind person's interest in the birds. The greeter seemed similarly intrigued. He turned around the guest-log notebook on the desk and asked for the man's name and address.

"Elvin Jones, 1437 County Road E, Minden, Nebraska, 68919." He held his cane propped against his arm and leaned on the desk.

"1437 Cow Knee Roadie? How do you spell that, sir?" The volunteer looked completely lost. Bobbie stopped to watch. Meant that practically anybody could have been here last night.

"1-4-3-7 C-O-R-D." Mr. Jones paused about a second then said, "E."

The volunteer transcribed the address. He must have had enough familiarity with the area to remember the town and zip code at least. He thanked Elvin Jones. Bobbie watched as Mr. Jones went toward the windows behind the desk. He seemed to know his route. Should mean Rowe gets lots of long time visitors, ones who really know there way around here.

The man tapped his way past the cash register to the viewing area opposite the entrance with its chairs and binoculars for watching the cranes and other birds. Bobbie looked at the birds that were feeding on the ground under a group of bird feeders. In the viewing area, where the blind man sat, you could hear their chirping.

"Those LBJs are Harris's sparrows," Frank said. "They're common here but are lifers for some of our visitors from the coasts."

"LBJs? Lifers?" Bobbie looked at them more closely.

"Little brown jobs--mostly sparrows, wrens and such." Frank pointed to the ones on the ground and several in a bush that Bobbie hadn't noticed. "The ones with the black forehead and bib are the Harris's sparrows. Most birders keep a list of all the birds they've ever seen, their *life list*. A new addition to it is a *lifer.*"

"These guys must be really serious. Wow." She looked at the LBJ and wondered at the finer distinctions. "Do you often have blind visitors?" She whispered the question to Frank.

"No," he said in a normal voice. "It is sad more impaired people don't come."

He went on about the support for people with mobility impairment while Bobbie thought about her investigation. It would have been very easy for a mob hit-man to come in here. Nobody at Rowe would have paid much attention to one out-of-place guy walking around. Oh. Frank finished his description.

"Incredible. Wonderful. I had no idea birding was so much more than looking at the pretty ones." New views of this bird watching world appeared at each turn. It seemed more than plausible that birding could be important to putting the puzzle pieces together.

The west or upriver end of the Nicolson Center had a long skinny viewing area along the river side. "Cope Hall" had an antiseptic smell from a recent mopping. The rest of the west end was a classroom with the touchy-feely collection of pelts, feathers and other bird parts. It smelled like a museum.

Bobbie stopped and looked at the maps on the wall. The world map had pins from dozens of countries and the US map looked like it had pins in every state. "I had no idea you attracted tourists from so far." She turned toward Frank. "Is that many years' worth of pins?"

"No, those pins are all from this year. Among birders, Rowe Sanctuary is no secret." Frank smiled at the maps. "It's only here in Nebraska we're unknown."

Bobbie turned from the maps and saw Ruth Bingham watching a large computer monitor. Six visitors were milling about and sort of watching with her. Bobbie walked over to see what was on the screen and realized that Ruth was operating the cam's control.

Ruth looked up from the screen. "Hello, Detective. Want to see anything in particular on our cranecam? Mainly it's the cranes we show, but I can move it to show anything you like."

Bobbie looked at the screen. "Is it a web cam? What's it showing now?"

"It's looking down the river. Here, I'll zoom out." The picture shrank rapidly so that it showed a river full of birds instead of a few standing in water. "There you can see the Visitor Center and a couple of the blinds."

Bobbie saw two blinds and a corner of the Nicolson Center. "Is it on all the time?"

"Yes, but I leave it aimed about the way it is now when I leave after sunup in the morning or after dusk in the evening—a general view down the river toward here. It's only early morning and late evening when I move it around so people can see the cranes. One Kearney boy in Afghanistan thanked us for the views of home."

"So all night it's left running showing the Platte from here up to about the photo-blind where Mr. Capodicasa was killed?"

"Yeah. Pretty much so."

"Can you tell me about it? Is the view recorded?" Bobbie spoke privately to Ruth. The detective looked around to see if anyone looked like they were paying attention. No tourist seemed concerned.

Ruth looked past Bobbie for the answer. "We make no recording of it," Frank answered from behind her. "We should get a newer, better cam, but we can't afford it. Right now the picture isn't bad, but rain often puts blots on the picture, wind jiggles it badly, and the cam's night vision is poor." Frank must have picked up on Bobbie's concern. He spoke so only Ruth and Bobbie could hear.

"How poor is it at night? Any chance it might help us?" Bobbie turned to look at Frank, but kept checking all the people in the classroom.

"My son calls the picture 'pixelated.' The darker it is, the worse the image. I don't know how to describe it any better."

"Can you see any better when the moon's full?" Bobbie recalled that the moon had been full at the beginning of the weekend.

"Some, I think," Frank said. "We'll have to check to see."

The first luck in the case. It had been fairly light most of last night. Maybe someone, somewhere on the web had been watching or recording. Bobbie turned back to Ruth. "Can you see the photo-blind Mr. Capodicasa was in?"

Ruth zoomed the picture out a little then panned and zoomed back in. "You can see part of the blind. It's to the right of Michael Forsberg's tower." She pointed to the middle of the screen.

"What's Forsberg's tower?" Bobbie studied the screen. Hidden in the picture by the trees was a tower that looked like a ham radio operator's mast with a sort of crow's nest on top. "Oh, I remember. It's just east of Capodicasa's photo-blind."

"Yeah. That's right," Frank said. "Michael Forsberg is one of the country's greatest wildlife photographers. He built that tower and put camo netting on it so he could get some specific shots of the cranes. We have some of his beautiful pictures and books in the gift shop."

Bobbie pointed to the monitor and spoke to Ruth. "Does that mean the Capodicasa photo-blind would have been visible as you left the cam last night?"

"I'm not sure how visible. It would have been in the field of view, anyway." Ruth looked at Bobbie as she spoke, the cranecam control in her lap.

"Thank you, Ruth, both for the cranecam info and for the sketch of Mikey. The CA will be on the news with it this evening. By tomorrow everyone in the state should be helping us find him."

Frank then led Bobbie back to the gift shop and out the main entrance. He pointed to a plaque on the wall behind the huge ceramic crane sculpture. "Paul was important to us personally and financially." The commemorative plaque honored "Paul and Sophie Capodicasa" for donating one million dollars.

Frank took Bobbie west, along the same path where she'd gone to the murder scene a couple of hours earlier. Most of the lights outside were red, all were dim. "We use the red lights so as not to disturb the cranes," Frank whispered. "Rowe really is about the sandhill cranes, though we provide sanctuary for dozens of other birds. We want to be very quiet outside." They were about 50 feet west of the Nicolson Center. "We shouldn't go any farther tonight. It might spook the cranes."

The two turned and walked back toward the parking lot. Small lights came on near their feet as they walked. Apparently motion activated walkway guide lights. "Tomorrow, or whenever you wish, I can give you a tour of the photo-blinds and the big regular blinds."

Bobbie saw two cars leaving the lot where she'd parked. The person at the gate looked like Vivian Lentini, the volunteer who had a 7-year service circle on her name tag. Bobbie had interviewed Vivian right after her talk with Bill Martinez. Vivian had been sent to reprimand Paul Capodicasa for allowing his telephoto lenses to stick out of the shack and was the last non-witness to see Paul alive. Vivian opened the gate for the cars and closed it behind them. "Why the gate guard?"

"Mostly to keep car headlights from unnecessarily shining toward the river. In the morning, the guard also helps our visitors find the turn-in to our lot. You should come back then to see it—Darth Vader with his light saber."

"What?" Bobbie jumped

"The volunteer who usually mans the gate, Ken Fader, dresses in a long black coat and carries one of those kids' light sabers you can get at Walmart. He uses it to direct traffic."

"Clever." Bobbie looked around and realized the low light also helped her night vision. "Do you have many kids in the blinds?" Kids see and remember different details than adults. More possible interviews. She could see the river, the trees on the far side, and a bazillion stars. The number of visible stars always amazed her when she was away from city and highway lights. Even those of a small city like Kearney drowned nearly all stars.

"We encourage parents with pre-teen children to use the viewing areas at Lowell Road or Fort Kearney because most kids are not patient enough to sit still for two hours. If a family really wants to go with us, we ask them if the kids will be quiet for two to two and a half hours with no phone, toys, iPads, et cetera. If the kids are used to long quiet periods without electronic support, we *may* let them go out to the blind with their parents."

"So some, but not many?"

"That's not a bad way to put it," Frank said. "Not even *some*, only a very few."

Bobbie couldn't think of any other questions about Rowe. Those would keep popping into her consciousness over the next few hours as she wrapped her mind around this complex part of her backyard. She hoped her discussions with Frank and Duane hadn't sounded like interrogations. She had to collect and assimilate all sorts of details because there was no way to know this early in her puzzle assembly what would be significant and what irrelevant.

She should have paid more attention to the people at Rowe. Mrs. Capodicasa warned Frank that any Buffalo County deputy would be too careless, and she had been.

Chapter 6

Mentes Petite

23 Years Earlier

Mentes Petite had one year to go in Law School. One year until he could join a law firm and pay off the debts. Dad could have paid for law school by skipping a new truck or combine one year. One year skip from his Old Man and he'd have had no debts. He'd have been able to work for the Public Defender, as he wanted. Well the community picnic today would be his last before graduation.

Mentes picked up a small glass salt shaker in the kitchen, an oblong half-inch thick one. He put it in his front pocket and walked across the yard to the tractor barn where his father stored all his unused or out-of-date farming materials. Lots of natural light from the open door. The shed smell had not changed in twenty years—dust, manure and grease.

He put on a pair of work gloves and checked the pesticides. He found some old rodent poison and carefully picked it straight up by the sides of the can so no dust on the shelf or on the can were disturbed. The label showed arsenic tri-oxide. He carefully unscrewed the top, touching only the sides of the cap, so the top of the container was barely disturbed. He flung the salt from his shaker, spreading it across the dirt floor of the shed, and half filled the shaker with the white powder. Mentes carefully returned the blue can with the skull and cross-bones to its previous position on the shelf in the dust-free circle where it had been. Only a very careful and thorough inspection would show it had been moved.

His research indicated that white arsenic had no smell or maybe a garlicky odor and that a few salt-shaker doses would be sub-lethal for his father. *With luck the egotistical bastard will get nice and sick with cramps and diarrhea. Wouldn't want to kill the dear old geezer. Perfect.* By the time anyone recognized the cause, if they ever did, salting his father's food would be forgotten. The shaker was barely visible, a slight bulge that might be excitement or a handkerchief.

Time to go enjoy the jiggle and wiggle at Minden's Labor Day Picnic.

At about 11:00 Mentes parked and walked among the throng. Too bad the bra-less style had barely made it to small-town heartland. The teenagers were the best, at least in the tit department. He went to the food shack and studied the Legion's menu and their food. "I signed up to help." He looked at Mrs. Longanecker behind the cash register. She was Mrs. Nebraska Farmer straight out of the '60s in her print dress and low heels. "Can you use anything now? I thought you might like someone to guide people and assist them to their tables. If Harry's got that covered, I'll help any other way I can." Mentes pointed to a big black man with tinges of gray in his hair and dressed in the uniform of a Civil War Confederate sergeant.

Harry was a fixture at the American Legion feeds, wearing a variety of Civil War uniforms. Sometimes he switched between the blue and gray in the middle of his shift.

"The crunch is coming." Mrs. Longanecker ran the feeds for the vets. "Harry'll need help soon." From years past Mentes was prepared to tell people their lunch choices and direct them to the correct lines. If anyone needed any special help, he would give them a hand.

"Sounds good. I'm on it." The aroma of baked beans and barbecue made him feel at home. Mentes stopped on his walk to the door. "Happy Labor Day, Harry. Uh, Harry Reb. Snuck past you. You must need some *meet and greet* help."

"Glad to have your help, Mr. Petite." They shook hands vigorously. Harry had the rough hands of a man who used them.

Mentes turned to the door as a family arrived. He invited the five-some in, pointed out the food and seating options, a pattern he and Harry repeated every few minutes as new families and groups of fair-goers arrived. They were far more solicitous, providing continuing help, whenever groups of young women came. Several times he checked the servers. Mrs. Longanecker seemed pleased and nodded approval when they made eye contact.

He met the two prettiest girls he'd seen all day. He told the unfamiliar twosome the prices of the food and the procedure for lunch. A couple in their sixties or seventies came right behind the young ladies he wanted to help. "Excuse me. I need to help the elderly couple." He left the girls and gave his pitch to the couple. "If you tell me what you'd like, I can bring your food to the table for you." He pointed to the food options and told them the prices. "No point in struggling with a cane *and* a tray."

Half-an-hour after delivering beans, ribs and coffee to that first geezer couple, he welcomed a group of girls. "Hey. You're Cousin Bobbie." He looked at the last of the trio. She'd look really good in a thin shirt. Unfortunately she wore a bra.

The yellow of her solid-color skirt matched the flower petals on her blouse. Bobbie fidgeted with buttons of the blouse. Mentes realized he was staring. He looked into her eyes. She looked awesome in her sunflower print blouse and short skirt. The sunflowers of the blouse outlining her tits, almost as good as bra-less.

"Hi, Uncle Menty. What you doing here?"

"Helping out a little." He paused but didn't stop looking at her eyes. "Save me a seat next to you." He leaned over on tip-toes and whispered to her. "I'll join you as soon as I can. Things should slow down soon." She wore a sexy floral perfume, but he wished she'd stop calling him *uncle*, it made him sound so old.

He heard one of her companions. "Is he your cousin or uncle?" Mentes did not catch the reply.

About ten minutes later, Mentes's parents came in for lunch. "Hello. Tell me what you want and I'll bring it to you. Go ahead sit down wherever you want." With his parents' order and money, he started to get in line. "I'll bring it over in a minute. Dad, you want some extra salt on your pork and beans, right?" he spoke from his position at the head of the barbecue line. The only way he would ever get anything from the old skinflint was when his dad died.

"Yes. Thanks." No smile. Really friendly. Could have been talking to one of his cows. The Petites sat at an open table while Mentes retrieved their food, paid for their meals, and put a little extra *garlic salt* on his father's beans. His father smelled of having come straight from work. Dirty hands and nails, too. The old coot didn't even bothered to shower.

He served his parents and returned to the cashier. "Mrs. Longanecker is it all right if I go talk to my cousin? Not so many people are coming in now and I'll be here to help if someone needs special help."

"Sure. Go ahead. Enjoy yourself. Today isn't a day for working." Mrs. Longanecker handed him a plate of ribs and beans and made a shooing motion with her hands. "Go flirt with the girls."

"Thank you." Mentes detoured from the direct path to Bobbie's table to check on his parents. "Everything okay?" he asked his parents. With satisfaction he noted his father was digging into his salty pork and beans.

His mother nodded and pointed to her mouth. She had just taken a bite of bread. His father grunted. Mentes smiled and went to Bobbie's table.

"How have your summers been?" Mentes looked at all three, but mostly at Bobbie. "Are you going to be cheerleaders? You're pretty enough." He decided Bobbie wore a lavender scent. Pretty.

The girls giggled and shook their heads.

"None of you? That's surprising. Is there some cheerleaders' clique that you have to be in?"

"Yeah, sort of." Bobbie looked more at her friends than him. She turned to Mentes. "What are you doing now?"

"I'll be going back to Lincoln for my last year of Law School in a couple of weeks." He saw their eyes widen and felt himself stiffen. "Heard anything about the pheasants this year? I've been wondering if I should come back at Thanksgiving to bag a few."

"Seem to be plenty in the fields." Bobbie turned from Mentes to the other girls. "What do you think?"

One of the high school juniors made a face, like she didn't want to think about hunting. The other nodded. "Been as many as last year, anyway."

"That's so far off. I'm going to get some of the rabbits tomorrow morning." Bobbie looked back from her companions to Mentes. "Anyway, I prefer a rifle to a gun."

"Yeah, me too." Mentes looked at Bobbie. "Do you ever go out during the bow season?" Mentes rubbed his chin.

Bobbie looked confused.

"You know, for deer?" Mentes splayed his fingers over his head.

"If I went bow hunting for deer you wouldn't want to be in the county. The deer would be safe, that's for sure." Bobbie shook her head.

"Oh. I hoped you might have one of those new compound bows. I've been wanting to see one up close. I can't believe they really work." How can all those gears and pulleys work fast enough to shoot an arrow so well.

"I'll take my 30-06 any day."

"Big rifle for a little girl."

"Yes. But it'll stop anything and its kick is nowhere near as bad as a 12-gauge."

Chapter 7

Paul but no Mikey

Wednesday, 8:15 P.M.

In the evening, after the tour of Rowe, Bobbie talked to several other volunteers and reviewed her notes. She told Duane she'd like to talk to Vivian Lentini again. He went to find the very tall woman who spoke like a ventriloquist and had been volunteering at Rowe for years. Vivian's interactions with the victim and other volunteers had been varied and somewhat confrontational but completely routine.

Bobbie must have been a little too much in the role of dumb blonde because she forgot some basic questions. Now she had to go back and complete her earlier interview with the volunteers' *Mother Superior.* Bobbie reminded Vivian that they were still in the middle of a homicide investigation and turned on her recorder. "Other than when you went out to the blind to give Paul Capodicasa hell, did you have any contact with him?"

"Yes. He sat out on the bench in front when I came in last evening. I try to make sure everything is set up for *everyone* going to a photo-blind because they contribute a lot of money to spend a night out there. Of course Paul makes huge donations in addition to the normal blind fee. I talked to him a little and asked why he didn't come in out of the rain.

Some rain drifted in through the pergola in front." She pointed toward the top of the office window.

Bobbie looked up, out the window at the huge wood slats of the open roof. They would not stop much rain, and it had been raining yesterday afternoon.

"He said he was well protected and dressed warm." Vivian's short salt-and-pepper hair enhanced her striking good looks. "He said he liked to smell the fields. Liked the rural things he never had at home. We talked about last fall's rainy season. I mentioned that rain had continued through the winter and until now—good for growing crops, bad for harvesting. I told him to take care of himself and came inside to check on everything."

"Was anyone with him?" Bobbie studied Vivian.

"Lots of people were around. I didn't notice anyone *with* him. " Her eyes had normal redness for 60 years exposure to Nebraska weather.

"Can you think of anything out of the ordinary?"

"Everything here is out of the ordinary." Vivian frowned for a few seconds.

Bobbie wondered if she would answer the question. First order is to wait and see.

"If you're not a Husker, the aromas here are unique. And, of course, the sounds of the birds are extraordinary. You must have noticed the cranes' noise when you were outside. The gabbing of the cranes is like that all night long. Never a quiet moment during crane season and if a coyote spooks the birds at night, all hell breaks loose for a half hour or so." Vivian didn't pronounce the final e of coyote.

Bobbie nodded and smiled. The birds on the river had been like a kindergarten class. Constant jabbering among them. "The yacking never stops? Goes on night and day?"

"Maybe quiet during the day when the birds are not here. But at night? I've never heard it quiet. I sleep with the windows open and I always hear the racket."

"Wow," Bobbie said.

"If you trust animals, like the OJ Simpson barking dog, then you might like to know that Ella Mae, the Stevie blind guide, reported seeing turkeys in the trees when they came back from Stevie at about nine. Like the owl I heard, I think if those turkeys had seen anyone near them, they would fly away."

"Even at night?"

"Yeah."

"They don't have set roosting spots? I thought birds went back to the same place night after night."

"I think turkeys move around." Vivian scrunched her eyebrows. She spoke slowly. "Like other flocking birds, if they didn't move we'd find huge piles of crap to tell us where they roosted. Even if they only used the same tree a few nights in a row, it would be obvious."

"Good point." Bobbie nodded and looked at her notes.

"Ask Frank, he'll know for sure." Vivian had a half smile and made some motions with her hands that Bobbie couldn't interpret.

"You said you talked to Mr. Capodicasa. Did you talk about his plans?" Bobbie again studied Vivian's eyes for any hint of dissembling. She used her hands while she spoke, but they never went near her face. Her arms never crossed and she didn't seem to moisten her lips or swallow any more often than usual.

"I'm sure we talked about it. Well, I probably knew he'd be going to a photo-blind, so we might not have even talked about that." Vivian frowned slightly in a way that Bobbie interpreted as indicating she had not yet related all of the story.

Bobbie waited a few seconds, hoping, unsuccessfully, that the silence would elicit more. "Wouldn't Mr. Capodicasa have told you which blind he was going to?"

"Probably not. He might have requested a specific one, but I doubt he'd do that. In general, we never tell our visitors which blind they'll be assigned to. They only find out when they're taken out." Vivian no longer frowned. "Even an hour-old list can be out of date in the evening, so I had no way of knowing which blind he'd be in."

"Who decides who goes where?" Bobbie tried to visualize the system that appeared rather baroque at the moment. That meant no list could be used by a murderer with any confidence. His target might not be where the list showed. Had the attack been meant for someone else?

"One of the staff," Vivian said. "I don't know how they do it. I've never been involved in that." Vivian frowned. "For example, if we decide a visitor may have trouble walking as far as the blind, we'll reassign them to Jamalee, even at the last minute, because Jamalee's the only one we drive too. In Paul's case I'm sure whoever does the assignments knows his preferences and accommodates them. I can't imagine anyone bumping him if we think he prefers the west photo-blind."

Bobbie looked at her notes again. She added "Possible someone beside Capodicasa was intended target?" Could the target have even been in another blind? "You said they contribute a lot to spend a night out there. How significant is it? Who do they contribute to?"

"I'm not sure of the exact amounts." Vivian twisted her mouth and frowned for a second. "I think Rowe charges visitors something like a couple of hundred a night in one of the photo blinds and twenty-five bucks per person for a morning or evening in the big blinds. Everything else is free." She smiled. "Well, not everything, just the trails, bird watching, and suggestions."

Bobbie thanked Vivian who did seem to think part of her job was to be sure that everyone else did theirs. The Den Mother of all the guides.

Before leaving Duane's office Bobbie reviewed the rest of her notes. She saw her quote from Vivian's first interview. "Cranes roost in the water because their feet can't clasp tree branches. No thumbs. Most birds roost in trees at night to hide from predators. Cranes stand in the water, using it as a sort of motion detector. If a coyote were to go after one, the splashing would alert the cranes to fly away. Nebraska's Big Bend has lots of shallow river water and lots of food. Perfect for cranes. And predators. Means that if anyone had been out there in the Platte he would have scared up clouds of cranes and probably some would have hit the power lines."

Bobbie was glad she'd made a note of that seemingly unimportant comment. At the time it seemed unrelated to the murder, just disjointed and garbled. She recalled that Vivian had made a three finger foot with her hand, using her thumb to hold her pinkie up against her palm to show how cranes couldn't roost in trees. Now it did look important. Very important She had to be sure she learned everything she could about Rowe and the cranes. It looked like some little detail with no relevance to the murder would make other parts fall into place.

On the way back to Kearney, Bobbie called Sheriff Leon Grayson, to brief him on the investigation's status. She visualized him watching the evening news to see the announcement of Mikey's disappearance. At five foot eight, Grayson was the exemplar of a person with short man syndrome. A good boss as long as things went his way. He probably wore a suit as he watched the news. Even in this community, where clean dungarees passed for Sunday best, he always dressed in a suit or freshly pressed uniform and smelled of Eton College Aftershave.

"Okay, Lee." Grayson's voice sounded like a Saint Bernard's woofing. "I'll meet you at my office in fifteen minutes."

"Yes, sir." A very long day, but dinner would have to wait. Starving or not. Hadn't even had time to think about food since she almost lost her lunch. Damn sugar low. Had to meet the Sheriff, which meant Grayson viewed the Capodicasa murder as his re-election guarantee.

Bobbie found Grayson waiting in his office and wearing a gray pinstripe suit and yellow paisley tie. She described the scene and the apparent openness of the volunteers and staff at Rowe. "The big missing testimony is from the man who was in the blind with the vic, the one you sent out the appeal on."

"That new CA, Petite, did the appeal." Grayson looked nonplussed. "If we don't find your guy by tomorrow, I think you better see if he could have crossed the Platte and headed north." Grayson's instincts were usually right on. "I know it's dangerous to try wading across because of high and cold water, but that expensive wet suit should make you safe. It should keep you warm enough. We've got to see if the river's crossable, and, if so, how easily."

Bobbie acknowledged the order and cringed at the thought of wading the Platte. Damn, this wouldn't be any walk in the park. When divers went into icy water, they wore two wet suits or a dry suit. From what Vivian said, it seemed unlikely that anyone went across. Worse than that, she would probably freeze to death despite the suit.

On the other hand, trying to cross the Platte would also show how difficult it would have been for the murderer to come from the river side of the blind. The more she thought about crossing, the more germane it seemed. No matter how cold. She shuddered.

Chapter 8

Paul Capodicasa

Thursday, 7:03 A.M.

The next morning Bobbie bungled her way to the coffee pot and poured herself a cup of her water of life. After showering she dressed, putting her bra on backwards as always. She hooked it, turned it around, slid her arms through the straps, and finished dressing. Her dog, Bear, awakened as slowly. Even though she never left clothes out of the closet and Bear never went in, his donation to her mornings was on her clothes. His main contributions at other times were comfort and protection. He was fiercely loyal and very much a one-human dog. As she left the apartment, she lint rollered herself, especially her butt, to remove his hair.

In her cube at the Sheriff's office Bobbie called the Central Nebraska Cremation and Mortuary Service in Gibbon, the next town east of Kearney. Fisk Eisenberg, the county's new medical examiner, had an office and forensic lab there. "Look, Dr. Fisk, I know you always do a conscientious job, but we've been told that the Capodicasa murder was a mob hit. Watch your back carefully even after everything's completed. I believe the mob wants no help or contact with the police. We have to be very cautious on this investigation. We were warned we can't be careful enough and that warning probably extends to you." She reworded and repeated her message so the urgency and importance would be reinforced. "Let us know of any threats or concerns, okay?"

"Sure. You know I'm always cautious." Fisk's voice sounded skeptical.

"Thanks, Doc. We want to be sure you're protected, if it comes to that. Be paranoid, at least for a few weeks."

"Hey, Bobbie, you're the one who needs to be more careful. I always watch around me, but I don't think you do. Be careful for yourself, too." They ended the conversation.

Crap. Fisk was right. She needed to check her house every time she came home and her car whenever she was about to drive.

She phoned Dr. Dom Chan, head of the computer forensics group in Lincoln, and passed the warning and explanation to him. Then, she got to the purpose of her call. "At Rowe they have a cam that pointed toward the murder scene. They make no recording. Is there any chance we can get a copy of the night before last's video or find someone who watched it?"

"Won't be easy. I'll see what we can find." No sign of optimism in his voice.

Thanks, Dom. The cam operator at Rowe specifically said they'd received thank yous from Husker soldiers in Afghanistan. Some homesick GI may have been watching the cam all night and seen something. If you find a recording somewhere or any watcher, please let me know."

Bobbie had to learn something about the victim and the threat. She could only think of one person she knew in the New York City Police Department, a fellow marine. After pleasantries when she called Patrick, she asked, "So how's my favorite SEAL? Still single?"

"Yeah. Still single. No love life. How about you?" He spoke with a clear New York accent, much more than she recalled. He dropped syllables and nasalized most of the vowels.

"Ditto." Bobbie paused a moment and visualized him. "Being a cop doesn't help me any." She'd first seen Patrick in a picture of an awards ceremony in DaNang when he received a Distinguished Service Cross for helping his unit recover from a direct hit on their boat. He'd been knocked from the captain's seat at the helm by a mortar round which landed amidships on their patrol boat. Everyone said that only a SEAL would have even survived the explosion.

Pat agreed that cops don't make good dates and paused a moment. "Can I talk you into a New York trip? Great city, lot's to do. Nice guy to escort you around."

"Ohh, good offer." She hesitated. "But if I came, I'd be really tired from the trip. Probably have to spend lots of time in bed."

"I'm sure the escort would help."

"What a guy." She recalled the last time. He was always prepared and cautious. And pretty good in bed—very gentle for a big tough SEAL captain. "In the meantime, I have some business questions."

"Shoot."

What can you tell me about Paul Capodicasa." She visualized her friend, able to take on any ten mortals.

"Be careful, Bobbie. This may be well out of your league."

"What?" She couldn't believe the apprehension in his voice. It could be concern for her, but it sounded more personal than that. "Christ, what do I have to do, Pat? Are you available as a bodyguard?"

"No. No. Be very careful. You need to call Quinn McKay. I can't really help except to say the rumors are scary. Quinn's a good man. He'll help any way he can. He'll know about Capodicasa. My work now is all with the gangs. Haven't looked at the mob in years."

Bobbie tried to pry something from Pat. What scared him? How could *he* be afraid? She had no luck. She disconnected the call. *What the hell? If a guy as guarded as Pat is scared, maybe I should get out of town.*

She reached Quinn McKay on the third call, to the last of the three numbers Pat had given her, his cell phone. After introductions and verifying that he had time to talk, she asked, "What sort of background information can you give me on Paul Capodicasa?"

"Let me call you back. Just a couple of minutes." He hung up before she could even acknowledge anything.

Twenty-four minutes later her phone rang. Quinn McKay introduced himself and asked, "Can you tell me about a retired Kearney County Sheriff and what he looks like."

"The one I know best is Alvin Beasley, we all call him Al. He's about 5 10" and probably weighs about 190. Bit of a beer belly. Thinning blondish hair and a round face."

"Okay," Quinn said. "Have you ever gone hunting with him?"

Bobbie Lee began to see where this was going. She knew Al had thought his re-elections depended on a macho, pro-hunting, Wyatt Earp image. "Yeah. What I think you're after is that he is not an enthusiastic hunter, doesn't care much for killing, and is not a great shot. I learned this when we went on a prairie chicken hunting trip a few years back."

"Okay." McKay sighed. "Capodicasa scares everyone here. I got to be sure you are who you said and I wanted to be talking from a more secure phone."

"I'm beginning to see." Bobbie started her notes with the self admonition, "BE MORE CAREFUL." She hadn't really believed the warning from Frank. Why would the mob bother her, way out in the middle of nowheresville. On her own home turf. She decided to try calming McKay. "I gather you know Capodicasa's dead. You're still worried that he can get you from the grave?"

"No, I hadn't heard he'd died. And no, I don't think he can get me, but I'm sure a power struggle will begin right away. Even knowing he's out of the picture, I'm sure you know ghosts can be dangerous. More so than gangsters. I don't want to be a participant in the fight to succeed him." He sounded every bit a New Yorker.

"Sounds cautious." Bobbie paused a moment.

"You know the difference between old money and new money."

"Yeah, think so. Family money versus newly wealthy, right?" *What's this have to do with anything?*

"Well, there are similar differences between old mob and new mob" McKay said. "Capodicasa is old mob, from Sicily, the ones who have at times run the Italian Carabineiri."

"Got it. Watch my ass. In fact when Frank Armstrong, the Rowe Sanctuary Director, notified Sophie Capodicasa that her husband was dead, she said she was sure it was a hit by one of his *business associates*. Given we're 1500 miles west of you, does that sound plausible?"

"Anything is possible for them, but it isn't their usual way of doing things." McKay spoke deliberately. It sounded like he was sorting through the mob hits he knew about, or something like that. "Sophie may know something. She grew up in a mob family and certainly still has close connections to it. She'll have sources of info as well as biases we don't."

"Okay." Bobbie tried to understand what this meant for her and her investigation.

"Wait a minute." Quinn's voice tone changed completely. "There are two Paul Capodicasas here. Which one are you talking about?"

"Let's see." Bobbie looked at her notes. "His driver's license said Paul Georgio Capodicasa. Does that help?"

"Yeah. At least he's the lesser of evils. Just recalled he's the one married to Sophie. He was a high roller, maybe involved in taking out some of his competitors, but we could never prove anything. We never even had any solid, unusable evidence. He gave lots of money to artistic and other causes. Even if we'd taken him to trial, he would be tough to convict because he's so well liked. He does have a great reputation." Quinn's voice relaxed, like he was trying to hide his original bad assumption.

"That Paul Capodicasa owns several night clubs, which is where he started, and now also owns some cleaners and small groceries. He's often seen with his wife, kids and grandkids. I think he has two boys and a girl, about a dozen grandchildren and maybe even some great-grand-kids."

"Sounds like a nice guy," Bobbie said. "The people here love him because of all the support he's given the Rowe Sanctuary." She nodded as she considered Capodicasa's generosity and complexity.

"You've got it. Typical Mafioso. Except for extortion, murder and bribing public officials, they're model citizens. We need more like them."

"Guess we're lucky. Those last traits were never seen here." She paused a moment. "At least not that I've heard of."

"He may be as upstanding as he'd like everyone to think," Quinn said. "I, myself, think he's at least legally clean. That's probably a minority opinion and I am sure he has friends who'd do anything for him at the drop of a hint."

"Anything?" Bobbie said.

"Yup. And another thing," Quinn said. "*Sophie's* in a position to call in a hit, or contract one out to someone in your area. She certainly knows people near you who owe her something. I wouldn't ignore her accusation but it may only reflect fear and family history."

"Nice people. Is there some signature action she or they'd use?"

"Yeah," McKay said. "They generally use a small caliber pistol to the head or rarely a machine gun and spray rounds all over the body."

"Just like the movies," Bobbie said. "The Capodicasa autopsy won't happen until this afternoon, but from what I saw, it looked to me like his injuries were from bludgeoning. Maybe some stab wounds."

"I've only seen *that* in a movie. Never heard of a hit like that. Wrong modus operandi." McKay spoke the Latin with a tone that seemed to say he was trying to impress a hick colleague, or maybe a female colleague. "Of course, if the hit was contracted out to a Nebraskan, it could be done however the sub wanted to do it."

Bobbie noted his thought in her journal. "What about his modus vivendi?"

"Touché," Quinn said. "Anyway, we can expect a local power struggle. Maybe Sophie will avenge his death. She may be moving to take over from him. She might drop a hint that gets her side of the family to start a bloodbath, something I do think they'd do for her."

"Well that's one the movies have missed."

"Yeah. It'll be a first here too. If she succeeds. But it also means that she may send someone there to find out what happened. Probably only reconnaissance to see who she needs to purge, if you believe the stories, or who she needs to watch, if I'm right. In either case she'll want to consolidate her position."

"Any idea who she might send? Who I should watch for?" She wished she'd paid more attention to the tourists at Rowe.

"Probably one of her sons. They're both tall, obviously Italian guys."

"Oh, yeah. She told the Rowe director she'd send out a son, Chuck I think." Bobbie thumbed through her notes looking to check the name.

"Chuck seems to be a good guy. Never heard anything bad about him. Not even his ex bad-mouths him."

They continued with flirting and small talk. Bobbie told Quinn she loved Nevada Barr mysteries. "It's something you can use as a quick identifier when I call—nobody will find that on-line."

"Okay, and I'm a Sci Fi addict. I've watched all the *Star Wars* and *Star Trek* movies many times and have seen all the Star Trek shows." Quinn made some thinking noises. "Hey, you're cute. Five foot six, 125 pounds. I like your hair."

Bobbie wondered where all this came from. Perhaps her driver's license file or the Buffalo County Sheriff's internal site. He could probably access either of them. Why did he like her hair? It was blond when they took her Deputy photo and longer and strawberry for the driver's license. "What color is my hair? How long is it?"

"Kinda blond with a tinge of auburn. Half way to your shoulders. I think it's what you'd call a page boy."

"That driver's license pic is pretty old. My hair is shorter, straighter and blonder now."

"Very good. When do you get off work? Want a beer?"

"Let's see. It'll take me about a day to get there, so we better not try to make it tonight." She wondered about her new best friend, *Flirty Quinn*.

They ended with an agreement to share info and to talk again within a week, but not go out for a drink that evening.

Bobbie headed for the equipment locker and shuddered at the prospect of going into the cold water. She took the wetsuit, weight belt, and a mesh bag with mask, fins and snorkel. "Damn I wish we had a dry suit. I'm gonna freeze my butt." Her time in the Marines had given her minimal preparation for diving, but Sheriff Grayson thought she was the expert. Maybe expert in the context of all her fellow "Great American Desert" cops. She lugged the moldy equipment to her Explorer. Apparently someone had rinsed it and put it away damp.

Hell, I'm only wading across the river, I don't need all this gear. She returned everything except the wet suit. *At least I'm better at non-S-CUBA work than anyone else because I can hold my breath twice as long as they can.* None of the other deputies were divers, not even any of the police from the area. Hell, there wasn't any water within a hundred miles that was too deep for wading.

She drove to Rowe. Only an idiot would wear a wetsuit in Nebraska. She decided to carry the gear to the murder scene to dress. The forensics trailer blocked the lane into the photo-blind. A perfect place to change. A few minutes later, after hellos to Scotty, she talked to Investigator Shirk. "Hi, Tom. Pardon the ridiculous outfit. Grayson wants me to see if it's possible for anyone to cross the Platte."

"Hey, no problemo. I always figured you'd gone off the deep end." He had a smile like he'd finished the better part of a six pack. From this angle the most ridiculous comb-over in the state of Nebraska didn't show.

Bobbie noted the ice floating in the water and stepped in. Involuntarily, her teeth started chattering and she started shivering. Shivering was good. It warmed the body. Yeah, sure.

Damn. Scotty and Shirk are gawking at me too. She waded in.

She felt secure walking in the current despite the slimy river bottom that seemed to ooze through the wetsuit's booties. She continued, leaning to the left to counter the current and occasional globs of snow and ice. She hesitated a few seconds when the water reached the tops of her thighs, letting the cold splash up on her rather than inserting herself into it. It was damn cold, even through the wet suit. She could feel the gooey bottom of the river, but at least its sliminess was masked by the suit.

At waist deep, the flow nearly knocked her over. A stutter step to the side made her right foot slip in the mud. She was swimming down the river. Should she try to make it across to the north bank? Ugh, not in this ice and snow infested water. Even with the wetsuit, the dry land was a long way off. A very long swim away.

Bobbie turned to swim back to the south shore and hit a large snag. It slowed her motion downstream but the current pushed her under the old cottonwood. Crap, now she was really cold. Her hand went through the Platte-bottom muck. Through the yucky slime where a branch or something scratched her hand. Another branch may have scratched her face—to numb from the cold to be sure, and it felt as if a large one poked her in the back. She relaxed and tried to look up through the murky water as the current pushed her along. But instead of clearing the log, all she saw was the thirty-inch trunk. A branch of the tree caught her suit and dug into the middle of her back. She could feel the current pushing her, digging the branch into her back and stretching the neoprene of the wetsuit.

Bobbie wiggled, hoping she would break loose or break the branch. The current held her under the huge tree. She pulled on the suit. Maybe it would rip free of the cottonwood? The tree did not release her. She reached behind her back, trying to feel how the branch tore into her wet suit. She could feel a stick poking through it, but could not pull it loose. She was hopeless to untangle herself back there. Of the many dangers of police work, this one had never occurred to her. Drowning by inanimate forces. What a way to go.

Again she reached behind her back and tried to pull the wetsuit off the tree, but she had no strength or dexterity in the middle of her back. Could she even make it to shore with no cold protection? Her lungs were beginning to burn so she'd been under water for more than a minute. Nearly time to panic.

Bobbie put her feet against the tree and pushed. The wetsuit stretched. Her shoulder hit the mud, but the only release from her trap, was her bra tearing. She had to hope she could stand the cold. She unzipped the suit and partially wriggled out of the top. The top turned inside out, releasing her torso, but not her hands. Her lungs were searing. How much longer could she hold out? Her core body temperature plummeted. Numbness, and a feeling of warmth. Delirium was beginning.

Must be way over two minutes by now. Turning toward the snag, she tried to pull the wetsuit free. Her hands came free easily, but her feet wouldn't budge. The sponge stretched but didn't tear. She tried to pull her whole body free of the neoprene.

Her fingers were too numb to pull the built-in booties loose. Why the hell had they bought one-piece suits? Her time was gone. She pulled on the log with all her remaining strength until her face cleared the water. Several gasps of air quieted her lungs, but she still had to untangle her feet. She had to free herself despite losing strength to numbness. What a wonderful headline, "Naked cop pulled from Platte." Lot better than "Dead cop fished from Platte." Or "Cop drowned by own wet suit." She had to stop thinking about the consequences and get free. Get free fast.

She took a deep breath and went down in the water to pull her feet from the wetsuit. With her feet untangled, she tried to pull herself up onto the log, but her arms were too weak to lift herself onto the cottonwood and her fingers were too numb to hold the tree even if her arms had been strong enough to lift her.

Bobbie slid along the tree, holding onto the trunk and thanking the gods of Nebraska for giving cottonwoods bark such deep crags that she could hold on with the current pulling her away. After two yards sliding along the massive log, her feet hit the slimy bottom. The water was only about four feet deep. She walked along the tree, holding it to steady herself against the rushing water.

She was saved, only about thirty feet to shore and dry grass. She looked down at her naked body. Scratches everywhere. The cold must have prevented her from feeling the branches ripping her skin. The scratches looked awful. She'd been shredded everywhere. Thank God there weren't any tourists gawking at her. Crap, O' cr Scotty would gladly hold her for observation. She hoped they weren't around.

The water wasn't so deep any more. She let go the tree and hugged herself for warmth and modesty. On the next step her foot caught on some willow or something under the muddy water. She slid in the ooze and fell.

Her arms spun like propellers as she tried to fly upright. She had to keep her bare torso out of the freezing river. She went down again.

The current forced her under a branch of the cottonwood. She caught the branch and pulled herself up out of the water, more numb than ever, but not gasping for breath. She wiped the muddy water from her face. Branches surrounded her. Unless she could climb up on the tree, she had no choice but going fully back into the water to escape her cage. She tried to dig her fingers into the crags of the old tree, but moss slicked its surface. Her fingers just would not hold. Perhaps if she could get a secure grip, her arms would be too weak to get her out anyway. She could not even climb out.

She felt with her foot to make sure the path was clear under the branch. Purposely, this time, she took a deep breath and went under the main branch of her trap into the wonderful air on the open side. She held onto the small branches as she worked closer to shore. Now she walked slower than before to avoid tripping a second time. She kept her eyes on her target dry grass on shore and her hand on the furrows in the cotton-wood bark.

How the hell could long distance swimmers endure the cold? At the edge of the water, she summoned all her strength to hold the willows on the bank to help her out of the Platte. Her hands were blue. The shoots on the bank were too slippery. As she tried to pull herself up the undercut bank of the river, the willows slipped through her hands and her feet got no traction on the mud. She skidded back into the knee deep water. Did she even have the strength to get out of the river?

She wrapped willows around both hands and with both arms pulling and both feet scrambling. She went up the bank like Wile E. Coyote and used her last energy trying for the haven of dry grass beside the river.

Chapter 9

Junior

Thursday, 10:15 A.M.

"We have a sexual assault victim. Maybe a homicide victim. White, middle aged female. Body cold and naked. Badly beaten."

Bobbie tried to think. What was that distant voice? If she wasn't dreaming, the message would be from her, not some disembodied voice in the distance.

"Vic washed ashore here at Rowe Sanctuary. Dressed only in panties."

Bobbie felt warm, even hot. She opened her eyes and tried to speak, but nothing came out.

"Oh, at least you're not dead," the officer said. The same voice she'd heard before.

She tried to see who was talking, but her eyes did not focus. All she knew was his voice. Some man. About ten feet away

"Victim is alive, get an ambulance here fast. Repeat get an ambulance to Rowe ASAP."

Bobbie's eyes and mind started working again. She started to understand. "Scotty, why are you calling me *middle aged*?"

"Lee? You're Bobbie Lee?" He stared at her.

Bobbie realized she was nearly naked and tried to draw her arms over her breasts. "Oh my God. I feel hot. Where am I?"

"You're about 100 feet from the Rowe Sanctuary Visitor Center, ma'am. We got a 9-1-1 call. What happened?"

"Stop staring at me for Christ's sake. I'm old enough to be your mother. Help me get up."

Scotty never took his eyes from Bobbie, but he did offer his hand to help her up. "You look pretty beat up, ma'am."

"Give me your damn jacket." She held out a hand for it. She didn't realize it was possible to shiver so violently.

Finally he pulled it off and handed it to her. "You're dressed in blood, Ma'am. Looks like you are wearing a blood shirt anyway."

"I've never felt so cold." She looked at her legs, which were also covered in cuts and were trembling like a dog scratching a flea. "How come I started out feeling so hot?" Why hadn't the lecherous son-of-a-bitch recognized her?

Scotty steadied her as he walked along side Bobbie toward the Iain Nicolson Visitor Center. He seemed to mumble something, but she couldn't understand. He called and canceled the ambulance. "Glad you're okay, ma'am."

"Thank you. And, this is a swim suit bottom, not panties. I lost my top and the wet suit in the river. I wasn't raped or attacked. It was all an accident. There was *not* another homicide. No crime of any sort. Just stupidity. And clumsy."

She realized she should soften her admonition in the interest of future cooperation. He wasn't responsible for the accident or for her being topless. "Thank you for your concern, Scotty. You did the right thing. It was my embarrassment that fueled my tirade." She turned away from the Visitor Center. "My clothes are in the evidence trailer. I'll go there. My bloody legs aren't ready to entertain the tourists."

Bobbie went back to their trailer, and washed as best she could with the basin of water and paper towels. She put on her uniform, returned Scotty Leslie's jacket, and headed for the Nicolson break room for some warmth and hot coffee. She took the largest mug she found. After several sips, she refilled it and cupped her hands around the mug to warm her hands. She headed toward the parking lot with the borrowed mug. She still shivered as she started the drive with the heater on high. It would be minutes before the Crown Vic fully warmed.

At least she had proved that no one could cross the river. Or had she? Maybe a seven foot, 350 pound guy could have made it. Bobbie had been so far from making the crossing, and it was so damn cold. For nearly anyone, the only way across was in a boat.

She looked at the wall of her office. A window would be nice. Hah. All she'd see would be the grubby parking lot and the window would need cleaning all the time. At least she no longer felt cold. What sort of office would Capodicasa have? Windowless, like in the movies? Below street level for security? With a window onto the stage of one of his nightclubs so he can keep an eye on everything? Maybe with an exit through steam tunnels so he can elude police and mob hit men. If he was even in the mob.

She decided to check her email and look up some Star Wars trivia for the next telco with Quinn. She rattled her mouse to awaken the clunker on her desk and watched the flash of her wallpaper—parents, brother and sister-in-law, two nephews and an assortment of pets including her overly protective Pomeranian. She logged in, cursing the new, slow, two-step login procedure.

Finally, her email popped up. The top item came from the office of Fisk Eisenberg, the ME. "The autopsy is delayed. It will be at 2:30, not 2:00." A half-hour stay of her sentence. She breathed a little easier. She hated the autopsy, hated the thought of having to look at Capodicasa's bloody head. She hadn't agonized much on the autopsies she'd attended. Little recollection and no obsession. For some reason seeing a corpse cut open was less unsettling than seeing a body badly mangled by beating or explosion. Maybe going to a lab prepared her for the blood and guts. Maybe the advance knowledge the person was dead made it more tolerable. Whatever the reason it was gory but not as bad as a murder scene.

Postponing the inevitable for a half hour wouldn't make it any easier, but at least it wasn't as soon. On the flip side, that gave her another half hour to stew about the autopsy. Just one of the perqs of being the lead investigator. She sneered at the computer.

Her phone rang. She answered on the second ring when the caller ID told her she had a call from 212, New York City, nothing more specific. She identified the department and herself.

"Hello, Deputy Lee. This is Chuck Capodicasa. I understand you're investigating my father's death?" His accent did not shout *New York*, but a few nasal sounds were there, with a touch of New England.

"Yes. I'm in charge of the investigation." She recovered her composure and realized he'd probably learned her identity from his mother.

"If possible, I'd like to talk to you." He spoke again before she could offer anything. "I'll be in Kearney about a quarter of one and hoped we could meet soon after that. Is there any chance you could join me for lunch or coffee this afternoon?" He pronounced her city's name correctly, with a short a sound, like "CAR knee."

"It sounds like you won't have had time to eat and I can wait." Bobbie tried to think of a good restaurant in Kearney. "Let's meet for late lunch."

"Thank you. Dad thought Gusto di Napoli was the America's Cup of Nebraska's restaurants. My recollection is that it's close to the airport and as easy to find as the next buoy." He sounded pleasant and educated, not at all like the New York thugs in movies. He pronounced the restaurant name as it should sound in Italian and spelled it for her. He apologized for not having the number to give her. "The owner's name is Valentino, if he's still alive. For that matter, I hope the restaurant is still there. The restaurant was on the way into town from the Kearney airport why don't we meet there?" Bobbie had never eaten at Gusto di Napoli because it looked too expensive.

"I remember seeing it, so I'm pretty sure it's still in business." Bobbie recalled a rather ornate and expensive looking place east of town. "Think they're open in the afternoon?"

"If they aren't planning to be open, tell them you're investigating Dad's death and I'm buying." He sounded sincere. "They may open for us. If they can't serve us, we can try any place you like."

"That'll be nice. I can make reservations, or at least check with the restaurant, and call you back with details."

Chuck gave her a call-back number. "My flight is due to leave DIA in about 15 minutes. If you don't reach me, please leave a message and I'll get it as soon as I land."

So the last leg of his trip is Denver to Kearney. "I must warn you that I have to leave for a meeting at about 2:15 so if your flight is delayed, I may not be able to wait." Bobbie took a couple of packages of almonds from her desk to keep her going until their late lunch.

They exchanged a few more pleasantries and Bobbie said she would not be allowed to answer some questions because of the ongoing investigation.

"Sounds good to me. If we're on time I should be able to get there by about one."

"I'll call you as soon as I contact the restaurant." Would he be like the Mafia hit-men in old movies wearing an overstated pin-stripe suit?

Chuck agreed.

When Bobbie called Gusto di Napoli, the restaurant's answering machine picked up. "This is Investigator Bobbie Lee at the Buffalo County Sheriff's Office. Chuck Capodicasa and I would like to have a late lunch at your restaurant this afternoon, at about one o'clock. If you get this message by a quarter to one and can accommodate us, please call me at 233-5200."

She ate a handful of almonds. *Wonder if I can catch Chuck Capodicasa before he leaves Denver?* She needed to tell him she hadn't reached a human being at Gusto's. The desk set rang. "This is Paul Valentino at Gusto di Napoli." Italian sounding restaurant name, the way Chuck had said it.

"Oh, thank you for the quick call-back."

"We would be delighted to serve you and Chuck," Paul Valentino said. "We were stunned to hear about Mr. Capodicasa's death and want to help the family any way we can." His accent showed New York and Italy.

Bobbie thanked Mr. Valentino. "I'm looking forward to meeting you. I haven't been in your restaurant. Sorry it's such a sad occasion." They commiserated over Capodicasa's death.

She ran to the ladies room to wash, brush her hair, and try to hide the scratches. It calmed some of the panic of meeting a Mafioso in a fancy restaurant. She had to learn about him, his intentions, and his mob connections. *Know your enemy.*

A few minutes after Bobbie arrived to an obsequious welcome at Gusto di Napoli, Chuck Capodicasa walked over to her table and introduced himself. He looked about 40, a doppelganger for the model Fabio but with darker hair. His long black hair complemented his Mediterranean complexion. He even dressed like the cover model for an old Harlequin romance with blue blazer, khakis, and his open neck white shirt showing two gold chains. Bobbie could not identify the aftershave he wore. Pleasing, definitely not agrarian. He wasn't from Nebraska.

From force of habit she showed her ID and expressed sympathy as best she could on his loss. His clothes were tailored so Bobbie could be fairly sure they hid little or no hardware. TSA would not have let him wear anything, anyway. She gave him her card and asked about his trip.

Chuck didn't seem to have much interest in small talk. After his monosyllabic answers he asked, "What can you tell me about Dad's death? How and where was he killed?" Chuck looked like he was on the verge of crying. "Do you have any thoughts you can share on what happened? I have extensive resources that I plan to use as I investigate on my own. I'll make sure you have whatever you need. But, please don't let Mama know I'm helping you."

When Bobbie assured him that she didn't need anything, he expanded on his offer saying he could help her get more manpower or up the political visibility so people or lab work would be quickly available. "My only request is to keep Mama in the dark," he repeated. "She is a tall ship among the motorboats and thinks we should never help the police or accept help. My generation is a little more Americanized, even Dad was. I want to help you."

"Thank you. If something like that arises, I'll let you know."

He again asked for details of his father's death, which Bobbie described using the most medical and sterile terminology she could think of. She gave some brief details of the photo-blind and Rowe and talked about the general area. "Have you been to Rowe?"

"Yeah. In high school and college I came out here with Dad. Several times." He paused, looked down and rubbed his forehead. "Up until I was about Mikey's age. You haven't said anything about Little Mikey. How's he taking it?"

Bobbie took a deep breath. "We don't know. We haven't found him yet." She studied Chuck's momentary frown.

He took out his phone, poked a couple of keys, identified himself and said, in New York City-nasal pronunciation, "See if you can find Mikey Ippolito. Put some effort into checking and let me know as soon as you find him." The cadence of his words indicated he was talking to a machine. "He may still be in Nebraska. Call me with progress reports." He hung up. "You see, I can do something for you." The New York accent disappeared with the phone connection. Again he was the urbane yachts-man. "As soon as Mikey gets back to The City, I'll let you know."

Bobbie wondered how soon Chuck would get the response to his voice-mail message. He continued being suave, flirting and talking about his father, their businesses in The City, and his passion for sailing. His hands were tanned and it looked like he'd recently had a manicure. He wore a school ring on his left ring finger, but she didn't recognize the college and couldn't read the inscription.

"Your mother warned Frank Armstrong not to investigate because of Mafia action. You said not to let your mother know we're cooperating. Are you warning me about mob vindictiveness too?" Bobbie watched closely to interpret any body language that might contradict his words.

"No. I'm sure the Mafia is not involved. It's possible, but extremely unlikely." All his gestures and facial expressions confirmed his words.

Before the check came he answered his cell phone. Other than iden-tifying himself and goodbye, "Keep checking and keep me informed," was all Bobbie heard. Right after finishing the call, he poked at his phone a few times then turned it to show Bobbie a picture of a boy and girl dressed in matching lady bug costumes. "These are my niece and nephew. Dad's only great grandchildren." He choked as he handed Bobbie the phone. "You can scroll through the album to see a few more if you want to. The call said Mikey hasn't been seen in New York yet." He looked down, closed his eyes and rubbed his forehead.

Bobbie took the phone and quickly checked the pictures of the kids ice skating in their Halloween costumes. "Twins?"

"Yeah, in fact they'll be four in about a week."

The rotund Mr. Valentino came to the table. "It's only a little thing, but your lunches are on us."

Bobbie decided the price was too high and put a ten on the table. She glanced back as they walked out and saw that Chuck had put a Grant under his mat. "Thank you for the lunch and trying to locate Mikey. If you hear any news or rumors about your father's death or about Mikey, please let me know."

"Don't worry," Chuck responded. "I'll give you everything I learn." He held up her card to indicate how he'd communicate. "And my sources, such as they are, will not get too busy with other matters."

Bobbie heard Chuck's cell phone ring as she got into her old Crown Victoria. *Could it be news about Mikey?* He did not call her.

Chapter 10

Forensics

Thursday, 2:20 P.M.

From Gusto di Napoli Bobbie drove into Gibbon. She turned east on Front Street, past Miller-Godberson Mortuary, City Hall, and Bond's speed shop. She parked at the nondescript gray metal warehouse labeled, "Nebraska Institute of Forensic Sciences Regional Center." The Central Nebraska Cremation and Mortuary Service faced the largest east-west railroad line in the country. Any effluent from the crematorium's two large smoke stacks would disappear in the exhaust fumes from the hundreds of diesel locomotives passing less than 100 yards north. It didn't offend the residents of Gibbon.

Most people did not want to know what happened on Front Street. Bobbie had no choice. Chain-of-custody laws and the possibility that seeing the necropsy would help find the murderer meant Bobbie should be at the autopsy. She arrived moments before Mr. Paul Capodicasa was pulled from the refrigerator onto the exam gurney. The ME, Dr. Fisk Eisenberg, Doc Frisky behind his back, stood at the head of the gurney, while the tech, Nancy Lu according to her ID tag, stood at the side. She prepared to make the Y incision. Bobbie stood two yards from the vic's feet, facing west where she could see the proceeding, but where the

75

body's bloody skull was out of view and she could easily avoid looking at the anatomical innards.

"Cause of death not initially clear," Doc Frisky intoned into his recorder.

"What?" Bobbie said in a breach of protocol. She hadn't spoken loudly, but the exclamation should never have escaped her mouth. How could Frisky not know how Mr. Capodicasa died? He was obviously beaten to death, as Frisky would explain in medicaleze.

"External examination shows massive blunt force trauma, puncture wounds, and signs of manual strangulation. All injuries appear to have been sustained over a short period of time. From the external appearance, almost any of them would have been sufficient to be fatal. Extensive trauma and lacerations on the ulnar side of arms and hands, consistent with defense against an attack."

You brat. She looked at Capodicasa's graying pubic hair. She didn't want to look at the head, but she remembered dark hair. Her quick glance at his face showed gray beard stubble and roots, though most of his hair looked noticeably darker. She'd missed the bruises suggesting strangulation. Maybe his shirt and jacket had hid them. Now they were obvious.

"The assailant seems to have wanted to make sure he was dead. No immediately obvious external evidence of gunshot wounds. Wounds are almost certainly not self-inflicted nor from fall of any kind."

Frisky was always cute. What would he do next, tell us he wasn't blown up in a nuclear bomb blast?

The tech, who had been watching Frisky, saw his nod to proceed and opened the abdomen. They took samples of many of the organs, remarking about the trauma. Usually Frisky remarked, "blunt force trauma" to the organ, but sometimes he said, "blunt force and puncture trauma."

Why didn't medical examiners call it a stab wound? Bobbie began to feel nauseous again, and she had a stomach full of spinach linguine, thanks to Chuck. She started looking around the room. A bulletin board to her right held dozens of business cards, mostly from local cops, deputies and funeral homes, but some from as far as Lincoln. The white board showed Doc Frisky's name, title and company name in neat block printing. Nothing to read there.

On her left was another, larger bulletin board with anatomical drawings and descriptions of various procedures. Next to a drawing of a stomach, was a page titled "Deflesh Process." She stopped looking at the boards. They were no better than the corpse.

She stared at the blank west wall and tried to imagine it as a television screen showing her lunch with Chuck. It worked a little and the nausea faded somewhat. What had she learned about the Capodicasas? If Chuck was connected to the mob, the movies and television shows have the details all wrong. Everything he was doing looked helpful. His denials of mob association sounded right. She needed to check on him. Was he Chuck or Upchuck?

Toward the end of the autopsy Bobbie asked, "Could the possible strangulation marks on the vic have resulted from the perp shaking him by the neck, perhaps banging his head against something?"

"Certainly possible," Dr. Frisky said. "The trauma to the back of his skull is consistent with that type of violence."

Bobbie worried she learned no more because she did not pay attention. The state lab in Lincoln would check the organ samples for a few drugs and toxic substances, but, as Frisky told his recorder, "no indications of drug damage." No gunshot wounds. At least Frisky and Nancy didn't find any.

Bobbie returned to the Sheriff's office in Kearney and went to Tom Shirk's cubicle. Empty. Not surprising. He probably hadn't finished processing all the blood splatters and collecting tissue samples a trial might require. If her hunches were right, they weren't going to find much directly. Nearly all the useful info would come from tissue analysis, and the DNA tests could take forever, if Lincoln bothered to do them at all. Damn. At least the requirement from the CSI television shows for DNA tests on every little case had not yet impacted the detectives procedures. Poor CAs.

As she got back to her office, the phone rang. She traded hellos with Tom Shirk. "Scotty Leslie said you had quite a swim this morning. I guess you're okay?"

"Yeah." Bobbie shivered. At least the chill was gone from her body, just not her mind. "Well, Grayson wanted me to see if someone could cross the river. I think I proved you couldn't get across. When I lost my footing, I tripped and went for a swim. My real trouble started when the wet suit snagged on the underside of an old cottonwood. I had to leave it there. It was so damned cold." Bobbie shivered again.

"Oh. Is that what happened? Scotty said something about forgetting to photograph a rape scene, but didn't elaborate. Sounded like he'll remember the eyeful for a long time."

"Yeah, I gave him a show. Anyway, I looked in your office for you about a minute ago. Were your ears burning?"

He laughed. "I know you want data before we know what we see. Figured I better check in to tell you I don't have much.

"Okay, not much, but what *do* you have?"

"Strictly off the record, you know, but we found fibers embedded in two of the telephoto lenses, a big scratch on one lens that is probably a match for the scratch and dent on the tripod and some black smudges on it that aren't blood. Oh, and, by the way, you were right, those are very expensive lenses—all have image stabilization and very small f-numbers. They are thousands apiece. Maybe in the ten grand range for some."

"What sorts of fibers?" She paged back through her notebooks to see what people were wearing.

"Can't tell much about the type, but the colors are earthy—dark blue, red, brown, black."

"In other words, you think a reasonable preliminary hypothesis is they came from the vic's clothes?" Bobbie couldn't think of more qualifiers to throw in so her hard-working criminologist colleague would divulge his preliminary thoughts.

"Well." He paused for several seconds. "I know you want answers faster than we can analyze the data we have, and this is a big mess to investigate. If you need something to keep you going until we have solid deductions from the blood and tissue analyses, you can probably safely use that guess."

"Yeah, okay. And the smudges on the lenses, could they be hair coloring? The vic appeared to color his hair."

"Hmm. Possible," Shirk said. "Can't say. Thanks for the idea. We'll start by checking for that."

Bobbie visualized Tom, overweight, short, with his hair combed from back to front to hide his balding head. The very image of an idler. His name enhanced the image. Nobody would guess how careful, thorough and conscientious he was until they worked with him. "Anything else that might be of help?"

"Yeah. Maybe. Like you asked, I checked the cars in the parking lot to see if anything showed?"

"Oh, good. What'd you find."

"On our third walk through the lot we found an old pickup with Nebraska plates that looked like it had blood on the steering wheel. We ran the plates and it belongs to a Mr. Eddie Stuart. I photographed the blood through the window, but we can't do anything more without his permission or a warrant."

"Okay, sounds really good. I'd much rather do it with permission, but if we have to, I'll try to get a warrant. Why don't you ask for permission first." Bobbie nodded and smiled. She wrote "If Eddie doesn't give permission, get warrant for blood in truck" in her notebook.

"What about fingerprints? They don't take long." Bobbie doodled a sketch of the photo-blind on the river. "What did Iris come up with? Anything usable?"

"Not many prints are usable from the lenses and other equipment. Lots of prints from two people, probably the vic and the kid with him."

"Please do keep me informed as you get further results *or guesses.*"

"You know I will. If it's any consolation, the DNA analysis should get a higher priority than usual."

"Oh, you think they'll actually do it without a trial looming over them?"

"Hope so. They do hate spending time unless a trial requires it. I'll give them my sweetest talk."

"Good luck. Use all the sugar and honey you got. I'm beginning to think we'll need DNA results to get anywhere."

"Bet we get some results." Tom's drawl added to the plodding image that often worked to his advantage in court.

"Wait a minute," Bobbie said. "You said you have Mikey Ippolito's prints? How do you know they're his?"

"We don't really, but we did find prints that weren't the vic's on the rear-view mirror in their car. I could be wrong, but I'll bet we learn Mikey drove the car. That's what I'm going on. Iris made the deduction. I think it's a good guess too."

"Great work. Thanks for the news. Talk to you soon." Why and how would someone smash Capodicasa's skull with his own equipment? This sounded even more bizarre than before. No mob hit man would go on a job with no weaponry, so a mob hit seemed even less likely than the improbable she had rated it. This had the earmarks of a crime of passion or opportunity

Chapter 11

Searching

Thursday, 5:47 P.M.

Except for the lunch with a suave, model-handsome guy and the best food she'd had in months, the afternoon had been useless. Bobbie had talked to the neighboring state patrols, the bus and airline companies without turning up any evidence of Mikey Ippolito. She checked her mail and found an envelope from Iris Goldman, the Forensic team's fingerprint specialist.

In her office she opened the *Preliminary forensics.* "Thank you, Iris," she said to her empty cubicle. A patrolman poked his head in and looked around. She put her hand over her mouth then shook her head. "Long day. Brutal case. Talking to myself." She turned back to the document.

> Casts were made of many of the tracks. Most appear unimportant. One set (or perhaps several sets) of new boots left tracks both in and around the blind. Tire and boot tracks and drag marks obliterated many, but it appears they belong to the person who dragged the vic from the blind.

"Okay, let's get serious," she said to the empty office. The one resource that always helped was her mentor, Sheriff Al Beasley, the retired sheriff of neighboring Kearney County. He had never been a detective, but he always seemed to ask the questions Bobbie had missed, steering her toward the solution to her problems. Sufficiently discreet and enough of an elder statesman, Beasley stayed below Grayson's radar. If Grayson had distrusted Sheriff Beasley, everything would have hit the fan.

She worried that she was shirking her duty to track the murderer. But she had to organize the growing mountain of clues, data and hunches to select the best path.

She called his home number in Minden. After her usual sports talk about his beloved Huskers' performance in the NCAA tournament, she admitted she had called for his help.

"You're working that murder at Rowe, I'll bet." She visualized his short gray hair and beard, the grandfather she'd wanted. In her image he wore blue denim coveralls, the Nebraska tux, and had just come in from inspecting his garden.

"That's it. Got some time to talk?"

"Of course, Bobbie. I always have time for you." His gentle approach was more like talking to a generous old uncle than to an elected and retired politician and a former sheriff, especially on the subject of murder. After some basics, Criminology 101 stuff, he asked about the suspects.

"The murder scene evidence points to an opportunistic crime of enragement," Bobbie said. "But I haven't found anyone who fits a crime of passion. Not a single person that I've talked to seemed at all excitable. Most just the opposite. Money, on the other hand, is possible, probably even likely. I don't think it's likely, but a power struggle with others in the Mafia is possible. One probable beneficiary of his death is Rowe Sanctuary, which is urgently trying to raise enough to buy several sections along the Platte near Kearney. Rowe urgently needs to acquire the land. So many farmers are moving to town because of the last few bad years, a lot of river-front land is being lost to developers." She paused while she pondered the money angle.

Any Nebraskan knew that *section* meant more-or-less a square mile of land, 640 acres, though the term was also used for the partial sections cut off by the river. The Nineteenth Century surveyors had marked the one mile grid all across the Great Plains. The roads and highways generally followed the old grid lines so Mid-westerners know compass directions and mileages. The surveyors were not paid for accuracy but by the mile. Roads often jog where the nineteenth century surveyors came to a grid point form several directions leaving more than one marker for the point.

"And whose career or job is on the line? Who would suffer most if Rowe lost that land?"

"Rowe's Director, Frank Armstrong. My guess is that his job wouldn't survive the non-acquisition of that land. He certainly knows how to move about Rowe without being seen. Like everyone there, he had the opportunity and offered no solid alibi, only his wife." She typed the notes into a spreadsheet as she talked to Beasley. "The only other money connection I've found leads to Eddie Stuart. He hoped to get money from the vic for the Kearney Youth Home. Tom Shirk saw what looked like blood on the steering wheel in Eddie's truck. Until we get a warrant or permission, we have no way to check it. Rumor has it that the vic often changed his will and that he planned to change it to give everything to Rowe."

"Okay, and what about power? You mentioned the mob connection. From the name I gather we have an Italian from New York."

"Not just Italian, Sicilian." Bobbie nodded. "I talked to two detectives in New York. They were both terrified of Paul Capodicasa. His wife said flat out that it had to have been a mob hit. On the other hand, the racketeering detective said he'd never heard of bludgeoning by the mob and he said my Paul Capodicasa was the cleaner of the two he followed. He was most concerned about the power struggle he saw coming rather than mob influence on the murder itself."

"Cleaner of the two? That's interesting."

"Yeah. He even thought my Capodicasa was a good guy, but he admitted this opinion was not widely shared."

"Okay, so what do you have left?"

"A bunch of the volunteers and employees at Rowe. Several of them had the opportunity, no alibi and acted guilty when I interviewed them." Bobbie mumbled the data to Al Beasley and made notes in her spreadsheet: Duane Mulcahy: Opportunity; no alibi offered. Bill Martinez: Messed up scene. Opportunity—maybe; only alibi is wife. Carole Sue Williams: Lied to me? Gut says she'd gladly have done it. Strong enough? Opportunity; no alibi offered. Some mob Rival (incl widow): Motive up the wazoo. Could they pull it off unnoticed? No specific perp known yet. Wrong MO.

Bobbie looked at the list. "Not many viable candidates. From it I get Director Armstrong or a mob or family hit as the most probable. Family, being part of a Mafia power struggle, not passion."

"Check them out, of course, but keep looking for other connections. What about the kid you're looking for?"

"He may be the key to understanding what happened. Worse, we *have* to find him for his own sake. If he's alive, he's probably in trouble." True to history, Beasley got Bobbie going in the right direction. At least it looked right now. She had a clear plan of where to spend her energy. She had to find Mikey.

Bobbie started to feel drowsy and was about to nod off as she reread the data. Ten hours did not seem like an unusually long day. She picked up her coffee cup and went for a refill, then decided to take a stroll outside to clear a headache, rare for her. Especially given all the little bruises and scratches from her swim. She walked around the county building and reveled in the cool clear evening.

As she passed the doors to the sheriff's garage directly under her office, she heard an engine running. Cars were running *inside* the closed garage. She ran to the man door expecting to find a suicide. She keyed in the combination and discovered two cruisers with engines running but no one in sight, either in or out of the cars. She pushed the buttons to open both overhead doors, shut off the engines and checked both trunks. No one. "If you want to kill yourself, you've got to stay in here with the carbon monoxide," she said to the empty room as she let out the breath she'd held for more than a minute. She shook her head. "Someone needs a lesson from the Hemlock Society." She made a much too ephemeral mental note to report the incident to the Sheriff.

"Hello Sheriff," Bobbie said to Buffalo County Sheriff Grayson, her boss. "I'm concerned that we've found no trace of the young man who accompanied Paul Capodicasa at the time of the murder. I think we should organize a search party for Mikey Ippolito. He has little outdoors experience, almost never been outside New York City. I plan to get some of the Rowe volunteers looking near the blind. Do you think we should get some local volunteers, like Boy Scouts, to start combing the fields around Rowe?"

"Bring me up to date on what's been done so far, Lee." Grayson's tone matched the formality of his words. Bobbie visualized him in a neatly pressed uniform with its brown pants a little too small. He loved sweets and it showed in his waistline.

"Yes, sir. We've had the plane up doing a FLIR search." The forward looking infrared camera on their plane would pick up any warm objects, like a live person, or one who recently died. "All the possibles we've seen were cows or deer. At first I thought the lack of IR sighting meant he'd fled the area, but the APB has found no trace and NYPD says he has not gotten back to New York City." Well, not actually the New York Police Department, but the victim's son. Chuck had assured her Mikey had not returned to The City. No corresponding word from Quinn or Pat. Too complicated to explain all that now.

"It'll be easy to get some searchers this time of year. I better run the plan past Petite so he doesn't feel left out." Sheriff *Madman* Grayson had no more use for the Buffalo County Attorney than Bobbie did. Uncle Mentes thought he should be the public face of any successful criminal prosecution so that he would get credit. Bobbie saw Grayson acting out the murder for the press, skulking up on an imaginary victim and bashing him the way he'd pound a fencepost with a sledgehammer.

"I'm going to get the Rowe people looking for him tomorrow, but if they don't find him and the APB doesn't get a hit, I thought we should try for a big crew on Saturday to search the fields. The murderer may have hurt him or he may have hid in the woods from the murderer and then wandered out into a field. Either way, we need to find him."

"Hmm. What's the chance he's involved in the murder?" Sounded like Grayson was trying to solve the puzzle himself.

"Eddie Stuart, he works with lots of troubled kids over at KYH, said he was quite sure Mikey could not be involved. He *was* worried about Mikey's safety."

"Sounds good. So what's the search area for tomorrow?" Bobbie saw Grayson acting out a Sherlock Holmesian search for TV cameras.

"Everywhere around the photo-blind. I planned to work out from it in all directions."

"Don't waste any time on the north side," Grayson said. "You proved he couldn't have crossed the river when you lost the wet suit. I'll get Scotty Leslie and..." Grayson paused and made thinking noises, "and someone to canoe downriver looking for him in or along the shores of the Platte."

"Good point, sir." Bobbie shivered. She hoped they would not get her dunking. They certainly would never receive the gawking-over Scotty had given her. "If Mikey Ippolito *is* in the river, I hope they can see him. It's so muddy. He'll be hard to see if he's caught under a tree the way I was."

"I'll make sure they check carefully. Are you sure Scouts will be okay on land? Do we need to get a SAR group?" Grayson's caricature led the Search and Rescue operation with a magnifying glass in his suit, power tie, and deerstalker hat.

"I think Scouts will be fine, sir." Bobbie suppressed the giggles from her Holmesian imagination. "We have a pretty good description of what he was wearing and a good picture of him. I only wanted them to search the fields. I guess the fields to the south down into Kearney county. My plan, with your approval of course, was to continue using the Rowe people and any deputies that show up for searching the riparian cotton-wood and underbrush scrub along the river, near the scene."

"Sounds like a plan." Sheriff Grayson sounded confident. He was competent, whether he acted out an event for the press or searched a field for clues. He would put 110% effort into helping. She knew Grayson would clear their search with Sheriff Brandon in Kearney County. Though similar to Grayson in stature and personality, she did not trust Uncle Mentes Petite. He was too antagonistic towards her and too intent on furthering his political career. If he needs to be informed, Grayson could do it. She did call Al Beasley, and let him know their search plan.

Chapter 12

A magnet will easily find your needle in a haystack.

Thursday, 6:50 P.M.

As Bobbie approached the Rowe entrance, the backup of cars waiting to enter the lot amazed her. Buzzards circled over the fields south of the river and only a few hundred yards west of the Visitor Center using the last hour of sunshine to look for a meal. Darth Vader directed the traffic into Rowe, talking to the drivers before pointing them into the Rowe parking area with his light saber. When she reached the gate, he motioned her through, but she stopped. "What do you ask them?" She pointed toward the cars in front of her.

This Vader was about six-foot-four in his cowboy boots. He was dressed in a black Stetson and black trench coat. "I make sure they have reservations for a blind. I check them off on the list and tell them where to meet their guide." He waved the clipboard in his left hand as he spoke. His right hand held a pen as well as his light saber.

Bobbie thanked him and parked her Explorer, the vehicle she preferred to drive at night. This time she went in correctly and parked properly. She still felt embarrassed at not deciphering the Rowe signs on Wednesday. *A cop turning the wrong way in a parking lot and going around the parking loop backwards.* She went to the main Nicolson Center entrance, which was almost impassable from the horde of bird watchers. She pushed through the crowd and saw a similar mob in the classroom where the cranecam video ran and a third flock in Cope Hall next to it. She turned and went past the *Staff Only* sign and checked for Duane and Frank. Neither were there. A few steps brought her to the breakroom door.

Bobbie saw a sign on the refrigerator with an inch tall headline, "Notice To Guides." She moved to read the memo, expecting it to relate to the murder. The print was quite large. "On all trips to the blinds, be sure to describe Rowe's desperate need to protect more habitat for the cranes, geese, ducks and other migratory birds. Encourage visitors to contribute to the Rowe Capital Fund for Protecting the Platte River. The very existence of our cranes and many other birds depends on this migra-tory stopover." It must have been covered by pictures or notes. No way she could have missed it the day before.

Rowe's finances seem to be perpetually in need of benefactors. She looked around the room and saw several people including Bill Martinez. "Hey, Bill. I'm looking for Frank Armstrong and Duane Mulcahy. Seen them recently?"

"I haven't seen Duane all afternoon, but Frank's around." He got up, coffee in hand and started toward the door. "I'll find him for you." Bill squeezed past Bobbie and started back toward the main part of the Center. His aroma of soap was unusual for a volunteer. He pointed into Frank's office. "If Frank was there and busy, his door would be shut. I'll be back in a minute." He pushed open the door to the main lobby and went out.

Bobbie followed through the door and watched as he checked the men's room, then walked toward the classroom with the large web cam monitor. He sipped coffee as he disappeared into the cranecam room. In a few seconds he reappeared from Cope Hall and came back toward her.

He shrugged as he passed her going back into the staff area and said, "Not there."

Bobbie followed him back through the door and watched as he quickly checked the East wing of the building. On his return from the storage rooms about 30 feet east of her, he stopped in the office next to Frank's. In a couple of seconds, he came out followed by a large woman. "He doesn't seem to be here, but Joanne should be able to help you locate him." Martinez took a sip of his coffee as he went back into the volunteers' breakroom, with the quick-breads and cookies provided by staff spouses.

"Come on in my office, Detective." Joanne had a husky voice and moved like so many obese people, more like a Pillsbury Dough Boy animation, than like ordinary walking. She was dressed in jeans that may have fit her a few sizes ago. She dialed the phone and looked up as Bobbie came into her office.

"Are you an employee?" Bobbie knew there were two employees she had yet to meet.

"No, no. I'm a volunteer." Joanne shook her head vigorously but kept the phone on her ear. "I work here for about six months each year, though, so I'm here quite a bit. I do the bookkeeping and lots of other work like that." She held up a finger and looked down at the phone.

"Hi, Kenda. This is Joanne. Is Frank there?" She listened a bit, thanked Kenda and hung up.

"Frank has a meeting tonight." Joanne started to pull a notebook out of the hutch on her desk. "He's probably trying to raise money for the Sanctuary, but whatever it is, we probably shouldn't interrupt him until either very late tonight or tomorrow morning. Let me see if I can reach Duane." She looked down at the cover of the notebook and started dialing the phone. She identified herself and asked for Duane. "Please tell him the detective wants to talk to him." She put her hand over the mouthpiece and looked at Bobbie. "Maybe we'll get lucky."

They talked about the wet weather as they waited. Finally, Joanne stopped and held up her index finger again and looked blankly at the phone. "Hey, Duane. Detective Bobbie Lee wants to talk to you." She handed the phone to Bobbie.

After the usual introduction and small talk Bobbie said, "I need some help. If Mikey Ippolito left Rowe, the APB or TV appeal should have found him by now. I need to organize as many of your volunteers as possible to see if we can find him tomorrow. I hope for a one or two day search, nothing more."

"We ought to be able to get quite a few people to help," Duane said in his unmistakeable down-under burr. "Is it okay if we start after about half eight?"

"*Half* eight, that's Adelaide for eight thirty? Yeah, that should be fine."

"Aussie for eight thirty, anyway. And that's as soon as it's fully light. As soon as the searchers will be able to work." He mumbled. Justifying his timing to her, not talking to himself. "Good." His voice had returned to normal. "Many potential searchers will be in the blinds till then anyway." She could see him, almost six feet tall, so slender his cheeks caved in, and dressed in the seemingly standard jeans and Rowe sweatshirt, but with his heavily-used leather jackaroo hat.

"Hmm," Bobbie said. "And as soon as we can search without disturbing the cranes, right?"

"True," Duane said. Bobbie could see him nodding pensively. "But it will only cost us a few minutes lost search time. We can't search in the dark."

"Right." Bobbie tried to assess how to get the most searching done. "I'll be back here by eight-thirty with Ruth's drawing of Mikey and descriptions of what he was last seen wearing so we can start briefing and organizing the searchers early."

"Yeah, no worries. I think that's the best we can do. I'll be there by then, too."

Bobbie wondered what would bring a person to Nebraska from Adelaide. "Thank you."

"Let me talk to Joanne," Duane said, "and I'll see if we can get some prep stuff done tonight."

"You've got it." Bobbie handed the phone back to Joanne. "He wants to talk to you."

After some conversation with Duane, she hung up. "I'll get the word out to as many people as I can so we have a good sized search crew tomorrow. Duane said to tell you to go home and get some rest. We'll do everything we can to get as many volunteers here by tomorrow at half past eight."

Bobbie felt skeptical. She worried they would not have enough people or time to find Mikey. The temperatures had been dropping below freezing at night; how long could the poor kid last?

Before she said anything Joanne spoke again. "Go on. Grab a glass of wine and a cookie in the breakroom and go home. We'll have a good crew here for you in the morning. I'll call the locals and Vivian will get the others."

Bobbie headed back to Kearney with a little more understanding of the operations at Rowe. While she was still on the unpaved V Road, her radio came to life. "Antelope County picked up a man on your APB. They've taken him into custody. Claims he is not Mikey Ippolito."

Antelope County? That was almost to the northeast corner of the state. Could Mikey have gotten all that way? And, even if he did, why? It's not on the way to anywhere. Disorientation and amnesia? Did they have the right guy?

The last time Bobbie had been in Antelope County, she had seen hundreds of 12 million year old fossilized animals trapped by the fallout of a Yellowstone super-volcano eruption. The visit showed many similarities between crime forensics and archeology. Even though it was a thousand miles away, the ash from the eruption had filled the air and covered the ground to a depth of several feet. She recalled seeing one of the largest collections of complete skeletons in the World: horses, rhinoceroses, camels and lots of smaller creatures. Birds were on the bottom, including a crane that is now only found in Africa.

Chapter 13

Try finding your needle in a needlestack

Friday, 8:28 A.M.

Bobbie Lee walked into the volunteer's breakroom in the Iain Nicolson Audubon Center at Rowe Sanctuary two minutes before her scheduled organizational meeting. She was surprised to see every seat filled and as many people standing as sitting—about 20 people, nearly everyone with a cup of coffee. The aroma of coffee overpowered that of sweat from the not-very-well-washed assemblage "Hi O'," she said to her fellow deputy whom she hadn't noticed at first. He was dressed in dungarees and work shoes, closer to the Rowe uniform than his deputy's. He looked ready to help.

Duane Mulcahy handed her a Rowe mug of coffee and said, "Some more volunteers will be available in an hour or so as they finish their guide work. I think only one more person is likely to come soon."

Bobbie thanked everyone for the early start. Following Beasley's suggestion, she began her briefing with a story. She was her own warm up man. "Last night as I returned to Kearney, I got a call from Antelope County for a hit on Mikey's APB. *Ah, no search necessary*, I thought. As I drove back to my office I marveled that Mikey could make it so far so quickly. By the time I called the deputy there, they had determined the man wasn't Mikey. Even though he matched Ruth's drawing, he had no tattoo and his alibi seemed plausible. They couldn't absolutely verify who the person they detained was, but we can be pretty sure we still need to search today. We've gotten no other hits on the APB, which should mean he has not used any public transportation."

Bobbie surveyed her eager-looking volunteers. "We're planning to have a really large search crew tomorrow, one that Sheriff Grayson is going to assemble." She taped a crude map of Rowe and the drawing of Mikey Ippolito to the refrigerator and wall. "If we're unsuccessful today, Sheriff Grayson's Boy Scouts will search the fields and easy areas like that." Bobbie pointed to the open fields on the map. "I hope you'll help search the areas near Mr. Capodicasa's blind, the ones that require better equipment, organization and a much more careful search. We'll start with the areas where the going will be tough"

Bobbie stepped next to the fridge and pointed to the picture. Another person walked into the meeting, following Duane' motions to a standing position in the southwest corner. "Our fear is that Mikey Ippolito may have fled your blind at the time of the murder and needs our help. Ruth Bingham drew this picture of Mikey for us after she talked to him on Tuesday. She also said he wore black and we didn't find any black clothes of his in the blind, so we can probably assume that's what he has on. The downside of his clothing is that Mikey will be hard to see. We're looking for a scared young man, dressed in dark clothes, perhaps with mud on them, hiding as best he can." Bobbie surveyed the searchers checking for understanding.

"Sheriff Grayson will have an aircraft with an infrared camera looking for anything warm. The negative results from yesterday's infrared survey mean we need to look under things where the aerial pictures can't see him."

"Do you think the killer could have gotten him too?" Duane Mulcahy stood near the door. He studied the picture of Mikey.

"Perhaps. But I'm most worried that he escaped the killer and isn't dressed for our cold, damp weather. If he ran off into the woods, he's likely to be in trouble. He's a city kid who already had a cold. Survival for more than a few days is a real issue, even with the kind of warm clothes that Mr. Capodicasa probably gave him." A few volunteers asked related and unrelated questions. Bobbie or Duane answered each. "Okay, let's go out and hope we find the man quickly."

As the search team prepared to leave the Center for their work, Bobbie reminded them, "Remember, if a person is scared and cold, he'll hide unbelievably well. We have to walk through the woods within arms length of each other and check under every bush and log. Make sure we don't miss him hiding in a hole or cowering under a leaf pile or branch. He may still think the killer is after him. One downed pilot in Bosnia hid for days as searchers passed within a few feet of him. Mikey may be as scared."

Duane held the main door to the Nicolson Center for the searchers as they left. Bobbie stood outside and thanked each one for his or her help.

"Shouldn't we also be checking the woods over there?" Bill Martinez pointed north, across the Platte.

"Yesterday I pretty well proved he has to be on this side of the Platte. I was dressed for swimming in the ice water when I tried to cross. He couldn't have been adequately protected against that cold. I didn't even come close to making it. Sheriff Grayson is going to have some Deputies canoeing downriver from the blind, searching in the water and along the riverbanks. It's hard to guess how far the river might have swept him by now if he did try to cross, so they'll probably be busy all day."

As the searchers neared the photo-blind where Paul Capodicasa had been murdered, Duane reminded the searchers, "Mikey was last seen wearing boots so we might find tracks to help localize the search. Also, his clothes were brown and black, so keep your eyes open for any dark bits of blood or fabric."

Bobbie looked into the photo-blind. Her flashlight showed a fairly clean interior. She was surprised at how neat it appeared and again was struck by its size, much smaller than a jail cell.

Duane arranged their 19 searchers in a line immediately south of the police-line-do-not-cross tape. They formed a row about 19 yards long. They moved south, scratching their way through the willows that were much taller than the searchers near the river. Fifty feet from the Platte the underbrush varied more, but was less dense and shorter. They checked everything until they reached the first corn field. Duane then turned the line around, and they searched the adjacent 19-yard swath back to the river, a yard east of the first search. He reminded his crew, "Talking may help Mikey find us, but be quiet from time to time so you'll hear him if he's moaning for help."

A Buffalo County Sheriff Office SUV with a canoe was on the path to the Capodicasa blind. Tom Shirk and Scotty Leslie walked around the area where she had started the searchers. "Hey, guys, got anything helpful for us?"

They both shook their heads. Tom inspected the ground around the blind. "I'm making one last check. No new trace of the kid. Mikey hasn't returned."

"Grayson got you two doing the search on the river?"

"Yeah, and we'll be starting in a couple of minutes." Tom straightened and looked at Bobbie. "As soon as we're done here."

She nodded and picked her way along the swath searched by her crew staying a short distance behind them, listening carefully for any sound Mikey might make. As the team made its 18 to 20 yard pass through the undergrowth, Bobbie put occasional pieces of yellow police-line-do-not-cross tape on the trees to mark sides of the searched section. "Thank goodness there's no poison ivy at this time of year. One little thing we don't have to worry about."

Duane nodded agreement. "I wouldn't be able to help much in the summer. I'm too allergic to that bloody American weed."

"You didn't grow up with it?" Bobbie looked at Duane. He shook his head. "Well, for what it's worth, we have three other plants with similar poisonous stuff: Poison oak, which I think of as a western version of poison ivy, poison sumac and poison tree. I think the poison tree only grows in south Florida."

"Australia has the world's most venomous animals, doesn't it? Don't you have your own wonderful toxic plants?"

"Not many. And I hope you keep them all." He looked disgusted with the topic.

The search party joked and gossiped about birds and the weather, surprising given the gruesome nature of the job they were starting. They seemed to view this more as a good excuse to spend a few hours in the woods, than as a search for a terrified kid.

Ella Mae, who had been the morning guide for the large blind closest to the murder scene, arrived at the second turn and joined the search. "Don't we need to check the fields?"

"It's not a high priority because the IR cameras should pick him up in the open. Also, we should have a much larger but less sophisticated teams of searchers tomorrow," Bobbie said. "I think the Boy Scouts will check amid the corn stubble as well as any group can. I don't really trust them to search the woods as thoroughly as you guys are doing now."

As the searchers approached the river the third time, Frank Armstrong called Bobbie to his end of the search line. "That looks like a Vibram sole print. You thought Mikey had new boots, right?" He pointed to a clear print on a little island hummock about a foot out in the river.

"That's what we think." Bobbie started putting crime scene tape around the area. She got out her kit, photographed the print, put a wood frame around it and mixed and poured dental stone into it. She didn't hear the conversation around her until the casting plaster was poured.

She studied the Platte. It was certainly not named for its character at this flooding time of year. A roiling, eddying mass of water. Nothing particularly flat about it.

Bobbie looked back at her setting boot-cast. "We're lucky this print happens to be out of the water."

"And away from where the searchers, cops and guides were walking because of those bushes." Duane waved at a clump of willows slowing erosion of the Platte's shore. Bobbie recalled when she'd slipped into the river on Wednesday afternoon and only encountered calf deep water. The Platte River had continued to rise. Now you'd have to wade more than knee deep in the Platte to walk around the north side of the blind.

She scanned the area. Surprising that any track was distinguishable amid all the other recent ones. She couldn't remember any signs of wear or cracks in the tread mark, but mud impressions are hard to read.

"Frank, why don't you keep looking along the bank for any other tracks. I have to stay here for about 45 minutes until my cast is dry."

They all agreed and continued their work. As Frank started walking west along the Platte, looking for prints, Bobbie called to him. "Frank, these fence posts don't look anywhere near strong enough to hold the blind in a high water. Have you lost any blinds during the Spring floods?" Bobbie referred to the principal spring floods from snow-melt, filling both the North and South Platte, and then the Platte all the way to the Missouri. Deep snow or a hot spring could raise the levels of all the rivers much higher than this flow from the lowering of Lake McConaughy.

"When they predict real flooding, we haul the photo-blinds back to the shop. They have to go in for maintenance every few years anyway."

While Bobbie watched her cast she wrote detailed notes about the work she'd done and the searching everyone was doing. When the searchers were out of sight and earshot, she measured the 107 feet to the blind and the seventeen inches to the Platte's edge, but always guarded the dental stone as it set. She mapped the location of the print in her note-book, labeled with her triangulation figures. The knew the print would not be very distinctive. Only old boots with cuts and cracks in the soles left truly unique tracks.

Without hope for quickly finding Mikey, Bobbie put her cast in an evidence bag and cornered Frank, Duane and O'Dell. "I'm going to try looking at the case from a different angle. If anyone finds anything, give me a call." She gave business cards to Duane and Frank and left to follow the money trail.

Chapter 14

Rowe's Survival

Friday, 3:15 P.M.

Bobbie Lee relaxed a little and started searching for information about Rowe Sanctuary and Frank Armstrong. According to Dun and Bradstreet, Rowe's finances were adequate, about par for a non-profit, donation-supported organization, not what the Notice to Guides implied. The income was meager but looked sufficient for ongoing expenses leaving little for expansion or protecting more habitat for the birds. Nothing unusual. D&B missed that Rowe, or was it Frank, was frantic to provide more space for the birds.

When she checked Frank's credit report, everything looked normal for someone who scraped by working for a non-profit. Google found several articles about his money-raising activities and news stories about his plans for Rowe. Most of the recent stories described his plans for a substantial expansion to permanently provide more habitat for the migrating birds, especially cranes, ducks and snow geese.

"There is an imminent need for expansion of the protected habitat." The *Kearney Courier* quoted the "Lillian Annette Rowe Audubon Sanctuary Director Franklin Armstrong," as saying. "Many of the older Nebraska farmers are quietly trying to sell their land because their kids have chosen less demanding jobs than farming. The low price of beef is aggravating their departure rate and encouraging Platte-side farmers to breakup and sell their developable land. Rowe Sanctuary is lucky that many farmers will give us sweetheart deals, but they cannot afford to donate their land. We have to buy it."

The article described how the cranes turned 1600 tons of wasted corn into fertilizer each year and eliminated the need for pre-emergent herbicides within a couple of miles of the Platte. It detailed the economic benefit from the thousands of spring visitors to the Big Bend of the Platte. "Even though sandhill cranes are not named for the Sandhill region of Nebraska and are not an endangered species, they are one of the oldest birds in the world," the article intoned. "Cranes were common in what is now Nebraska 12 million years ago, as shown by the fossils at Ashfall." *Come on. Interesting, but none of this is important. I've got to focus on the case.*

She couldn't find any motivation. She needed to bounce some ideas around. Lucky for her she reached retired Sheriff Beasley on her first call, to his old office. She asked if she could see him in 30 minutes. He agreed and she left for a leisurely drive to Minden. Time to think about the murder. She went straight south out of Buffalo County into Kearney County then east on unpaved farm roads. She relaxed on the drive, except for two puddles she powered past so the car wouldn't wallow in the mud. Maybe she should have driven the Explorer instead of the Crown Vic, or even one of the newer Chargers. Nah, none were as comfortable.

She tried to pay attention to the birds and wondered how many more she missed. How many would an ardent bird watcher see? When she passed a pond with a couple dozen ducks and geese, she realized that someone like the victim or the Rowe volunteers would probably identify each one. These guys were just BBJs, big brown jobs, except for two white geese, snow geese to her.

She pulled into a parking slot on the north side of the Kearney County Municipal Building, facing the Minden Opera House. "Hostetlers 1881 Opera House" was carved in a large white stone at the top of the red brick facade. If the murderer was as incongruous as an opera house in Central Nebraska, they should be able to pick him out easily.

She walked past the Kearney County WWI Veterans Memorial with its "water not drinkable" fountain and into the imposing Courthouse. The massive granite building topped by a white dome was as unusual as the opera house. Neither one seemed to make any sense in this agricultural town of about 3000 people in a county of only 7000. They were magnificent, enduring monuments to the wealth and culture that Kearney County once had, a bit of history the City of Kearney apparently lacked, even though the city was now much more prosperous.

She went upstairs to Al Beasley's office in the musty-smelling Courthouse. Al was seated with his feet up on the old oak desk reading *Farm Journal.* Bobbie started with small talk about the Husker's basketball season. He looked relaxed. "Retirement certainly seems to agree with you," she said.

"Gardening is much better for the body and soul than politicking."

"I'll bet it's also much better for the soles." Bobbie pointed at his shoes.

"Okay what's your problem with the murder investigation?" He surprised her with the abrupt change of topic to the one she came for.

She described the credit reports. "My initial top suspects included Rowe Director Frank Armstrong because of the benefit Rowe should expect from Capodicasa's estate. The Sanctuary is desperate to acquire several sections along the Platte. As the possibility of development looms, Armstrong has some motivation to hasten the endowment from Capodicasa."

"That sounds pretty tenuous to me. Is there any reason to think Armstrong expected *he* would benefit from the estate himself? Would he be absolutely sure that Rowe would benefit?"

"Tenuous is putting it mildly. I need to determine how voluble Capodicasa was. He might have promised Armstrong something or Armstrong might think he'd been given a promise, even if it isn't in his will. I haven't heard of anything like that. I should be able to get a peek at the will." Mrs. Capodicasa would probably make it available.

"Who else you got?"

"Well, the other big possible money swing is to or from Eddie Stuart's favorite org, the Kearney Youth Home. I forget who, but someone told me Capodicasa was about to cut KYH from his will and give it all to Rowe."

"Remember, Bobbie, in a case like this it doesn't matter what the will says. It only matters what the perp thinks it says."

"Yes." Could anyone be so gullible as to say to another, *I'll give you a million when I die.* It does provide an incentive to kill. Much better would be to put it in the will and tell people the opposite. Especially for someone in the mob. Pay them well and tell them when you die, their income is gone. Was Capodicasa a clever or devious enough braggart to fabricate like that?

"You've got to follow the money trail. Not the real one, but the one people believe is real." Beasley looked at her sternly, but Bobbie hardly noticed and ignored the lecturing glare. "Remember reading about the Clutter murders down in Holcomb, Kansas, in '59? Hickock and Smith thought they'd find a ton of money, but there wasn't any. In fact the lack of money may have contributed to the violence of the perps' actions. They killed because they expected money, not because they found it."

"Yeah. Yeah." Bobbie rubbed her holster. "Any ideas on how to learn what people think?"

"Has anything been released about the will?"

"No, not that I've heard of, anyway. It's awfully soon for anything."

"Ask people what they think will happen to his estate. You can see how it varies from person to person and you should be able to learn how close their opinions are to the reality of the will. Once it's released, you'll never know what people thought at the time of the murder. Find anyone who might benefit from his death. So far, I can't see anything close to a motive for murder in any of this."

Bobbie nodded and wrote herself a to-do list.

"I think your real problem is to follow up on Mrs. Capodicasa's fear. You seem to have stopped checking Mafia connections completely." Beasley leaned back in his chair and put an index finger on his chin.

"The one mob cop I talked to in New York wasn't convinced that Capodicasa was in the mob. He seemed to think the vic was clean. I'll follow up on that idea, though. Also, the way I read Chuck Capodicasa, the vic's son, there's no way the Mafia is involved."

She added, "Check Mafia connection both with Quinn McKay and Chuck Capodicasa" and "Watch butt" to her to-do list. Calling Quinn at the NYPD and talking to Chuck should be fun.

Chapter 15

Fabio

Friday, 6:30 P.M.

Bobbie Lee stepped into the shower and thought about her date. Tall, dark and Sicilian—close to a girl's ideal—and suave, rich and maybe in the mob—nothing more for a cop to want. Chuck showed no evidence of recent wedding band wear, but the class ring could hide the mark from one. She wondered what he planned. Kearney didn't have much beyond his motel room. A romp in the sack with Chuck wouldn't be all bad. Hell a romp with any guy would be good right now. Maybe she could be the dumb blonde with a minor witness, but not with her sheriff and not with the victim's son.

Bobbie had to learn about mob connections and about this Fabio. He had dismissed mob action, but what about him and his family? Would Chuck confirm Quinn's background on Rowe's Paul Capodicasa. If he contradicted it, she'd know a lot more about him. What about his treatment of women? Of course, abusive men often hide their abuse from the law so the lack of record was certainly no assurance of good behavior.

Her cowboy boots provided space for her Ruger LCP pistol and her bra hid a shiv. From Quinn's guess and her own analysis, Chuck Capodicasa seemed to be a gentleman. She should not need any weapons. They were more for her detective paranoia than defense.

In addition, she protected herself and her privacy by meeting Chuck at the Sheriff's office in Kearney, diagonally across town from her apartment. He could probably learn where she lived, but not easily.

She drove the ten minutes to the Sheriff's Department. How can she pry reliable information from Chuck about the mob connection?

She found no messages in her office, so she went back to the County Building lobby in time to see a black Lexus sedan park in front.

"Your yacht awaits, mademoiselle." He opened the door of his rental for her. "Is there someplace you can suggest? The only place I know is Gusto di Napoli."

"I'd love Gusto di Napoli. It's not one of my usual diners—cop's don't make enough." She wished she had a nicer wrap. She hoped Chuck did not find it as ugly as a Mae West.

Before their entrées came, Chuck asked about her name.

"Actually my name *is* Bobbie. It's not a nickname or anything else. I think my father wanted a boy, so he gave me a boy's name. In fact, the way he tells it, he told the nurse *Bobbie* meaning *Roberta,* and never noticed when the nurse put down exactly what he said on the birth certificate."

She paused while their entrées were served. "And what about you? Is Chuck short for Charles?"

"Yes. Charles must have been popular 40 years ago, because I had a couple of classmate Charleses in first grade. I think 'Chuck' was easier for the teachers so I've been Chuck as long as I can remember. When I first went to St. Lawrence, I told people I was Charles because I thought it sounded more mature. It didn't last. I especially didn't like the French pronunciation with an sh sound instead of ch. After a couple of weeks in French classes, I told everyone my name was *Chuck.*"

"Cute story. This afternoon you said you were sure your mother was mistaken about Mafia connection to your father's death. Can you tell me why?" She had finished about half of her dinner so she studied him while he responded.

"You've read enough novels and seen enough movies to know the mob was brought to New York by Sicilian emigrants. Mama does have a number of relatives who are inside, but no one in our family has any connection to the House and no one on Dad's side of the family has any connection that I know of. I've heard stories about being able to get cars for practically nothing. By the time I was old enough to fantasize having my own car, I knew I couldn't afford to take a free one from Uncle Marco. Actually, the scariest story I heard concerned someone complaining to Uncle Marco about being cheated on some business deal. I'd guess there was no cheating, only an insult or something like that. Anyway, the guy apparently whined to Uncle Marco. 'I hope that bastard Carl's house burns down.' A week later it did."

"So why was your Mama so sure the murder had been mob action? Why are you so sure she overreacted?"

"In her family's world, murders are never random and any death that isn't with a doctor at bedside and at an old age isn't either. She's sweet and wonderful and was a great mom and is a great grandmom. But she does have a blind spot for La Casa Nostra. She had a brother who died when his car skidded on ice and rolled into the Hudson River. I'm sure she still thinks that some enemy of Poppop orchestrated his murder. By the same reasoning, she'll never completely believe Dad's death wasn't murder by some Sicilian connection." Chuck frowned a little and seemed to study the table cloth.

"Do you know why the detectives I talked to in New York seemed so scared of your father?"

Chuck still frowned at the table, now cleared of their dishes. He looked up and met her eyes. "Dad has often been hassled by the NYPD. To make matters worse, there's another Paul Capodicasa, Short Paul, who is no relation to us. He survived an assassination attempt when I was in college and has probably meted out some revenge. We have many common friends and business associates and the police have seen many coincidences, like one Mafia hit being right outside Dad's first restaurant. Some guys in NYPD will never believe Dad is really clean." Chuck hesitated and rubbed his forehead. Bobbie waited to see if he'd elaborate. She wondered if Paul Valentino was persecuted by the New York City Police Department.

According to the history on the menu, he'd brought his training and recipes from New York City. She thought about Tall Paul Capodicasa and Mafioso Short Paul Capodicasa, and decided that Paul Valentino must be Round Paul.

"That's probably claiming too much. No businessman is a saint. Nobody in the restaurant business in Manhattan, or at least no Italian, can be completely clean, completely free from mob connections. I'm sure he's been mixed up with or contacted by the mob at times, but I'm sure the only contacts would have been minor extortion. Like insistence that he pay them for protection and things like that. At times, no small business could operate in The City without Mafia *protection.*" He shook his head, but offered no more for many seconds.

He brightened and looked up at Bobbie. "Why don't we try Tiramisu for dessert? It was Dad's favorite here."

Bobbie put her hand to her throat to see if she could feel her heart pounding. Did it show? She wanted to jump into Chuck's lap. "Sounds right." Her voice sounded normal, to her. She hoped it was not the squeaky one in her head.

Round Paul came into their private dinning area. *How'd he know we're ready for dessert?* How had Chuck signaled him? Had he been given some sort of signal or sign? Round Paul Valentino was the image of a successful Italian restauranteur. Medium height, borderline obese, dark hair and complexion, perpetual smile, and his clothes are permeated by the cloying aroma of fresh-baked pastry and the savory one of marinara sauce.

"We'd like two Tiramisu and a bottle of your Alzeyer Rotenfels Riesling Eiswein."

Round Paul nodded and retreated. "Good pairing, sir. A memorial for Paul? We'd been saving it for your father. I'm sure he'd approve of using it on this sad occasion."

Chuck looked at the table and rubbed his forehead, probably to hide his moist eyes. In a few seconds he looked up. "Bobbie, you look confused."

"Yep. What's ice vine?"

"Eiswein is a sweet wine, invented by the Germans, that will be perfect with our dessert. The evening has been fun, so I thought we should finish with the best." His smile amplified how wonderful the evening felt. "The name means ice wine. The grapes are not picked until after the first frost and they're picked while still frozen when they have the most sugar. It yields a delectable dessert wine."

Bobbie was surprised how well the sweet white wine complemented the Tiramisu on Gusto di Napoli's striking red dessert plates. "I haven't had a sweet wine in years. I was really skeptical when you described it, but it's wonderful, like everything." She was interrupted by a phone ringing.

"Excuse me, I forgot to shut off my phone." He turned it screen-up. "Uh oh, I better see what my daughter wants." He hello-ed and listened. "Damn. Everything always happens at once. I've come out to Nebraska to see about Dad. In fact, right now, I'm at a meeting with the detective. If your mother can't help, my Mama certainly will get carried away and help, probably more than you want." He talked a little more, goodbyed and hung up.

"If the old saw is true, something else bad is due. That was number two. Somebody tried to attack Nicola. She was not hurt, but it was only her fast unlocking of their apartment door and her security behind it that saved her. She described a creepy guy following her. When she ducked into her flat, he actually pounded on the door trying to get in."

What was it with the Capodicasa family. Two attacks in a week? "Rape is so horrible." The chill mad Bobbie's stomach muscles spasm, and she felt a headache starting and banished her own story from her mind. She shook her head and looked down at her clenched fists. "So often the cops blame the victim instead of sympathizing. She probably needs a shoulder to cry on and an ear to bend more than anything."

"Yes, and probably a female one. She and I are close, but this is the sort of thing I cannot possibly identify with. At least not as much as she needs."

Chuck looked up at her, his eyes clearing. "I cannot do anything more now and probably couldn't do anything more even if I were there." He nodded decisively.

After dinner, he took her back to the Sheriff's Office. She had to learn more about him.

Chapter 16

Hi, Mom

Saturday, 7:40 A.M.

Bobbie looked at the clock and gasped. She was supposed to be at Rowe in 35 minutes. She showered, put out breakfast for her overly protective Pomeranian, Bear. She drove east on I-80 at about 95. She could slow down. This wasn't such a big deal. A few minutes late wouldn't bother anyone. Yeah, but would Madman Grayson think it's okay to be late? He was bound to be there giving electioneering and pep talk to the searchers and press. Damn. And obnoxious uncle and new County Attorney Mentes. He would be there. Uncle Mentes had gone ballistic when she stopped him two days after he was elected. Hell, he even blew his top at Bobbie for a six months old parking ticket she hadn't issued.

Family rumors attributed the meanest actions to him. Some even blamed him for his father's suicide. Bobbie knew all the stories and had too many of her own. She had tried to suppress the most personal ones. He also volunteered at the Kearney Youth Home where he helped troubled teens find their way and often helped the KYH financially. She had long visualized him as an angel with horns and fangs.

She called Sheriff Grayson to tell him where to find the search-area map and other materials he'd need for briefing the Boy Scouts, in case he wanted to start right away. She did not apologize or give any indication that anything was unusual or that she expected to be late.

As she pulled into Rowe Sanctuary, she saw two school buses. Either Grayson had been extraordinarily successful at rounding up people, or Rowe was having a great season. She parked and went toward the Nicolson Center, where Leon Grayson worked the crowd in the parking lot. Actually he performed for the adults in a ritual of talking to their kids that reminded Bobbie of politicians kissing babies. When she started making her way through the throng, he quieted the 75 or so people, mostly Boy Scouts and Scout leaders in uniform. He introduced Bobbie. She walked to the easel where the map was propped—her nervousness at addressing such a large group made her headache disappear. At least that meant it wasn't a hangover.

When the Scouts left to search the fields near the photo-blind, Bobbie went into the volunteer's breakroom and found twenty people waiting for her. Most faces were familiar. "We thought we'd wait so we don't overlap with the other groups," Duane said. "Where should we search today?"

"Thank you for showing up again. We need to continue yesterday's search. Sheriff Grayson will have the Scouts going through the cornfields to the south of our area and Deputies Shirk and Leslie will continue their search in the river. I'd like most of you to continue widening the search in the woods and underbrush. A few of us will search the woods near the blind again, in case Mikey moved during the night."

Today Shirk and Leslie would start at Route 10 or Warp Drive, the next bridge upstream from Rowe and look for any trace that Mikey might have been there. Sheriff Grayson had asked the Corps of Engineers about stopping the release of water from McConaughy to lower the river for the search. They'd pointed out that it would take a long time for the lowering to have much effect at Rowe, more than a hundred miles downstream. He did not press the issue because the searchers might still find Mikey. Hiding somewhere around Rowe. Dead in the river. Back in New York or on his way there.

Soon the Rowe volunteers, joined by three more of Sheriff Grayson's deputies and seven cops from Kearney, set off to scour more of Rowe Sanctuary's woods. After an hour in the woods, the Troop Leaders and Scouts described their wonderful finds: several badly decomposed rodents and a wedding ring. "The ring should make the farmer glad we came out here looking," one scout leader told Bobbie.

On the third turning around in the field, Carole Sue Williams drove up on a Rowe ATV. Its trailer was filled with thermoses, cups, cookies and breads. "Perfect timing," Carole Sue said. "Hoped you'd be where I would find you but no Scouts. Got coffee and cocoa to warm you. Keep you going. Some bread and cookies, baked last night. My recommendation: the bread Kenda baked." Carole Sue pointed to a large-casserole-size plastic container full of quick bread. Looked like carrot bread and zucchini bread. "Even without the chocolate chips it's good enough to kill for. And better with them." She licked her lips and spoke the last sentences with more passion than Bobbie had heard before.

Everyone thanked her and grabbed a half-slice or two of bread. Carole Sue took one of the two garbage cans off the trailer, put a piece of wood on it. Most members of the crew took a cup of coffee. "Save your cups." Carole Sue took a box of pens from the trailer and put it on the ersatz table. "Stow your cups here if you like. Gonna take some goodies to the Scouts. I'll be by again in little while so you can get a refill."

Bobbie squatted and looked at the search map. The only trace they'd located was one boot print. She would have to talk to Chuck, because he might know where Mikey got his gear. If Paul was as generous as Chuck, then he would have bought Mikey's gear for him. She took another sip of coffee, emptying her first cup.

"Ms. Lee?" Bobbie looked up to see a woman in stylish clothes, heels and other accouterments of cities not sanctuaries. She looked to be fiftyish and had a Mediterranean complexion like Chuck's.

Bobbie stood quickly. "Yes, I'm Deputy Lee. May I help you?"

"I was told you were in charge of the search for my son. How can I help? I have to do something. I got here as fast as I could."

Damn. Bobbie had forgotten to call her. Hadn't even tried to contact her. "Oh. What's your name?" Bobbie held out her hand. She studied the woman the way she watched people she interrogated. Too much makeup. Trying to hide something.

"Oh. Excuse me. I'm Martha Ippolito, Mikey Ippolito's mother." They shook hands. The size 12 woman did not look much like Mikey. She was darkly complected with black hair, like most of the Italians Bobbie knew. Her hair was curly, in a way that must have been done by a salon, not her genes.

Chuck must have given her the word that Mikey was missing. "We're doing as much as we can out here. Where'd you come in from?"

"From Little Italy. They sent us all over the place. We went through both Chicago and Denver." Martha stood on a rocky bump in the terrain that kept her shoes out of the mud. It was hard enough that her heels didn't sink in.

The Capodicasa's were from Little Italy, Manhattan, so that must be where she's from. "Basically, we've found nothing so far. If he'd been killed when Mr. Capodicasa was, I think we'd have found him, so we think he's alive but terrified of the perp and hiding from him." Bobbie bit her lip and wished she had used euphemisms.

"We have about a hundred people out today—75 Scouts searching the corn fields and a couple dozen Rowe volunteers, deputies and cops searching the woods and river for the second day." She pointed to the group of Scouts who were visible several hundred yards to the west and waved an arc indicating the Rowe-cop search team. "We also have a canoe on the river and a plane with an infrared camera, which should find anyone in the open. Because the FLIR plane didn't find him, he must have hidden himself very well." Bobbie stopped her description abruptly. No need to tell her a body in the Platte would cool so off fast it would not show in infrared.

"Just a sec." Bobbie held up her hand.

She turned to the searchers. "Frank, O'. Can you start the next search? I'll catch up as soon as I can. I need to talk to Mrs. Ippolito." Bobbie watched as Frank started organizing his line of searchers.

"What can I do?" Ms. Ippolito had a large ornate cross on a silver chain around her neck and understated earrings. Her fake fur coat had a stylish cut and watery eyes showed behind her tinted glasses.

"Do you know what size boot your son wears? What kind of boots he brought?"

Martha looked on the verge of breaking down. "He doesn't have boots. He only wears Air Jordan Nike's. Size twelve." She started crying and fell onto Bobbie's shoulder. "You've got to find him. He's got to be okay. He's worn nothing but Mikey's shoes for years, out of loyalty for the name, I think." Martha shook her head and clutched her purse so tightly her hands blanched. "Wait a minute. You may be right. I think I did see some new boots with the stuff he packed for his trip."

Bobbie wished she had a chaplain or priest. How should she have handled a distraught mother? "If you just got here, that means you must have gotten up very early this morning, right?"

"Yes," Martha said, "I had to get up at 2:30 to catch my flight. I must look terrible. Thank God Anthony is not here. He'd kill me for looking like this."

Well, her eyes were red, as though you've been crying since 2:30, or 12:30 Central time. "No you look fine, maybe a little tired. You probably could use some rest."

Should Bobbie have tried to keep Martha busy? At least that would have taken her mind off the more macabre possibilities. So far Bobbie's big mouth had only made things worse. "We found a boot print that looked like size twelve or so to me. Can you think of anybody who might know what type of boots he brought? Do you think Mr. Capodicasa bought Mikey some boots? Could you make some calls for me to check that out?" Bobbie patted Ms. Ippolito on the back. She noticed a lavender scent, like she'd expect from expensive soap or cheap perfume.

Martha stood up straight and started fumbling in her huge fake-leather purse. She pulled out a small phone and stared at it crying. "Mikey gave me the iPhone. Must've saved for months to buy it." She stared at its screen. She poked it with her index finger a number of times then held it for Bobbie to see a picture of Mikey.

"Thank you for showing me the photo. One of the volunteers here at Rowe drew a picture so everyone would know who they were looking for. Her drawing *is* very good." Bobbie realized that she ought to give Ruth's picture to Martha. "I'll try to get the drawing back. Sheriff Grayson used it when he talked to the media about our search. If I can get it, it's yours." Bobbie frowned. How much and what should she relate?

"We did put out an APB. Sheriff Grayson and County Attorney Petite made appeals on television for Mikey." Bobbie tried to look as sympathetic as possible, not one of her strengths. She felt cramps in her stomach. She didn't have the right thing to say or do.

Martha Ippolito thanked Bobbie. She pointed to the iPhone that Bobbie had returned. "He preloaded it with photos of all of the family. He was a perfect son." She sobbed. "He taught me how to use my computer and always fixed things when I messed them up."

"I'm not very good at helping, Ms. Ippolito. May I get a priest or chaplain for you?"

"Thank you. I guess a priest might help."

"Okay, let me get you someone." Bobbie took out her own phone and dialed her mentor, Al Beasley. "Hey Al, we need a priest or chaplain. Preferably a priest. Can you find someone to come in and help Mikey Ippolito's mother? She arrived a few minutes ago and needs sympathy, not me."

In a moment she hung up. "An old friend is going to try to get a priest. I'll do everything I can, but that means working out here." Bobbie pointed to the fields and woods. "The priest should help. You need someone to talk to more than anything, don't you think?"

"Yes, Detective. Thank you. I think that'll help." Her taut jaw muscles showed in her round face in a way that said she tried to control her crying.

"Martha, call me *Bobbie*. I'm Bobbie Lee. I think the best help I can offer is ensuring we're doing the best search we can. I'm not much good at comforting people—cops usually aren't."

"Yes, thank you, Bobbie. I didn't mean to be such a cry-baby. I was determined not to let this happen." Martha snuffled and stifled another sob. "I'm not very good at being a stoic New Yorker, am I?"

"You're doing fine, Martha. No one could do better. I can't begin to feel the anguish a mother must feel." Bobbie continued comforting her.

When her phone beeped, Bobbie talked for a moment. "Sheriff Beasley found a priest who's on the way. Why don't you go back to the Visitor's Center to meet him." Bobbie pointed toward Nicolson, a third of a mile east. "Actually, wait a minute. Let me go with you and I'll get you Ms. Capodicasa's number. She may be able to help you find out if Mr. Capodicasa bought Mikey some boots for this trip."

"Oh. I know you're right," Martha said. "I remember that Mr. Capodicasa said that Mikey didn't have to worry about bringing anything. He said he'd help him and they went shopping a few weeks ago. Mikey told me about it. He was so excited. That's right, I remember now. He said Paul had gotten the boots for him when he was packing."

Bobbie nodded and retrieved Sophie Capodicasa's number. "Here's is Ms. Capodicasa's number: 212..."

"Thank you." Martha spoke softly as she interrupted Bobbie. "I have her number in my phone. The Capodicasas are old friends. They're our neighbors, several floors above us." Martha turned to walk back to the

Iain Nicolson Visitor Center with the phone to her ear and holding onto Bobbie's arm. She cried as she left a message.

"I hope Ms. Capodicasa can tell you exactly where he got the boots."

"I'll be sure to ask her when she calls back," Martha said.

"Then we can ask the store for the exact type of soles Mikey had."

Bobbie steadied Martha and guided her away from the muddiest spots on the trail. "If you want, I'll find someone to stay with you until the priest arrives."

"Thank you, Bobbie. You're a dear."

Bobbie answered her phone to a return call from Al Beasley. She was no closer to finding Mikey or the perp, but was delighted to find Ruth in the Gift Shop. The perfect shoulder for Martha until the Father Ed Miller got there. Bobbie could get back to her important tasks.

Chapter 17

Always Tell the Truth

Saturday, 7:30 P.M.

Bobbie Lee picked up a romance she'd bought at IGA a week before, and looked at the cover model. Chuck must have looked like him a few years ago. She tried to read but kept getting cramps in her abs from working on a case with Mentes. She would have to work with the creep. The only bright spot was the promise of a good dinner with Chuck.

Chuck seemed antsy about something from the moment he picked Bobbie up at her office. Seeing his agitation started her head throbbing. After they were seated but before Round Paul asked about drinks or appetizers, Chuck spoke. "I haven't been able to learn anything about Mikey. No one's seen him. I'm pretty sure he couldn't have gone back to The City." He looked at the tablecloth and shook his head.

"His mother arrived here today." Bobbie shook her head as she wished she'd been better prepared to help Martha Ippolito. I wish I had more skill dealing with people. I did get her a priest, but it seems like I should have been able to do more for her."

"I think a priest is perfect," he said. "I see her in church every Sunday and I think she often goes during the week as well."

"Oh, good. Thank you. It's nice to know I guessed right." Bobbie scratched at the napkin under her water goblet. "About all I did when she came to Rowe today was keep my feet in my mouth. I was really gauche." She ground her fists into her stomach to quiet her cramps.

"You couldn't be gauche even if you wanted to." Chuck frowned and shook his head. "Did she join the search?"

"No. She had no clothes for that. She was still in heels. I sent her to try to find out what kind of boots your father bought Mikey. Martha felt sure Mikey's new gear included boots."

"Sounds like Dad." Chuck's voice cracked. He squeezed his temples.

"I need to find out exactly what kind. Is there a specific store where he would have bought them?"

"I suspect so. He tends to be very loyal. Mama'll know." Chuck texted his mother for the information. Bobbie thanked him for his assistance.

"The psychological strain of an attempted assault is severe. How is Nicola doing?" Bobbie's cramps became worse as she contemplated Nicola's escape.

"She's okay as far as I've heard. Her mother says she's fine." Chuck shook his head and shoulders.

"When you get back to New York, keep close tabs on her. Make sure her mother knows there are others to help Nicola. The effects of an assault are likely to increase over time. I know. I've been there." Bobbie's cramps started easing.

"You've been there? What happened to you?" Chuck studied Bobbie. His concern seemed completely genuine.

"When I was a teenager, I was raped."

Chuck slowly shook his head. "Oh my God." He spoke distinctly, staccato.

"Yeah, it's horrible. It's made it harder for me to relate to men." She mustered her most questioning expression as she looked at him.

"Thank you. I'm beginning to sense something special." He squeezed her right hand and soothed the back with his thumb.

"If I do something weird, please let me know so I can correct it." She looked into his beautiful brown eyes. She studied the symmetry of his face, the characteristic that made her think he could be a model. She realized her eyes were getting wet so she looked back down at her wine.

Chuck nodded. "Rape is so horrible." He seemed to want to wait much longer but thought a long pause would be a strain. "You may be surprised, but I actually feel at a loss for words."

"I understand. This is not a great dinner conversation topic. I wanted you to know you had a friend here who *may* be able to help you understand your daughter."

"Thank you. May I let Nicola and her mother know about you?"

"Yes. But what we really need is to find Mikey. At least I have not found anything that remotely looks like motive for murdering your father. Do you have any speculation you'd care to share?"

"No. I've come up with a big zero." He pounded his fist in his hand.

Chapter 18

Rapist Mentes Petite

23 Years Earlier

Bobbie Lee got in Mentes Petite's car. He was ashamed of the twelve-year old red Dart, but at least it had no dents and the scratches had rusted so they barely showed. He hoped that it was as clean as any of those from her high school friends, even if it was older than theirs. It would be a year or two before he could afford a new one. As soon as her legs were inside, he closed the door. Nice legs.

"So what's this new rifle I hear you got?" Bobbie barely turned her head as she spoke. "Sounded impressive."

"Yeah. Great Christmas present. A left-handed Ruger M77 .300 with a Nikon scope." Mentes couldn't recall the scope's model.

"Must've been expensive. Who gave it to you?"

"Mom and Dad. I'll bet Dad wrote it off on his taxes. That'd help quite a bit."

"I'm sure it's beautiful. I'd love to see it."

"Deal. You can even shoot it. I made a range at the farm." At the Petites', Mentes jumped out and ran to open Bobbie's door. She was already out when he got around the car. Damn. The view would have been nice. Still not bad.

As they walked toward the house, he put his arm around her. "You smell nice. Is it a spice?"

"Yes. Thank you. It's from potpourri." Bobbie stood straight.

Mentes could only feel her hip and shoulder. He dropped his hand and opened the door to his one-room loft. Her tight ass went up the stairs three steps ahead of him. What a cute butt. "The Ruger is the cabinet to your right."

She turned at the top of the stairs and was stroking the rifle when he came into his room. He stood behind her. He looked around his loft. It was clean and neat and the red slip cover on the couch went nicely with the multicolor curtains. He put his arms around her. She leaned into him.

"Great action. Want to check it out?"

Bobbie picked up the rifle and spun it around so the barrel was pointed down and away from them. Mentes kept his arms around her. She reached over the stock, pulled back the bolt, glanced in the breach then clumsily drove the bolt home. "Wow. Really awkward for me with the bolt on the left. Excellent balance and heft. A lot lighter than mine. "

"It's all in the hands of the user." Mentes took the gun from her and laid it on the rack. He slid his right hand up to her breast. She didn't resist when he turned her around to hug her, holding onto that cute butt with both hands. They kissed in a way he was sure was new to her: mouths, tongues, bodies. He pushed her on his bed.

"No. No." Bobbie's voice was far away.

"You'll love it." Mentes pushed her skirt away and pulled her panties down. *I can't stop now, anyway.* He drove into her. "You're so nice and tight." She tried to get up, but he held her down by both shoulders.

Bobbie cried. Her "nos" were far apart. Mentes timed his thrusts to them. He finished and collapsed on her. He did not let her up or withdraw. She was quiet except for slight periodic spasms. She had loved it. She tried to rise again, but he was not ready to finish.

"Twice is better." He knelt, lifting her butt onto his thighs so he was still inside her and opened her blouse.

"No. No." Her voice was so far away some part of him wondered who talked. She was telling him not to stop. No stopping.

He pulled her bra off and started massaging. Much firmer than older big-titted girls in Lincoln. As he came back to life, Mentes started again. This time it would last longer. Better for both of them. He kept rhythm with her body. *She's really grooving with me.*

At the second climax he again collapsed on top of her and held her. Girls don't like fast withdrawal. After several minutes he rolled to the side. *She's crying with joy.*

"Please take me home." She pulled her clothes back into position with her free left hand.

"Don't you want to try the Ruger?" He stood.

"Take me home. *Now.*" She pulled her bra into approximate position but didn't rehook it, and buttoned her blouse. She pulled her panties back on and tried to smooth her skirt. "Look what you've done to me." She pointed to some blood on the yellow print skirt.

"You can clean up here." He finished buckling his belt and pointed to the bathroom door. "Oh. You're having your period."

"Take me home." She headed for the door. Her voice trailed into a mumble. "You're a beast. It's not my period. That was a couple of weeks ago."

Chapter 19

Never Tell the Whole Truth

Sunday, 9:30 A.M.

Bobbie Lee had knots in her stomach. The worst since she'd taken her first rescue tests at the State Patrol Academy. Worry about dragging a 200 pound dummy a hundred feet was nothing compared to telling a mother her son was lost. Not just missing, but lost.

Should she say he might be dead? She nearly threw up at the prospect of giving Martha that news. He might have amnesia and be almost anywhere, terrified that the killer will come after him. She rubbed her forehead. How could she dispel the headache from that thought. Mikey could be hiding in the woods, far from Rowe where they would never find him—he'd have to find himself. Mikey, Mikey, where are you? She shook her head and wondered about something like an Amber Alert for him. If he walked out to I-80 and hitch-hiked west, he could be lost until his amnesia clears. Maybe that's a story for Martha.

She called Sheriff Al for the name and contact info for the priest he'd found and then called the priest. It took several tries, but she finally reached someone who gave her Father Ed's cell number. She called, "Do you think it's okay for me to call Martha Ippolito? I don't have anything much positive to tell her. I thought we could gab some, but pretty soon

I'm going to have to tell her Mikey's lost, at least that we can't find him, and possibly he's dead."

"Talking is probably the best thing anyone can do for her. Thank you for volunteering." Father Ed Miller sounded soothed, as though he was now relieved of an unpleasant duty.

"I've some positive speculation. Should I share that or stick to facts?"

"I wouldn't share any speculation, positive or negative. You'll be setting her up for greater disappointment if you're wrong." Father Ed made some sounds indicating he was mulling the best approach. "I would think you'd want any background on Mikey you can get. Some obscure tidbit might help you find him, even if he's passed into the hands of Our Lord. Starting her talking is probably best for her and with luck she'll offer some bit of personal history that will help you locate him."

Bobbie collected additional suggestions and thanked the priest. She called Martha's phone and got to her voicemail. Bobbie identified herself and said, "I'd like to chat, girly talk, not police talk. If you need an ear or a shoulder, please call me." She decided to go to Rowe, hoping to either get a call from Martha Ippolito or to bump into her at the Sanctuary.

As she pulled onto I-80 from Second Avenue in Kearney, her phone rang with Martha's return call. They agreed to meet at the Nicolson Center in about a quarter hour.

Bobbie decided on a leisurely drive to the Gibbon Exit and south. She opened the windows and looked at the fields, full of cranes. She felt sure she saw tens of thousands, and these were all in the twelve mile long, one-mile wide strip that she could see from the Interstate.

Bobbie sat with Martha in the Nicolson Center viewing area, hoping to learn that obscure fact about Mikey that would give her the clue leading to him. Martha seemed oblivious to the two rug rats who were playing a squealing game of tag around the clothes displays beside them. Bobbie pointed to the river, 50 feet in front of the center. "The Platte is very high for this time of year."

Martha nodded but didn't say anything. Today she was dressed much more sensibly. She still wore heels, but shorter, and her dress was gone, replaced by slacks and a blouse.

"When Director Armstrong gave me a tour, he called these birds 'LBJs,' for 'little brown jobs.' Do you share Mikey's interest in birdwatching? Can you identify any of these guys?" Bobbie pointed to several sparrows on the ground and in the bushes.

Martha shook her head. "Birding not birdwatching, Mikey always told me." Martha's mumbling was barely audible, a remembrance, not a correction to Bobbie.

After a few more tries Bobbie ran out of small talk about the birds and weather. "You told me that Mikey was good at computers. I could sure use him. But tell me more about him. His hobbies, likes, dislikes and so on."

"He always behaved well and had good manners," Martha replied. "Just the sort of son anyone would want. He always did well in school, but was so patriotic that he wanted to be a soldier. I think he knew Anthony and I were terrified of him going to Iraq or Afghanistan. But he did get a full scholarship to Fordham, where he could take ROTC. He planned to enlist after he finished, in a couple of months. He kept assuring us life was safe for the officers, even over there."

"It must be very hard to be the parent of a soldier. You're so proud of him serving his country and so afraid that something might happen."

"Yes, I think that's it." Martha was on the verge of crying again. She wiped her eyes with a tissue. "You asked about his hobbies. Mostly they relate to computers. He loves computer games. He plays some sports, but not much. He's always liked birds and had decided that he wanted to be an ornithologist instead of a soldier. Thank God." She crossed herself.

Bobbie tried to think of a diplomatic way to ask for juvenile troubles that would not show in any records she could see. Perhaps ones that had been sealed or never made it into any legal documents. "Can you tell me about his background? Was he any trouble for you?"

"I'm going over to John's house, okay?" Mikey was 17 and responsible.

"Of, course, Honey. Don't stay late, please." She and Anthony never saw any need to set curfews for Mikey on Fridays, even when he left at 9:00.

At the start of the evening news, Martha answered her phone. Weird for someone to call so late. Maybe Mikey needs a lift or something.

Her *Hello* was greeted by a very official sounding "Is this Mrs. Martha Ippolito?" She acknowledged with the wariness of a cat approaching a live meal.

"This is Zeke Bruto at the Office of Children and Family Services. Are you Michael Ippolito's mother?"

Oh my God. What has happened to him? Children and Family Services chase parents of abused kids. "Yes. Is he okay?"

"Yes. He is okay but in trouble. He was picked up along with about ten other teens at a party where alcohol was being served. He admitted to drinking wine." Zeke's voice was deep and coarse.

"Oh dear." Well, he'd had wine at communion. That didn't sound so bad, but Martha would need to hide his arrest from Anthony.

"We are calling all the parents because we take this very seriously. We think putting them in jail overnight will be a safe way to teach them the severity of breaking the underage drinking law. We want your permission to lock him up with the other kids."

Martha agreed. At least Anthony would not be able to get to him.

She went to bed. No need to stay up any later. "Anthony, Honey, I got some bad news."

"Thought I heard the phone ring. What the hell happened?" Anthony's snarl said *I'll kill him if he's in trouble.* He never hesitated to use his belt. His hands and fists were too ready.

"Someone served the kids wine at John's. The cops busted the party. Mikey's at the station and they want to lock them up overnight to teach all the kids respect for the law." Martha looked for her husband's reaction. He seemed to think the punishment was suitable. "I told them to keep Mikey overnight so he could think about what he did."

"Is that enough so he'll remember?"

"I hope so. Since he has wine at Communion, it wasn't a wild, first time fling. Locked away from his computer and everything seemed fitting."

"Maybe you're right." His snarl added several expletives.

"Right now this tough love may be perfect for him." Martha watched Anthony closely to guess his actions.

The next afternoon, Zeke Bruto called again. After introductions, he told her that some of the kids from the party were being picked up. "We recommend keeping them here for another night. They had one big party last night. I'm not sure they understand how serious it is to break the underage drinking laws. If you agree, we'll keep Michael for another night."

Thank God I answered the phone. Anthony might have gone to get him. Poor Mikey if that happened. "Yes, that will be okay. Will he be out in time to go to mass tomorrow afternoon?"

"I'll make sure you can pick him up whenever you wish tomorrow." Zeke sounded pleasant for the first time. Decidedly more avuncular and less punitive.

She found Anthony. "I talked to the cop. I must have been so upset and worried last night that I misunderstood him. Mikey will be home tomorrow, not today."

"That should teach him." Finally he sounded like he thought the punishment was adequate. Less snarl.

Bobbie nodded and tried to think of something to say.

"I hope we did the right thing. He wasn't bad before but he's been perfect ever since. I think it was the right thing to do. He never talked about the time in jail." Martha started crying. In a few moments she had controlled herself. "He got a therapist afterward. We paid for the visits, so we know there weren't many. We know the lesson worked because he rarely attended parties after that, especially at his friends houses."

On her way back to the Sheriff's Office, Bobbie smelled exhaust fumes. Her first reaction was to roll the cruiser's windows all the way down and swear at herself for not driving one of the Chargers or Explorers. When it became uncomfortably cold she stopped to see if she could fix the problem. Sheriff Grayson always found better use for his budget than routine maintenance on older cars in the fleet so Bobbie suspected a hole in the muffler—that would explain both the noisy engine and the fumes. She tried to look under the car, but couldn't see anything. Then she saw a hole in the floor in front of the fiberglass prisoners' seat. She found a bag of sand in the trunk and tossed it on the floor in back where it blocked the hole, but she still drove with the windows cracked until she arrived at the station.

In the garage she wrote a note so no one would drive this Crown Vic until it was repaired. Then she lifted the sand bag and checked the hole. It wasn't rusted through, as she first thought. It looked like someone had broken a hole in the floorboard. Some of the raw edges of the metal were rust colored and others were shiny. Some perp or drunk must have smashed a hole with the heel of his boot, probably while cuffed in the back.

That evening Bobbie made shoofly pie to take into the volunteers at Rowe. She snitched a taste of pie. She would have preferred it quite a bit moister, as her grandmother had said. She made a note to go with it "My Mommom gave me this Pennsylvania Dutch shoofly pie recipe. I remembered it from when she made it for us as children. Better in my memory than in reality. You may prefer it with copious ice cream."

Chapter 20

Mommy DNA

Monday, 8:30 A.M.

Bobbie's email showed some preliminary DNA results were in. *Wonder why he didn't give me the results?* She called Huy Ng who insisted that they talk face-to-face. He suggested the Back Alley Bakery in Hastings, a long drive for him and about an hour for her. A wonderful excuse to get away from Kearney for a few hours.

When Bobbie walked in, she didn't see Dr. Ng, but the Back Alley Bakery had the best bread in central Nebraska, so she selected a baguette, a pecan sticky bun, and a cup of coffee. She scanned the other offerings. She thought something Italian for Chuck would be appreciated, so she picked out a pane dolce di Pasqua to share with him.

Dr. Ng came in and walked up to the counter beside her. "That's why I suggested here." He pointed to her bread. "This is best bakery around. I'm going to get some things to take back. Get a table and I'll join you in a minute." His Vietnamese accent made his suggestion a little difficult to understand.

She selected a corner booth in the back. Bobbie tossed her jacket on the adjacent table. Dr. Ng joined her. "I thought DNA results took months and you only did the test when a trial required it." She bit the tip of her tongue. "Did 'CSI' or some other TV show kick some butts in Lincoln?

Can you analyze samples as fast as TV shows now?" She'd recently read that one big negative effect of "CSI" was that juries now expected definitive DNA proof of everything. One of the Sheriffs had joked that the CAs were now CYAs. County Attorneys: cover your ass ... for everything ... with lab tests. Even in non-felony cases, juries expected to see DNA proof, so the CAs were asking for more tests all the time. Soon: DNA on speeders? On speedometers? More DNA-processing bottlenecks and costlier prosecutions. Next juries would want DNA tests for DUI convictions.

"It may have helped, but main thing is the technology for DNA testing has been improving rapidly." He frowned in thought for a moment. "In last decade, we've gone from months to days for tests and sample size we can analyze has decreased from milligrams to nanograms."

"Okay, so what's wrong with the DNA results? Why not mail or email them? Or tell me on the phone?" She spoke very quietly. The isolated booth gave them more privacy than most coffee shops and there was traffic in and out but few customers sitting down in this old brick warehouse that housed the bakery. Because Bobbie had monopolized the whole corner they were private. "Or maybe you wanted the state to pay for your trip to buy bread?"

He looked irritated at her comment. "What do you know about DNA?" He pulled a couple of paper napkins from the holder on the table and a ball point pen from his shirt pocket.

"It's damn good identification but slow and expensive. Oh, and that 'CSI' is horribly exaggerated, at least compared to any capability we have here."

"That's about half right. We have a cheap fast DNA check, but only on mtDNA. Nuclear DNA is expensive, takes longer, and we rarely do one except when a case is about to go to trial. When we have to nail perp for sure."

"Okay. Speak English." She looked him in the eye. His black eyes were clear. She wondered if his Vietnamese genes protected him from whatever caused most people's eyes to get bloodshot with years of exposure to the Nebraska sun and wind. They certainly made it harder for her to judge his age.

"You know cell has a nucleus and a blob around nucleus, right?" He drew a picture on a napkin. It looked like her third grade amoeba lesson, like the ones she'd always seen of cells. He continued after

Bobbie's nod. "DNA in the nucleus is the type you usually hear about." He pointed to the cell's nucleus on his napkin. "It's good for identifying someone. Analyzing nuclear DNA is slow because it's hard to analyze and there's very little in each cell, but it *is* very distinctive. It has one-in-billions accuracy you hear about." He looked up at her nod of understanding.

"Also DNA out here." He stuck his pen in the blob around the nucleus.

"Okay. And?"

"This outer DNA is mitochondrial DNA or mtDNA. It's not much good for identifying people because nearly everyone's is same as their mother's. It's rarely used in criminal cases because it's too generic. But it can tell you something about the family of the person. It's inherited from person's mother and doesn't mutate much so you, all your brothers, your mother, her mother, your mother's sister's children, and so on, normally all have identical mtDNA. You can think of it as mommy DNA. And there's lots of it in every cell." Dr. Ng studied her and must have decided she didn't really follow all this. "It's how they proved that Jefferson had an affair with his slave. You heard they've shown that he did father some of Sally Hemmings children, right? And how they proved the identity of the Richard III skeleton they found in Leicester, England after more than a half-millennium."

Bobbie nodded. "Yes."

"So if we analyze your mommy DNA, we can tell about your mother's side of the family. It's what many of the DNA genealogy labs analyze."

"Oh. A friend sent a cheek swab into one of those." Bobbie frowned as she tried to recall the details. "The lab told her she had pygmy ancestors. Surprised her and gave her something to laugh about."

"Right again." Dr. Ng nodded. "Because we are all descended from Africans, everyone probably has some pygmy ancestry. Another possibility is lab did lousy work. DNA analysis is not easy. Is easy to contaminate. Maybe the cells were small. Pygmy cells?" He laughed at his joke.

She joined his laughing and studied the drawing. "Okay. You can tell my brothers, but not my father?" Bobbie frowned.

"Right again, your brothers and maternal uncles, but not half-brothers with different mother." Dr. Ng drew a family tree and put circles around the mommy lines. "They also used mommy DNA to find hypothetical Eve you heard about a few years ago."

"Okay."

"It can be useful in criminal identification, even though it doesn't identify the individual like a nuclear DNA match."

Bobbie nodded. "But if it can't identify a person, how is it used?"

"Well, it was used in a case in England to identify a rape suspect. They couldn't get DNA samples from possible perps because that would have been fishing by cops, as inadmissible in England as here. The courts wouldn't order it. But the possible perps' families gave the police samples and mtDNA analysts were able to pin down the rapist. Their small group of suspects were not closely related—they all had different mtDNA. Then the courts ordered the nuclear DNA testing. The testing needed for conviction."

"I think I understand." Bobbie had not yet figured it out. "With it narrowed to only one perp, the courts were willing to order him to give a DNA sample?"

"Right again. Now brace yourself." His Vietnamese accent seemed to increase.

"Okay." Bobbie nodded. What's the big deal? Tom Shirk must have sent in hundreds of samples. He would have collected blood all over the blind and tried to get some of it from most parts of the scene.

"Our machines do 96 samples at a time so when we do a run we often add a few known samples to be sure everything works properly. We try to use a sample relevant to case. For this one we used sample from you for one of our known."

Bobbie put her hand to her mouth and slowly took a deep breath.

"And all mtDNA from your murder scene we've analyzed either matches vic's or yours. Did you know we have your DNA on file?"

"Oh. I remember giving a sample to NBI. You used that?" The list of same-mtDNA started to fill her mind. Eddie and all her cousins on her Mom's and on Mommon's side of the family.

"Right again.

"I'd forgotten all about it."

"Our first guess is that your child, sibling, mother, or your maternal fifth cousin three times removed left hair and blood at scene."

Well, Dr. Ng, I don't have any children, never even been married, and my brother and mother are in Lincoln. But ... Then Bobbie spoke, "My family has been in America for generations, so some tenth cousin might be the perp, but nobody like you could be. Right?"

"Right again."

Bobbie stared at him. She clenched her fists and put them to her face. "No." She could feel the tears trying to come. She had managed to push the thought from her mind for years. It came back. She had been exiled to Kansas by her family for what should have been the second semester of her junior year in high school. She'd put the infant boy up for adoption when he was less than a day old. Was it possible? There were thousands of maternal cousins, but there was also one child. The unadmitted child. The adoption records were more than twenty years old. *Oh my God.*

Bobbie put on the best smile she could muster. "So now I need to find some cousin who hates bird watchers."

"One approach. Or have someone else do it." Dr. Ng studied her.

She couldn't show any emotion, but she had to learn if Mikey was her son. Bobbie fidgeted. "How soon do you expect to have the DNA testing done?"

Ng indicated it would not be soon because of the cost and probable uselessness. They discussed options and schedules.

As soon as Bobbie reached her office she picked up her phone and dialed Patrick, her SEAL friend in the New York Police Department. "No, no." She hung up then dialed Quinn McKay, the NYPD Mafia cop. On his machine she left the message, "Quinn, this is Bobbie Lee in Nebraska with more of a personal than professional question. Can you get me any information on Mikey Ippolito? Was he an adopted child? Any background like that." She hung up after some false starts then a *thank you.*

Now is the time to see if Chuck can get me something. Martha had hinted about Mikey being an only child. With no trace of him for almost a week now, she couldn't ask Martha about adoption. If she went to Court, how long would it take to get her son's adoption records unsealed? Could she even do it? "Dear God, please let Quinn or Chuck get me the answer," she said to her empty office.

She tried to conjure all the possibilities. Mikey could be her son. Any of her local or non-local maternally-related cousins, including her son, could be the murderer. Mikey could be a distant cousin and either a witness or the murderer. And those were just a few that came to mind quickly. Considering the possibilities made her head hurt.

Chapter 21

Better lucky than good

Monday, 2:23 P.M.

Bobbie's phone rang. The caller ID showed State Police IT Division in Lincoln. *Aha, maybe something to nail this coffin shut.* The caller identified himself as Dom Chan in Cyber Forensics. After introducing himself he apologized for not having better tools, "Our group is small and our resources are quite limited." In other words, Capodicasa's murder was not their top priority. "Homeland Security is making us do all sorts of irrelevant stuff that gets in the way of doing any of the work we need to do. It even gets in the way of the stuff they want done."

"Tale of two governments." Bobbie realized he was probably trying to help her. "Sorry, I didn't mean to sound so unappreciative."

"No offense taken. We did send an appeal to a number of commanders in Afghanistan to try to locate any soldiers watching your cranecam, as you suggested." Dom spoke with a pronounced Chinese accent. He paused, apparently considering how to describe their results. "We located a few candidates and sent requests directly to them." Bobbie visualized Charlie Chan, talking to her. Does Dom have a Fu Manchu mustache? Is he as stocky as Warner Oland's 1930's Charlie. No, Dom would be more likely to have a knife made out of a circuit board than any kind of blackjack. Or maybe a mouse-cord garrotte.

"Sounds like good police work." Bobbie was speaking more to herself than to Dom.

"Yes, ma'am," he said. "We try. We have just now received a reply email from one of the soldiers in Afghanistan. I think he may be the same one who told the people at Rowe that he liked the cranecam because it reminded him of home." Dom sounded like a teenager. His accent seemed to be getting stronger, worrying Bobbie that she would not understand everything he said.

Bobbie stifled an urge to ask, *Are you Number One Son or Number Two Son?* That thought changed her vision of Dom. He took on a slim physique. "So did this soldier remember what he saw last Tuesday night?" Bobbie turned to her computer to find the time difference to Afghanistan. +4:30 to Kabul and -6:00 to Central. 10½ hours difference.

"Last Wednesday morning, about 1100 hours, he guessed, the cranecam showed a big disturbance. The soldier thought he saw a coyote or something that scared the birds. He remembered something was splashing across the river. Not chasing the birds, only scaring them as it crossed."

"Yeah. I've seen a flock of geese parting for a coyote like that. At least this gives us an interesting start. Did he have anything more? Is there any chance there were two disturbances, like two coyote's close together?"

"We didn't ask that specifically, and I will check on it, but I'm pretty sure he said he only saw one animal, or maybe a single person, disturbing the cranes."

Bobbie had hoped for much more than a coyote in the early evening. No wait a minute, it would be... "That does mean about 9:30 in the evening here, right?"

"No ma'am. Not if he remembered the time right. Eleven hundred hours there is 12:30 here, about a half hour after midnight."

"Okay, that means the moon was up so he had about as good a view as the cam could provide at night, right. Did he say anything about the quality of the picture?"

"He said it had lots of squares. We've checked overnight and can confirm that the picture is not very good. In fact if the moon hadn't been quite bright, we doubt he would even have been able to see that the cranes were upset."

"So the full moon allowed him to see almost enough to be useful?" Bobbie asked.

"Yes, ma'am. As I said, we did check, and the pic's not great."

"This is very useful, Dom. Please excuse my snide comment. It was unwarranted." Bobbie shook her head and wished some of her body language showed to Dr. Dom Chan. "Oh, and please let me know if you're able to turn up anything more. You've probably fixed the time of the murder. That will help me a lot, I'm sure. Now if we can get some solid leads on either the witness or the perp. That's what I was hoping for, what I really need."

"I'll email the report with all the details we have as soon as it's available," Dom promised.

"Thanks, Dom." Bobbie knew she'd have to be lucky to be within six hours on her time-of-death guess based on the state of rigor mortis. The body temperature, which the coroner checked, might yield a time of death to within a couple of hours—she did not recall that exact time, but both of those data had led to the wild ass guess of about midnight. "Oh, that information does conform to our wag of the time of murder." She hesitated and hoped Dom would understand her slang term for a wild-ass-guess. "I think your soldier may have seen our witness or the perp escaping. It's also given me some new ideas. Thanks again for the data and please relay my thanks to your group. I owe you all a lunch."

"Well, thank you, Bobbie." He sounded very pleased, as though her pat on their backs was a completely new occurrence. "We hope the information is of some use. We know it isn't much. By the way, I like Cantonese."

If the "crane disturbance" was the perp, maybe the river meted out justice for us. If it was a witness, maybe the river wiped out all chance of solving the case.

Bobbie decided on a walk. That would help her concentrate on the issues she needed to sort out. She headed for the back door and left the county building. Walking east along Railroad Street, she visualized Chuck's always neatly coiffed black hair and realized she was visualizing him in a Tux and started analyzing her dream pattern. Was she hoping for wedding bells? Nah, probably the image from one of her romance's covers.

Where could Mikey be? Was there one or more than one person besides the victim in the blind? How could she find him, or was it every-one? Or was it just a coyote the soldier saw?

Chapter 22

The Fat Lady Sings

Monday, 3:35 P.M.

Bobbie's phone rang. Her heart jumped. She hoped it would be another invitation from Chuck, but the caller ID showed Madman Grayson's office. "Investigator Bobbie Lee," she answered the phone in her most formal voice.

"Hello, Lee," Grayson's secretary Hank said. "Sheriff Grayson wants to discuss the Rowe murder investigation." His voice was pleasant —none of the gruff and authoritative tones that Grayson often used.

"I can brief him on the progress whenever he wishes."

"That would be good. I think he has some other issues too. He wants you to come to his office."

"Oh, okay. Right now?"

In response to Hank's "yes" she collected a few notes and walked up the stairs to Grayson's office. Hank told her to go right in and closed the door behind her. Grayson motioned for her to sit down at the round table beside his desk. He finished some paperwork and joined her at the walnut table.

"I've been talking to Al Beasley and Huy Ng. Do you think you should investigate this case? Are you a completely disinterested party to Capodicasa's death?"

"Yes, sir. I have no connection to it, at least none I know of. Is there some specific issue that's been raised?" Maybe she had no connection in a legal sense, but her son or some cousin might be involved. Damn, she had to stay on this case. And what if Eddie or some close cousin like him is involved. She was in the best position to understand all the issues around her family.

"I've been given two specific issues and two vague ones. Dr. Ng thinks a cousin of yours may be the perp, as he told you this morning, right?"

"Yes." Bobbie drew out the answer. At the Hastings bakery meeting Dr. Ng had obviously been concerned, maybe apprehensive. He certainly acted exactly as he should in disclosing the possible conflict of interest to her boss.

"The other one, which may or may not be important, is that Petite seems to be trying to make me remove you or to quash the whole investigation. I've been isolating you from that until now, but I don't know how determined he is to stop you."

Bobbie could feel herself start. "What does Petite want?"

"That's what I wanted to ask you. Could he have any connection to this case?" Madman Grayson studied Bobbie. Was he looking for hints of prevarication?

"Sir, two pieces of background information you may not know. I stopped Petite for speeding about a month ago. I never wrote it up, but he was vocal, even vicious. He seemed to blame me for a parking ticket he'd gotten a few months ago. I hadn't heard of the parking citation until he bitched about it." Bobbie frowned and tried to think of connections he might have to Capodicasa.

"He's also my uncle. Come to think of it that means his mtDNA is like mine. I haven't talked to him, outside of legal stuff anyway, for years and years. I haven't turned up anything connecting him to Capodicasa or Mikey Ippolito. Or to Rowe Sanctuary, either for that matter. Maybe I should look into that more?"

"Possibly, but if you do, be very discreet, even secretive." Grayson seemed to be pondering some new and unexpected information that had not previously been available to him. "I don't want him even hearing rumors that someone may be checking on him."

"Yes, sir. I'll be very careful and do anything involving Mentes by myself so there's no chance of a leak."

Grayson nodded.

"Can you tell me what the vague concerns are?"

"First, Beasley is concerned that you're close to everything. Nothing definite, just his gut telling him something didn't feel quite right. His intuition was a strong enough for him to call me about it. He didn't suggest you're not doing a good job, he gabbed about the case and mentioned his feelings while we talked."

Bobbie nodded. She wondered if the call was like locker room talk. Perhaps there's more to Beasley's instincts that Grayson had picked up on.

"And the second one is the possible Mafia connection. If they're involved, we need an investigator who is more careful watching their back than you. You're always very intent on your cases. So much so that you forget to watch around yourself."

"Sir, the last issue is moot. I'm almost certain there is no Mafia connection, despite Ms. Capodicasa's certainty. Chuck Capodicasa, the vic's son, is helping in a way that says no mob connection. Second, the NYPD Mafia detective said nothing in the murder fits the mob's MO." Bobbie spoke decisively. She suspected her investigation depended on convincing the Sheriff. "In fact, and third, Quinn McKay, he's the New York Mafia cop I talked to, said *our* Paul Capodicasa probably has no Mafia connection."

"Are you really sure? Do you think you've got good data?"

"Quite certain. In fact, both Quinn and Chuck said," Bobbie paused momentarily, with the realization that she revealed more about her meeting than she intended, "there are two Paul Capodicasas in New York and it is the other one who's in the Mafia. They both also said Chuck's mother does have relatives who are involved in illicit activities. According to Chuck, his mother sees the mob's influence in all sorts of places where it doesn't exist." Bobbie stopped for a moment. Did she want to add more details, or would additional arguments weaken her case? Better to stop.

"Families have ways of doing things." Grayson nodded as he continued studying Bobbie. "Clean father, clean son. Usually."

"Yes, sir. Those were my thoughts too."

"And conversely. Remember that. If Chuck Capodicasa is clean, then his father probably is too." Grayson mumbled in thought. "Do you know anything about the young Mr. Capodicasa himself?"

"Everyone says he's okay. For what it's worth, he's a Harvard MBA."

"That's good," Grayson repeated several times, trailing off.

"I did all the on-line research I could about both the father and son and everything corroborates Quinn. I'm quite sure they're clean."

"Okay." Grayson looked Bobbie in the eye. "You're watching your butt better than I expected."

"Thank you, sir. And, sir, I think Dr. Ng is overstating the connection. The maternal DNA analysis he's done only says the perp is probably a cousin. It could well be a tenth cousin, someone I don't even know I'm related to. That mommy DNA is the only type he's had time and resources to check. It's the same for generations. It's probably the same for me, my mother, her mother and so on back to 1639, when Richard Lee came to America. I calculated I have something like 50,000 of these same mommy-DNA cousins."

"Don't you think you might be overstating how many people have similar mommy DNA, as you call it?"

"Remember that skeleton they found under a parking lot in England? The scientists did mommy-DNA checks on two of Richard III descendants'. One had an exact match to the skeleton's and the other was almost exact. And these guys are something like 20 generations later. King Richard III died more than 500 years ago."

"Okay, I take your point. You really want to stay lead on the case."

"Yes, sir. I do." *And if someone in my family is involved, I'll be in a better position to understand and solve the case than anyone else.*

Bobbie soaked in her shower and enjoyed the fruit smell of her Pantene Shampoo. She looked at her body, at the faint ladders on her nearly flat tummy. Stretch marks. She usually avoided looking at herself because it reminded her that she had been pregnant. *Who am I trying to kid. Maybe Mikey Ippolito is my son.* He may have been deeply involved in the murder. Perhaps he was an accessory after the fact. Maybe before the fact. Maybe a conspirator. Maybe a principal. Had she been lying, even to herself? She washed her whole body. At least the data and picture for the TV announcements were completely accurate so she didn't have to revise and reissue the APB.

She put on a fresh uniform and headed for Rowe. Instead of the usual seven miles to the Minden exit and then back roads to Rowe, she went 12 miles east on I-80 and turned south at the Gibbon exit toward Lowell Road.

Like any investigation this one was a puzzle and all she had were a few of the jigsaw pieces. Missing pieces were likely as were pieces that belong to some other puzzle. Or, maybe it was a crossword puzzle with some mis-numbered clues, some Shortzian red herrings. Maybe it was a crossword puzzle and she was looking for jigsaw pieces.

A fun enigma. Some bits of evidence did not fit. *Facts are facts, the story has to fit them. If it doesn't, the story, the theory, has to adapt. The alternative is illusions and delusions.* She could look at any number of clues for any kind of word puzzle and none would help assemble a jigsaw puzzle.

She had to have missed something. Now was the time to start checking all those improbables she had skipped. Somewhere she had to find a missing piece. She turned west off Lowell Road onto Kilgore, the only road between the freeway and the river, putting her on the north side of the Platte, across from Elm Island Road, the lane into Rowe.

She pushed the button on her odometer to reset the trip distance to zero. She knew she had to go about 2.1 miles west. In 2.4 miles, which allowed for a jog south on Kilgore, she parked. If her mental map was correct, she was only a little over a mile north of the Capodicasa blind and about a third of a mile of that was the Platte. At a low river time, the Platte would be more like 100 yards wide. She climbed through the barbed wire fence along the road and started walking south toward the river, toward Rowe Sanctuary and toward the photo-blind where Capodicasa had been murdered.

Bobbie looked around the field, which had not been planted in corn last year so weeds filled it—no corn stalks. She walked toward the cottonwood trees and willows bordering the Platte. Thousands of cranes in the air, making the gargling noise that Frank had pointed out to her. A few hundred cranes were in the field behind her, across Kilgore Road. She realized that every corn field had a few hundred Sandhill Cranes with their gray to brown bodies, white heads and long necks, and striking red foreheads. She looked back at the cranes and remembered Frank had told her what looked like the crane's body and tail was almost entirely wing feathers, its bustle he'd called the part that looked like a tail. The weight of a chicken but a yard tall, she mumbled as she studied them. And he said these are the *lesser* sandhill cranes. What little fact would make some of her puzzle pieces fall into place?

Oh, he'd also said the brown color on their bodies was from mud they smear on their feathers. Could Mikey have used mud to hide?

She turned and continued her walk south and heard snarling and grunting from the trees. Sounded like pigs. She turned a little to the east toward the noise. *What the hell was that pair of dogs fighting over?* Something was in a willow thicket and under a massive cottonwood log. At about 50 feet away, she saw the black object that interested the dogs. She jogged toward them and waved wildly. "Get out of there. Go away. Scram. Beat it."

When the larger dog didn't abandon his dinner, she fired a shot into the cottonwood above the dog. Bobbie knew that a shot fired in the air had to come back to Earth somewhere. Too dangerous. By shooting at the fallen tree, the bullet would safely bury itself in the log and because her pistol was aimed in the direction of the dog, its noise would actually be noticeably louder, deafening to the dog. The damn rottweiler mix looked at her but stood its ground. No tail wag. She picked up a stick and approached the large dog.

The dogs' interest looked like an otter. She approached and saw bloody flesh at both ends. The black was leather. "Oh my God. It's an arm." She spoke aloud. She couldn't bring herself to examine it more closely, at least not yet. And not with the snarling rottweiler wanting it for its own.

She looked around. *If this is part of Mikey, he should be close. God, what a gory thought. Can't think about it. Got to find him if he's here.* She pushed at the willows to see what hid under the huge tree. A growl greeted her, but she couldn't see anything. And another from behind her. She hit the rottweiler with the stick, which broke. Damned cottonwood. The dog retreated a few steps from the arm, but continued baring its teeth and snarling. Cramps clawed at her stomach.

With her pistol in her right hand, she pushed the willows to the side with her left. More fierce, deep growling from in front of her. Then the eyes. A mountain lion. She quickly took a step back and fired above the animal. She knew a wounded lion was much worse than a healthy one. Less of a threat to her and to the two damn dogs. The dogs were so close, they must have found the body only minutes before Bobbie arrived.

She heard the cat move. Not much sound for a big animal. Sounded like it was moving away from her and toward the river. Another step back. She stretched as tall as she could and looked over the tree. Some movement on the other side. Then she saw the lion retreating downriver. She inhaled and realized she hadn't taken a breath since the cat's first grumble at her.

She turned to the growling behind her and saw the rottweiler snap at the arm. "Stop. Sit." she yelled. The dog made a lunge at the arm and grabbed it.

Before the dog could go more than a few steps, Bobbie shot. The dog grabbed the arm more securely and started to retreat. Bobbie shot at the dog this time. Two fast shots, accurate despite her dizziness. The dog spasmed, dropped the arm and collapsed. She doubled in an attempt to stop the nausea. Bloody bodies had sickened her before, but this was worse. What could be worse than a seeing a young man being eaten? Her muscles heaved again, but nothing came up.

She pushed at the willows where the lion had been and saw a large black patch not far from the cat's location. It had a bloody stump where the jacket's left arm should have been. The body wore black pants. At least the only smell was the typical moldy Platte underbrush. She wretched, turned to the side and lost part of her lunch. She looked at the remaining arm and saw the parrot tattoo.

She called dispatch and had them patch her to Sheriff Grayson. "I think I've found Mikey Ippolito, can you get a coroner here?"

"I'll get right on it. What do you have?"

"Possible mountain lion kill or scavenge. Some dogs had a part of him. Thank God they had just found him. I'll call his mother. It is not pleasant, but not as bad as the vic. More grisly." She filled in the details for Madman Grayson and saw him miming the finding of the body and shooting to chase the animals away. He would act out the body's protection so it was more like a scene from Rambo, but no one would correct the impression.

"Why didn't our FLIR plane find him?"

The images Bobbie had seen from the forward looking infrared camera on their plane were amazing, but nothing like photographs. "Two reasons, I think. First he's on the north side of the Platte. Until I came over here today our searching was strongly concentrated across the river." Neither of them thought anybody could cross the Platte. "Second, he was under a huge cottonwood, I wouldn't have found him when I walked past if the dogs hadn't been fighting over his arm. If he hid there all along, he would have been completely concealed from our plane."

"So, you got lucky, huh?"

"Yes sir, if you can call it luck. The area even has thick willow growth all around it further obscuring the IR and making him harder to find." She gave him directions for the coroner.

"How could he have crossed the river when you couldn't?" His tone showed no doubt of her competence. Did she read him right?

"I remembered that O'Dell said the river was rising rapidly while he was at the murder scene the first day. Mikey crossed in the middle of the night before, when the Platte was a low, winter river. Maybe he got so cold he hid himself under this big tree for warmth. Poor kid probably froze. At least I hope he froze before the cat got him."

On her cell phone she called the motel where Martha stayed. No one answered her room phone. She started to leave a message, then decided to try the more personal approach of several more calls before leaving impersonal notes. She called Rowe and asked for Martha by name and description. This time she was rewarded. "Hello, Martha. I'm afraid I have very bad news. I think I've found your son."

"Oh, God. No. What do you mean exactly."

"I'm with a body that is dressed the way Mikey was. It's in awful shape. If it weren't for your need for immediate closure, I'd suggest you not come see him, but wait until the coroner has tidied him up. Do you want to come right over?"

"Yes. Of course." Martha cried as she spoke. "I'll come as fast as I can."

"I'll stay here to keep animals away until you get here and the coroner arrives. Your positive ID will help us." She broke a branch from above the body and swished it past the arm-less shoulder to chase the few flies away. Why do those horrible things come out in this chilly weather?

"Yes. I'll come right away. Where are you?"

"Maybe I can get one of the Rowe guides to bring you over. I'm about a mile north of you, across the river, but you have several miles of driving and a couple hundred yard walk off the road." She continued waving the willow switch over the exposed parts of the body to prevent flies from landing on it.

Martha said she'd find someone. Bobbie could hear her asking for assistance. Soon Duane Mulcahy was on the line identifying himself. "I'll bring Martha over, if you tell me where you are."

Bobbie gave him directions. She looked around for the mountain lion and shooed the flies from the remains. She called the priest to bring him up to date. With her duties done and a few minutes to wait, she looked at the body, defended her site against the small dog and watched for the lion.

Damn, could this have been her son? How could she even think about that? How would Martha handle it?

Chapter 23

A parents worst nightmare is losing a child

Monday, 4:15 P.M.

After Martha identified Mikey she collapsed next to her only child. As she sat on the soggy ground she lifted his remaining hand and showed Bobbie and Duane his wrist with the parrot tattoo. Dusky was lettered under it in an overall pattern that gave it a vague resemblance to a skull. "Dusky is our pet. He's the same age as Mikey. They were best friends." She carefully set his hand down and looked away from his damaged shoulder and face. "Did you know parrots are often single-person pets?"

"No. I've never had a parrot." Duane shook his head and turned away. He avoided looking at Mikey's body.

"If you want to go, go." Bobbie spoke very quietly to Duane hoping Martha wouldn't hear. "I can bring her back."

He nodded. "Thank you," he whispered. "If you need me or anyone else for help, call Rowe."

"Thank you." She touched his hand.

"Dusky may never accept anyone to replace Mikey." Martha's voice was reedy. She looked up at Duane and Bobbie.

Duane didn't move. Martha looked down at her son and Duane walked quietly away. Bobbie squatted next to Martha and put an arm around her shoulders.

"It would be normal. I hope Dusky can understand about him." Martha's body shook from the suppressed sobs.

Bobbie started to feel some of Martha's anguish, but knew there was no way for her to really understand what Martha felt. "No one can replace him. Do you want to talk to me about Mikey? You said he was a senior in college, so he was about 22?"

"Almost 22. He would have been 22 in two months, on the 31st." She was crying again.

Bobbie's son had been born at the beginning of the weekend. Her recollection was that it was the 29th. Was it possible that the date had been changed? It seemed like everything else could be changed, why not the date? Could she have mis-remembered it?

Martha took out her cell phone, tapped a couple of keys, and shook the hair from her ear. She spoke quietly. "Are you sitting down?"

She covered the phone's mike with her palm and held the rust colored telephone to the side. "He's capable of great violence," she whispered.

She uncovered the phone quickly. "Yes they found him a few minutes ago. I'm here with him." Pause. "I can't talk anymore now. Call you later when I've recovered." She cried aloud as she tapped several times on her phone, apparently all to disconnect the call.

Bobbie knelt so she could stay next to Martha. Martha collapsed onto the cop. Bobbie had never felt more supportive in her life, both literally and figuratively. Martha's body heaved, but no other evidence of crying. Bobbie wondered if she had cried herself out. Could someone cry herself out? She vaguely recalled that Memorial Day weekend 22 years ago when she'd cried herself into the decision that she'd have to give her baby away. She decided to give the baby to a stranger even before she went into labor.

She knew that no one in her family would ever admit that she'd had a boy. No one would believe she'd been pregnant, well they'd believe it but never admit it. No one would believe or admit she'd been raped. A secret the family would sequester and suppress.

Martha started telling stories about Mikey, about being on the Dean's list every semester, about making sure she was able to use the computers and other e-gadgets she had. He had been the only real comfort for her when her mother, Nana he called her, had a stroke and eventually died. Martha started to dial again then stopped. "Mom's dead too. I can't talk to her or tell her Mikey died." Her body convulsed. Again she collapsed against Bobbie.

Martha sat up and started messing with her phone. "This is the last picture I have of Mikey and Dusky together." She showed Bobbie an 18 year-old Mikey with a dark gray parrot on his left arm. He looked like he was talking to the bird. "I'm sure his relationship with Dusky is part of the reason he treasured this trip to see the cranes. He told us during Christmas Break he had applied to Cornell graduate school. He said they had the best avian department in the world."

Bobbie patted Martha on the shoulder as she heard a car door slam on Kilgore Road. "I'll bet that is the Sheriff." She wanted to stand to show them the direction, but she couldn't do that without disturbing Martha. She stayed kneeling, supporting Martha.

A man came into view about thirty feet away. No one Bobbie recognized. He carried a rifle or shotgun. "Why the hell are you shooting on my property?" His shotgun was still pointed down, but aimed only a short distance from Bobbie and Martha.

"Oh my God. Don't shoot." Martha stood. "My son's been killed. I came to identify him."

The farmer waved his shotgun. At times it pointed directly at the women. "What are you talking about. Get away from there." He waved his gun and followed its aim.

Bobbie tried to believe he was only motioning stupidly. She pulled her pistol out of its holster. The farmer could not see the pistol or much of Bobbie because Martha hid her.

"What the hell's this. You killed my dog." He raised his gun to a threat position, but looked at his dead rottweiler.

Bobbie moved several steps to the side, away from Martha. The farmer could see her uniform for the first time. She went into a crouch, pointing her weapon at the farmer. "I'm Detective Bobbie Lee, Buffalo County Sheriff Office. Drop the gun immediately."

The farmer raised his hands but held the shotgun all the time. At least now it pointed at the sky. "I didn't shoot nobody." He paled. "Do you think I had something to do with that murder over at Rowe?" He waved his gun in the direction of the Visitor Center.

"Drop your gun, sir. Don't do anything fast."

His face seemed to show understanding, finally. His eyes widened. He looked up and reacted as though he didn't know he held the 12 gauge.

"Oh. Don't shoot, officer." He carefully pointed the gun toward the road, away from Bobbie and Martha and set it down on the ground next to his feet. "I heard some shots fired and thought some tourists were poaching on my land."

Bobbie stood and saw three men about 100 yards away coming toward them from the northwest, from the direction of her car. A deputy and the coroner followed Duane Mulcahy. She collected info from the farmer, Ulam Eskay, and told him she'd run a check and return his shotgun if he came up clean. He retreated northeast, in the direction he'd come.

"The big round guy behind Duane is Deputy Scotty Leslie and the beanpole is Assistant Coroner Smithson," Bobbie said to Martha. "The law requires an autopsy, which'll be done in Gibbon, only a few miles north of here. You may want to give the coroner details of how to treat Mikey when they have finished the examination."

"Thank you. Paul was so good to him. He showed Mikey that ornithology made a respectable career. I think Paul wanted to be an ornithologist and was disappointed that his kids never took birding seriously."

She patted Bobbie's hand and shook her head. "The rich businessman telling a young man that the scientists' vow of near-poverty is okay. That science is a respectable career. That being a bird nerd, as he called himself, is a compliment. The two of them were so happy together. Mikey because of all the places Paul took him birding and Paul to have a serious birder in his *family*. Paul's own boys are wonderful, but neither shared his mania for birding the way Mikey did."

When the trio arrived, Bobbie introduced everyone. "Do you know anything about Mr. Eskay?" Head shakes from all three. "This is his farm." She and Martha stood back.

"Hey, Bobbie. You want to be the department's bloody situation specialist?" Scotty spoke in a loud voice, like he was telling a joke.

Bobbie gritted her teeth. "That's enough. His mother doesn't need your comments." She waited a second to make sure Scotty looked at her. Without moving her jaw and with her teeth still tightly closed, she spoke in a very low voice. "Keep your damn mouth shut."

Scotty did not look happy about the reprimand.

With no change of manner or tone of voice, Bobbie said, "And pick up the vic's arm. Hide it with the rest of his body." She pointed toward it as Smithson positioned Mikey on the litter.

Smithson and Scotty stood with their burden and started walking back toward the vehicles. Duane walked up to take a handle from Smithson, who had the heavy, head-end of the litter and who looked less capable of carrying the weight than Scotty. Martha and Bobbie walked beside Mikey.

"Do you know the difference between birding and bird watching?" Martha asked Bobbie.

"No," Bobbie lied.

Martha explained the difference again.

"Oh." Bobbie tried to sound sympathetic. Probably the best thing she could do for Martha was to listen.

"Did you know there's pretty good birding in New York, even in Manhattan? One of the, uh, flyways Mikey called it, brings lots of migrating birds through The City each spring and fall." She cried and stroked Mikey's hair as they walked. Bobbie looked away, afraid that she would also start crying.

Bobbie steadied Martha as they walked back to the car.

No witness. She lacked the chutzpa, or maybe it was courage, to ask Martha about Mikey, at least not for many days. The one thing Bobbie had to do was to get blood samples from his clothes and body. Then, at least for a few thousand bucks or so, she would be able to privately settle all the questions about her relationship to Mikey.

Chapter 24

When in Doubt, Mumble (Bureaucrats' Law #2)

Monday, 7:00 P.M.

Bobbie noticed that Chuck got into his Lexus and sat down more slowly than he had two days ago when he'd taken her to dinner the first time. He set the dolce di Pasqua she had given him on the back seat. She no longer was confident that she didn't need his help. In fact, she knew his help was likely to be necessary to answer questions about the Ippolitos. At least necessary for her to avoid asking Martha questions that would seem to denigrate her son. The pain in her tummy told her she better make her admission and ask her questions fast. "I got pregnant as a result of that rape in high school and had a boy." The secret that not a single person remembered.

"Oh, no." Chuck slowed the car as they pulled onto twenty-fifth street. That sounds much more traumatic than Nicola's experience.

Bobbie nodded. "I immediately gave him up for adoption. That was 22 years ago."

Chuck slowed his black Lexus. "Twenty-two," he repeated slowly.

"Yes. I remember it was Memorial Day weekend."

Chuck nodded. Bobbie couldn't tell what occupied his mind. At Gusto di Napoli he exited the car. He walked around the car to the passenger's door more slowly than his usual pace. Or was it her apprehension making the time seem much longer than normal.

Did Chuck know Mikey's birthday? "Martha told me that her son's birthday is May 31st. He was about to turn 22." Bobbie paused. She tried to guess Chuck's thoughts.

Chuck shook his head. "Oh dear Jesus, Joseph and Mary. Mikey reminds you of the son you gave up. He even looks like you. No wonder you're so attuned to Martha's feelings."

Bobbie looked at the restaurant's sign. "There's another possibility." She nodded.

"Another? What's your first choice?" Chuck's voice said surprise, almost panic.

"Mikey looks like me and is the right age, but his skin is dark and Martha said his birthday was two days late." She checked in Chuck's eyes. "I wonder if I could be Mikey's biological mother."

He met her gaze. "Oh, Dear Lord."

"Yeah. And I can't ask Martha if Mikey's adopted or anything like that. She is so fragile right now. She needs support, not more worries or questions. I hoped you could get some information without Martha knowing I'm prying into her son's life." Bobbie clenched her teeth and looked straight ahead trying to shake off a headache that wanted to ruin her evening.

"That sort of information should be easy to locate. Consider it done. Martha will never know of our stealth investigation." They slowly walked to the restaurant's front door. "You might be right. Mikey does look Italian, but he doesn't really look like either Martha or Anthony. I can't remember Martha being pregnant, but I doubt I'd have noticed it back then." Round Paul showed them into the private dining room in near total silence.

"Thank you. I need pretty detailed info. Even if he was adopted, was he really born on exactly May 31st?"

He appeared to be making notes to himself as they sat at the table in their private dining room. "I may have to call back with results. I talked to the priest and Martha after Mass yesterday then Mama called a little later as I drove home. The sharks are circling and the lawyers have been bugging me, too. All sorts of problems, both in The City and here."

Sharks wanting to pick over his father's businesses? Lawyers about Paul's estate or about Paul's murder? Or was this something about

Mikey's fate? The priest wouldn't have anything to do with Paul and Chuck's business interests, but lawyers would only bug him about the arrangements for his father or Mikey, wouldn't they? She sought a comfortable way to ask for clarification.

"I'll call my friends in The City and get them started on your questions." He tapped a finger on the place-mat. "I'm trying to attend to all the business issues that are arising, but the distance makes it difficult, to say the least." Chuck made a phone call.

They sipped the Chianti that appeared without any order Bobbie saw. She felt a warmth and security she'd never felt before during a time of such crisis. The week felt like a month, as though the time between their dinners together had been a week instead of a few days. Bobbie couldn't reconcile any of the nastiness his Sicilian ancestry suggested with the man she saw. His mother's certainty of a mob connection didn't fit what she saw. "When Frank Armstrong called your mom last Wednesday morning, he said her immediate reaction was fear and caution. She felt sure that he'd been whacked by someone in the Mafia and I ran into similar reactions when I called cops in New York. Can you tell me what's going on?"

"You've read enough novels and seen enough movies to know the mob was brought to New York by Sicilian emigrants. Mama does have a number of relatives who are inside, but no one in our family has any connection to the House and no one on Dad's side of the family has any connection that I know of. I've heard stories about being able to get cars for practically nothing. By the time I was old enough to fantasize about having my own car, I knew I couldn't afford to take a free one from Uncle Marco. Actually, the scariest story I heard concerned someone complaining to Uncle Marco about being cheated on some business deal. I'd guess there was no cheating, only an insult or something like that. Anyway, the guy apparently whined to Uncle Marco. 'I hope that bastard Carl's house burns down.' A week later it did."

"So why was your Mama so sure the murder had been mob action? Why are you so sure she overreacted?" She reached across the table and touched his hand. She wanted to be sure he thought of this as a friend's question, not a police grilling.

"In her family's world, murders are never random and any death that isn't with a doctor at bedside and at an old age isn't either. She's sweet and wonderful and was a great mom and is a great grandmom. But she does have a blind spot for La Casa Nostra. She had a brother who died when his car skidded on ice and rolled into the Hudson River. I'm sure she still thinks that some enemy of Poppop orchestrated his murder. She'll probably never really believe Uncle Mario's death wasn't murder by some Sicilian connection." Chuck frowned a little and seemed to study the table cloth.

"Do you know why the detectives I talked to in New York seemed so scared of your father?" *Actually they feared the other Paul Capodicasa, but let's see how Chuck explains this.*

Chuck still frowned at the table. He looked up and met her eyes. "Dad has often been hassled by the NYPD. To make matters worse, there's another Paul Capodicasa, Short Paul, who is no relation to us. He survived an assassination attempt when I was in college and has probably meted out some revenge. We have many common friends and business associates and the police have seen many coincidences, like one Mafia hit being right outside Dad's first restaurant. Some guys in NYPD will never believe Dad is really clean." Chuck hesitated and rubbed his forehead.

He always massages his temples when he is really torn about some-thing. Bobbie waited to see if he'd elaborate. She wondered if Round Paul was persecuted by the New York City Police Department. According to the history on the menu, he'd brought his training and recipes from New York City.

"That's probably claiming too much. No businessman is a saint. Nobody in the restaurant business in Manhattan, or at least no Italian, can be completely clean, completely free from mob connections. I'm sure he's been mixed up with or contacted by the mob at times, but I'm sure the only contacts would have been minor extortion. Like insistence that he pay them for protection and things like that. At times, no small business could operate in The City without Mafia protection." He shook his head, but offered no more for 30 seconds.

Bobbie broke the silence, well after it had become awkward. "I noticed you called your grandfather *Poppop*—I call one of my grandmas *Mommom*." She hoped Chuck liked the coincidence.

His family history must have created all manner of biases she had not noodled out. "It sounds like you feel embarrassed by being the white sheep in a herd of blacks. Like you've been dirtied by the others you don't approach, but can't escape. Or let me change that, you feel like a yacht in a fleet of scows you can't escape."

"Yeah, I guess. I've thought of it as if we're the kids on the play-ground caught up in the Narcs' sweep. The clean speedboat that gets caught and searched by customs. Sometimes it's even felt like they planted stuff on us. We may be culpable, but we aren't guilty."

Bobbie wanted to believe Chuck. If this was an accurate portrayal of his family, then the mob connection could be taken off the table and she might be able to see him after the investigation.

Chapter 25

Kicking Cousins

Tuesday, 8:15 A.M.

Bobbie asked Eddie Stuart to come into the sheriff's office to talk. She could go to his condo or school, but she wanted to be on her own turf. Also, if he came into the County Building no one at Kearney Youth Home need know. He would avoid the disruption of being taken from or even leaving school or home. It was far from conclusive, but the Kearney Youth Home stood to get a couple million bucks. Eddie supported the KYH so faithfully that a million dollars of Capodicasa's beneficence would certainly rub off on Cousin Eddie. If he brought in that kind of money, no way his teaching job would ever be in jeopardy.

He also knew the sanctuary and wildlife in a way that would make it easy for him to move around without disturbing anything. He had volunteered at Rowe for so long he'd have no trouble learning the photo-blind they'd assigned to Paul for the night.

She kept thinking he would get some money for himself as well as for KYH. Just the thought of a million bucks had been more than enough for Hickock and Smith to murder four members of the Clutter family. Was it enough for Eddie?

Eddie sat in front of her at a table in the Sheriff's garage. Compared to the interrogation room, this was a quiet and friendly place to have a chat. "You were at Rowe last Tuesday night. Were you with anyone?"

Eddie, dressed in chino slacks and a broadcloth shirt with a teal and blue check pattern, hadn't taken off his denim jacket, normal for the cool garage. "No, not with anyone. I did talk to a bunch of the volunteers who were there that night and guided one of the groups of birders to Strawbale."

"Strawbale? What's that? Where's it?"

"Oh, sorry. That's the old name for East Blind. They changed the name when they rebuilt it. It's the only one east of Nicolson Center."

"The only one? I thought there were two or three at least." She studied his eyes.

He stopped making eye contact. "You're right. I guess there are a couple of photo-blinds and one old regular blind that they still use if they have a really big crowd. All three of those are downstream from Strawbale, I mean East Blind."

"East Blind isn't a much better name than Strawbale. Why didn't they rename it after someone, like the others?" Bobbie hoped a conversational tone would keep Eddie gabbing.

"My guess is they're trying to sell the naming rights. A hundred grand, or whatever they want, will go a long way in their budget."

"Makes sense. So what time would you have brought the visitors back from East Blind?"

"Normally we bring everyone back as soon as it's too dark to see. By then the birds shouldn't see us. The dead trees and straw bales beside the blind make it easy to sneak in and out without bothering the cranes on the river, but we like to have the cover of darkness as well. Last Tuesday, the cranes were only about 50 feet from the blind, but it was very cold, so we left early. Several of my people were freezing." Eddie fidgeted and scratched his hands. "We tell people to dress warmly when they make their reservations. And I always warn them to take all their extra clothes before we leave Nicolson for the blinds. Many end up without enough clothes to keep warm, which happened last Tuesday for a bunch of my East Blind group."

"Doesn't it stay pretty warm in the blind? Straw bales are awfully good insulation, aren't they?" Bobbie realized that trying to play both the good cop and the bad cop would not work. But she didn't want another officer present because that would make the interview feel like an interrogation. She had to keep this friendly. A difficult self-assignment with Weird Cousin. He probably was not so weird in this family. He'd never win a weird-cousin contest with Uncle Menty in the running.

"No, the blind is a plywood shack. It is not made of straw bales" Eddie brightened considerably.

"Oh. I assumed from the name it was built like the visitor center. Didn't you say there were straw bales there?" She should have spent more time learning about Rowe. "Even so, with dozens of people in it, I'd expect it to warm up quite a bit."

"Good guess on the name. It comes from the fact that the first blind on that location *was* built from straw bales. Because the blind has a big viewing port for each person in the blind, that's twenty-five one by two foot holes, no heat is held in. The cold blows through the blind as though you're outside. A few straw bales are beside the blind to hide visitors from the river."

"Oh, so it was never made like the visitor center? No real insulation?" She tried to visualize the blind. It sounded like a large version of the photo blind.

"Yeah." Eddie nodded.

"Oh. Thank you." Bobbie bit her lip. "When you bring them back, if it's too dark to see, how do you lead them out?"

"We have several things to help. First we stay on the mowed road so it's a fairly smooth path with high weeds on both sides." His voice had no defensiveness, but reminded her of a teacher talking to a class. "Second, I have a flashlight to lead everyone and the other guide will be at the back of the group with a flashlight to make sure nobody gets lost. Third, there are tiny lights along the paths at each turn so the guides and visitors with good night vision can see where to go."

"Why don't the flashlights bother the cranes?"

"We have red filters on the guides' flashlights. It seems to work. The cranes are never bothered by us as we sneak the visitor groups in and out. Actually, I think we'd do better with blue filters because birds see red better than we do and some can even see in the infrared. I don't think they see blue as well. At least the red filters cut down the amount of light and remind the guests of the need to be slow and quiet. We tell our visitors to stick together and try to look like a giant millipede, not people. Except for

Nebraska every crane state has a hunting season. The birds are very skittish when they get here."

"And what did you do after you came back from the blind last Tuesday?" Bobbie studied Eddie's face and listened for the tone of his answer.

"I stood around outside talking to several of the visitors for 10 or 15 minutes and then went into the breakroom for a cup of coffee and a bite of Kenda's carrot bread." His tone seemed less confident and he was back to fidgeting. "I stayed in the volunteers' lounge, the breakroom, for quite some time, talking to Ruth and Carole Sue. I didn't pay much attention to when I left, but I probably got home about eleven."

"And the rest of the night?"

"I was home alone until I left for work between 7:15 and 7:30 Wednesday morning." He frowned. He looked as though he realized he was a suspect.

"Please think carefully, Eddie," Bobbie said. She knew she frowned, that her police interrogator personality was obvious. "As of now, you are a person of interest, if not yet a suspect. You have the knowledge and strength to have committed the crime, and you have a multi-million dollar motive."

"What motive? I had no reason to hurt Paul. He was a good friend." Eddie did look genuinely surprised. "We've even been birding together nearly every spring when he comes out here."

Seemed to be defending himself a little too vigorously. "He had named your employer and favorite charity, the Kearney Youth Home, in his will and the rumor I heard is he planned to change it and give everything to Rowe. Several people here have said you were aware of both those facts."

"*I* wouldn't get anything from him." He continued to protest with too much sincerity. "You're grasping at straws because you have nothing on anyone, right?"

"We have quite a bit on you. If KYH viewed a Capodicasa donation as your contribution, it would immeasurably enhance your career and position. And we saw blood in your truck." She studied him. "May we look in your truck and house? You know, for fingerprints, blood samples, anything tied to Mr. Capodicasa? The evidence might clear you completely. What do you say?"

"I don't like the idea of cops prying into everything, let me think about that."

"Please don't leave the county without notifying us where you're going. For the time being I want to know where you are all the time. On the other hand, I want to keep this as quiet as possible for your sake." Was he as innocent, as he pretended, or was he deluding himself, confident he had thoroughly buried everything incriminating?

Chapter 26

Mentes Petite

22 Years Earlier

Mentes opened the letter from his father. The envelope was the ivory watermark paper he used for his business correspondence and he'd applied his special red foil return-address label. Handwritten address. The paper matched the envelope. Nice texture, but why did he write? No salutation. No signature. Handwritten. "You little bastard. You not only raped your niece, you knocked her up. You may be able to live with that, but I can't." Mentes reread the letter several times before he really believed it. He called home.

"Hi, Mom. Is Dad there?"

"He's dead. I don't know what you did, but he said you are never to be allowed in his presence, especially in the hereafter. Don't call again. Good bye."

The call disconnected. Mentes looked at the table and phone.

It hadn't been rape. She wanted to. It was consensual. She enjoyed it.

Chapter 27

Candy is dandy, but liquor is quicker, and incest is ...

Tuesday, 7:30 P.M.

Bobbie met Chuck in the foyer at Gusto di Napoli. When they were seated, before any wine had been ordered or delivered, Bobbie asked, "You said you occasionally go to Nicks' games. Are there other teams you follow?"

"No. Not really. Nicks are the only team I go watch." He seemed distracted. Round Paul took a wine order, which Bobbie noticed because the previous times the wine had appeared with no apparent request. "I've been to a few baseball and football games. I think I've see all the New York teams at home, but those were for family or business reasons—the game was secondary, or even irrelevant."

Bobbie studied him. She wondered if he would wear the blue blazer, gray slacks, and open neck shirt in New York. Probably not. Air travel presents so many challenges, he probably left everything but a basic change at home. Wait, he could have also shipped clothes here, something she could never afford to do. Where he's staying? Are his digs as posh as his Lexus? Something more to find out.

She finished the wine in her glass, another sign of Chuck's distraction. "You've been out here crane viewing with your father several times. Were all your visits many years ago?"

"Uh, yeah. The last time I was here must have been almost 20 years ago." He smiled. "Dad's the only birder in the family." She noted his jacket was not new so he probably hadn't received or bought any new clothes yet. She hoped that didn't mean he planned to leave soon. They ordered dinner.

Before the salad came, she tried again. "I've been to some of the sights in New York, but only the big name ones. Which others do you like?"

"I think the memorial and building on the World Trade Center site is worth a trip. Some of the other Lower Manhattan tourist traps are fun too. That's where I live, Lower Manhattan, near Wall Street and Greenwich Village, the fun part of The City." The salad arrived. Chuck motioned for some freshly ground pepper then waved Round Paul off and shook red pepper flakes from the table's shaker on it.

She savored her arugula-carrot-radicchio salad with Gusto di Napoli's house dressing and studied the bright red tomatoes and radishes in it. She had to ask. "How's Nicola handling the attack aftermath?"

"She's scared for the first time in her life. She's blaming herself for being cute." Chuck looked disgusted.

Bobbie looked down and shook her head. "I wonder how many times I've told victims not to blame themselves." She paused studying the wine and thought about her reasons for blaming herself.

"Damn it. Victims are never to blame." He frowned.

"You're right." Bobbie shook her head. "Maybe it's some worry about not be quite careful enough that makes us want to blame ourselves." *Oops.* She hadn't meant to use first person. Maybe he wouldn't notice she implicitly admitted to being a rape victim.

"Good point." He rubbed the bridge of his nose.

After a little too much wine, several minutes of embarrassing silence, and several attempts to restart the conversation, she asked, "So, tell me what your boys do?"

"Tony's majoring in sociology and I think Marc will be a computer geek or something like that." Bobbie saw the scene in *Gigi* when Louis Jordan sang "She's not thinking of me." Gaston, Jordan's character, poured his glass of champagne, or whatever it was, down his vivacious date's cleavage because she had completely forgotten him. Maybe Chuck-'s change of subject showed gallantry or embarrassment instead of inattention. And he was certainly not the life of everyone else's party, as Gaston's date had been.

Bobbie tried several more subjects but couldn't engage Chuck. She felt sure her behavior was not the cause. It must be something else. She wanted their relationship to flourish and to learn more about him. Maybe it was family or business problems in New York.

After the too-quiet dinner, Bobbie watched as Chuck's Lexus pulled away. She turned toward Round Paul Valentino. "Since you're not very busy tonight, can we talk about Paul Capodicasa for a few minutes." She explained that she hoped to find some tidbit of information to help under-stand what had happened a week earlier.

Paul Valentino completed his culinary training when Chuck was in sixth grade. He then apprenticed as a sous-chef in one of Paul Capodicas-a's night clubs for several years. Even if he could round up the financing for a restaurant in New York, the violence worried him. New York seemed like a poor place to raise kids.

One winter evening Mr. Capodicasa ordered a Tiramisu. Valentino looked over his specialties, the ones that had been started for the evening, picked the best and finished preparing it. He drizzled a small amount of dark chocolate sauce and dusted it with chocolate powder. He drew a bird with more drizzle of several colors. Outside Mr. Capodicasa's office he waited for a response to his knock. He tried to calm himself. No use.

"Come in."

He opened the door and presented the dessert to his boss and watched.

"Very good, Paul." Mr. Capodicasa took another bite.

"Sir, if you have a couple of minutes, I have a business question I'd like to ask."

"I always have time for such a question. Shoot."

"I'd like to start my own restaurant, but way away from The City. My ideal location is a city barely big enough to support one outstanding restaurant. A good place for raising kids"

"Actually, I have a recommendation right off the bat, Paul. I like to go the Kearney, Nebraska, for my spring break each year and I would like a good restaurant. I'll be there in about a month. Maybe you should come out at the same time. You could look around and size up the area."

"Thank you, sir." Valentino smiled and bowed slightly as he took a step small back.

"The one downside of such a move would be us losing some great Tiramisu." Paul Capodicasa smiled.

Four months later Paul Valentino moved to Kearney, Nebraska, to oversee renovation of a defunct Mexican restaurant into the Gusto di Napoli. Paul Capodicasa had suggested the name and cosigned for the financing he'd need to get started.

At her condo Bobbie found a brown lunch bag by the door. She stooped to pick up Bear and the bag. A single slice of shoofly pie, Mommom's shoofly pie. Mommom was always so gracious. She put the pie on a small plate, nuked it for 30 seconds and sat down to enjoy a second dessert. Her first bite of Mommom's shoofly pie in years. The real thing.

She turned on the TV and sat to savor the pie. Something was wrong. She retched and spit the pie into her cupped hands. That wasn't a dry taste but a metallic one. She washed her hands and threw the rest of the pie down the garbage disposal. She rinsed her mouth several times. Spoiled food sure had an awful taste.

She returned to her living room and stared at the TV. Maybe she should have saved the pie for testing. No point, the health department only tests restaurant food. She called her grandmother. After exchanging hellos, she asked, "Did you send some pie over?"

"No. I made two pies after you asked about it, but I served it all Sunday. I told everyone you asked about it and that I was sorry you missed it. Why do you ask?"

"Somebody brought me a piece of your shoofly pie. It must have turned. Probably been sitting out too long. It tasted funny. I threw it out."

"Can't imagine it would spoil. It'll keep for days, even in warm weather."

Chapter 28

When to recuse

Wednesday, 8:20 A.M.

For a decade Leon Grayson had been reelected every other year to Sheriff of Buffalo County. Bobbie never considered running for any political office, but Grayson's performance for the press had started her thinking in terms of including details of her investigations that would lend themselves to his performances. For the last three years she gave him the sort of interesting, sordid or juicy details he liked. The ones that inspired his performances.

He'd earned the fond nickname *Madman* from the Fourth Estate for the lively way he entertained them at briefings, like the ones for the Capodicasa murder. He aped the killer's stalking of the blind's inhabitants and the bludgeoning of Paul Capodicasa. He reminded them of the way Crocodile Dundee had foiled the mob on his home turf in Australia and showed how snipers and spies would protect Central Nebraskans from Mafiosi. Bobbie had no doubt that his antics guaranteed his reelection, abetted by local television's love of the caricature he was.

Bobbie Lee walked into Grayson's office to find the Sheriff waiting for her. She'd prepared the sort of details he seemed to like. First term County Attorney Petite sat at the round side table, lost in the burgundy-leather covered chair. She hadn't noticed him at first. He held a legal pad in his right hand and made notes or doodled on it. "Good morning Sheriff, Uncle Mentes." Mentes wore a slightly musky scent, probably his deodorant.

She was glad she felt well prepared for the briefing. Here were both of the men who were doing their damnedest to guarantee future reelections based on her investigation. She wasn't bothered that they would garner the credit from the television reporters for solving the case. Conversely, she was aware they knew poor police work would cost them dearly in November.

"Sit down, Lee." Grayson looked stern.

She sat and turned to look at the County Attorney. He was no happier. This wasn't her briefing, after all. She had only a week on the investigation, they couldn't already be feeling pressure to solve the case, could they? She turned back to see the Sheriff motion toward the CA. Did Menty insist on pushing her aside? This was the most interesting case she'd worked on. It'd be years before another puzzle like this came along.

"Bobbie," Petite said, "There is nothing prejudicial about reassignment. No negative connotation, not even the slightest personnel record smudge. But, conflict of interest and failure to pursue leads appropriately would cause all sorts of negative legal and personnel results."

Bobbie nodded toward Petite as he spoke, acknowledging her understanding. She realized her frown showed them she knew she was about to be removed from the investigation. She tried to think what conflict of interest they thought they'd found. With only a week since the murder, they couldn't be worrying about missing some lead. Oh my God, maybe they disapprove of my dinners with Chuck. Her mind lasered onto the dates, the ones she hoped would lead to something after the investigation. Even if Chuck lied about his divorce, there wasn't anything illegal or inappropriate about eating with him. Unprofessional and dumb, maybe. No, worse, not maybe, definitely anti-professional.

She had other sources that confirmed the divorce. Could he have remarried and she missed it? No, no sign of that. Legal and stupid. Moral but hormonal. Damn.

"Mr. Petite, the Sheriff and I discussed the issue of impartiality a couple of days ago. Is there something new that has arisen?"

She pressed her hands against her gut to calm herself and studied CA Petite's tie, a yellow paisley power tie. The type he always wore when he might be on television. It billowed out in a sensuous loop above his trademark red vest, draped with a gold watch chain, though she had never seen a watch. Small man syndrome clothing of the sort she expected on a male politician of her height. Two Napolean-complex politicians in her county, and they were both here. Each was sure he was her boss.

"We're concerned that your primary suspect is your cousin," Grayson said. "You may be subconsciously ignoring facts or focusing too many resources on him. And even if there is no bias in your investigation, the appearance is bad. We need to be sure no hint of conflict of interest shows."

Bobbie felt confused. True, Eddie Stuart was her cousin, but she hardly knew him or others in his family. Except for the interview last week, she'd had no conversation with Eddie of more than 20 words in almost 20 years. Only family gossip about the Stuarts. She knew nothing about her mother's relatives. "I thought everything was settled Monday. Sir, if you don't mind, can you tell me what has changed?"

Madman Grayson turned toward the County Attorney. "Mentes?"

"I guess there's no reason not to lay my cards on the table, Bobbie. We received a direct complaint from your grandmother. She thinks you're persecuting her grandson, Eddie Stuart." CA Petite slouched in Grayson's easy chair. He had a half smile.

"Mommom does dote on her grandchildren, but she's over-reacting. I have to check all leads." Bobbie hesitated for a moment, wondering if it was Mommom, or Grandma Lee. But Grandma Lee wasn't related to Eddie. Easy to rule her out. She turned toward the sheriff. "Also, sir, Cousin Eddie is practically estranged from the family." Grayson won't know about the family and he's the person I really have to convince. "In addition to the fact that we are not a close family, Eddie is so obnoxious that I avoid him whenever possible. Mommom may be reacting to that." She could discern neither politician's attitude. "Sir, may I make a request?" Bobbie decided to tell Grayson about Eddie's employer, the Kearney Youth Home, when Menty was not there.

"Yes, okay." Grayson glanced at Mentes, apparently assuring himself of the CA's support.

"Talk to Eddie or watch him in a crowd. He cannot stand not being the center of attention. He'll walk into a crowded conversation and loudly start talking about himself, so the conversation will change. He's doing great work at the Kearney Youth Home, but the real reason he teaches is because it guarantees him a devoted audience six hours a day, every school day."

"You don't like him much, do you?" Petite still sported the smug look of someone with secret information about the discussion.

Mentes was one of several members of the family she had good reason to detest. She wondered if he was still mad about being stopped for speeding. Perhaps this was just to get her. "I have no like or dislike for him," Bobbie said. "I hardly know him. I do know that he will complain to everyone within earshot about any perceived injustice or negative remark. I suspect he complained to Mommom about the fact that I asked him for an alibi. I'm also pretty sure that he would rather be the subject of the investigation than outside it looking in. I'd bet anything he'd prefer to be accused over being ignored."

"No alibi, huh?" Madman Grayson said.

"Like everyone connected to the case, sir." Bobbie turned to face her Sheriff. "No alibi and the two people with at least some financial motives are Eddie Stuart and Frank Armstrong. Both have, at least at times, had their favorite charities named in Capodicasa's will, and they knew it. Both their careers would be greatly enhanced, maybe saved, by the sort of megabuck bequest they expected Capodicasa to make." Bobbie turned back toward Petite. "Mentes, my gut feeling is neither of them is guilty, but I haven't ruled them out." How'd a rapist like him ever get to be CA, anyway. How could he go on about her. Menty couldn't be objec-tive about anything she did. Give enough money away and you buy all the right friends.

"Well, we still have problems," Petite said softly, more to Madman than to Bobbie.

Bobbie straightened to attention in her chair. What problem? What will appease Grayson and Petite and at least buy me a few more days. "Sir, I hope the decision to take the case away from me is not final. I think I am very close to finishing it, which I would like to do." What details will give Petite the feeling he's controlling the whole show. "I have hardly spoken to Eddie Stuart until last week when I interviewed him. Except for a few words at Thanksgiving or Christmas, I don't think I've spoken with him since before I became a deputy. I have nothing for or against the Stuarts—I hardly know them. I have been and will continue to be impar-tial in judging any facts regarding them. I would like to continue leading this investigation for at least a few more days. We are that close to tying up the loose ends, even without the DNA results from Lincoln."

Grayson looked at the CA. Some communication went on. He turned back to Bobbie. "Mr. Petite and I need to discuss this before we authorize you to continue. At this point in time, please prepare to relinquish your role. Bring Tom up to speed so he can take over for you. If the change of investigative lead has to be made we want the transition to be fast and perfectly smooth." Grayson paused. "We'll make a final decision soon. So for now you and Tom will be joint leaders."

"Yes, sir. I'll start briefing Tom immediately." She looked at Grayson to see if she was dismissed. Probably not. "If you have a few minutes, sir, I'd like to bring you up to date on the investigation. If he has time, Mr. Petite might be interested also." Maybe he's worried that his felony will come to light. If so, this will calm that fear.

Again Grayson checked with Petite before answering. "Okay. What have you got?"

"I thought you'd like to know that when I found Mikey Ippolito's body, it was in pretty bad shape from several days in the woods, and it was being eaten by a mountain lion and two dogs. I had to chase them away. I fired shots to scare one of the dogs and the cat. I finally shot the rottweiler when it came back to get Mikey's arm and I couldn't scare it off. Mr. Eskay—he owns the section north of Rowe—was more than a little perturbed at losing a vicious dog." Bobbie paused and studied her Sheriff. She felt sure he'd have a cap gun or some blanks in his revolver so he could fire a shot for the press. Anything to get on the evening news.

"Thank you. Anything else?"

"Yes, sir." Bobbie looked back and forth between Petite and Grayson. "Actually, two more things. The first: Tom saw blood on the steering wheel of Eddie Stuart's truck. I don't believe we've gotten a search warrant or permission to search the truck. We haven't yet followed up on that." Searching Eddie's truck should buy her some time. She studied both men. "Tom did think the blood was old."

"And the other one?" Grayson smiled for the first time since the interview began.

"The other item is less important. I called Ms. Ippolito to let her know I'd found her son and to ask for a positive ID. She stayed with me until Scotty and Smithson arrived. I think you know everything else, sir. I had not included those details in my report. Dr. Eisenberg's report on

Mikey Ippolito should be coming out soon. It will have many details that you'll probably want to know and that should help reveal his role in the whole thing."

"Yes. Thank you, Lee."

Bobbie was unhappy at her dismissal. If she tried to do more it would weaken her argument and probably shorten her tenure as lead investigator.

After briefing Tom Shirk on the assumptions and leads for Capodicasa's murder, Bobbie and he drove to Rowe so he could be introduced to key people there. As they walked in the main entrance to the Nicolson Visitor Center, Bobbie saw Chuck sitting across the lobby watching the birds at the bird feeders. "Since Chuck Capodicasa is right here, let's start with him." Bobbie looked at Tom as she pointed to Chuck.

When the introductions were done and the two cops were about to leave, Chuck spoke quietly to Bobbie. "I tried to call your cell, but got no answer. I have to leave soon. When you have a minute, can we talk?" The tone of his voice did not promise anything good.

After the morning's bad news, Bobbie felt the return of the foreboding pain in her stomach. "Let's meet out in front in about ten minutes." Bobbie waved toward the main entrance to the visitor center. "Is that soon enough? It'll give me time to show Tom around."

"That's good. That's about all the time I have."

Seven minutes later, Tom spoke to Bobbie. "Go see what Chuck wants. I'll look around in the gift shop. I think my girls would like some stuffed cranes."

Chuck stood near the double doors and walked out with Bobbie. "We'll have better privacy if we go for a walk." He pointed down the path to the west, toward his father's photo-blind. They walked west, past the classroom of the Nicolson Visitor Center.

The knots in Bobbie's stomach worsened. She tried to think of some positives, but all she came up with were concerns that she had never been able to make a long-term connection with a man. She vaguely heard him apologizing for his request. *I have to listen.*

"I know things here are very different from New York and even more different from CSI and such, but I'm worried about the investigation. Could you be so close to some of the suspects that you won't do a good job? Should you consider stepping aside?"

Bobbie could feel herself jump. *Et tu, Chuckie*. She felt sure nothing showed and she still had some hope that she would not lose her investigation. She might be replaced, but nothing definite had happened and it might not. This came from Chuck to her personally, not from familial prompting. Does he have sources inside Grayson's or Petite's office? "What do you mean that I'm too close? Is there something specific that concerns you?"

He frowned and made some thoughtful faces. "I don't have anything specific. Your list of possible perps includes some of your relatives, doesn't it?"

"Yes, but that will not in any way impede the investigation. It isn't as though I feel any sibling rivalry or anything like that. I'm not after anyone. My family won't stand against outsiders." Should she ask about his attitude? She never liked whiners and asking him for support would sound like a complaint not a request.

"As I said, it's a gut reaction to what I see here. Or maybe to what I *think* I feel." He directed their stroll so they looped back around toward the parking lot. "I'd wait longer, but I have to go back. I have to return to The City to attend to dozens of business and family problems that have arisen in the last week." He paused for a few seconds and looked at his watch. "I know you'll do what is right. Keep your objectivity in mind." He stopped as they reached his rented Lexus. He opened the door and pulled out a gift bag and handed it to her.

"Here's a little something for you." He shook her hand. "I'm sorry I have to go, but I really have to run now."

Bobbie felt her abs cramp. Her vision was down to a tunnel on only Chuck and his black car. Had she been dumped? She forced a smile and tried to make eye contact as he got in his car. She didn't manage to say anything before he closed the door. He opened the window and she finally managed to speak. "I hope you make it back to Nebraska soon."

"Hope so." He looked at Bobbie, but she couldn't read anything in his mechanical reply. She could barely see it.

Bobbie's vision blurred. She hoped he couldn't see her wet eyes. She had to be strong. No whining. Why'd she make that lame, come back to Nebraska remark? Maybe he thought she was an item with someone else. Oh, damn. He backed his car out of its slot and she looked into the bag. Next to the two bottles of Chianti was a red Rowe coffee mug. He waved as he pulled forward to leave Rowe. Maybe this was his attempt to establish a relationship. Maybe she expected too much from a guy. Maybe. Maybe Maybe.

Chapter 29

Eyewitness accounts—Provably unreliable

Wednesday, 1:00 P.M.

Eddie Stuart claimed he gabbed in the break room until about 11 and then went home. Time to talk to his friends and co-workers. What would Carole Sue and Ruth recall about his temperament? Only a patho-logical murderer could beat a man to death then go to class with no discernible change in demeanor. Obnoxious was not even in the vicinity of neurotic, even further from psychotic.

His behavior to her said *innocent,* but she needed more evidence to rule him entirely out of the picture.

Bobbie looked in Mulcahy's vacant office as she walked toward the volunteers' break room looking for either woman. Carole Sue, dressed in a forest green Rowe tee shirt and faded dungarees, was in the office across the hall where reservations for the blinds were being taken on the phone. As Bobbie waited for the end of the call, she smelled the coffee burning behind her.

The phone call ended. "Carole Sue, do you have time to answer some questions?" As always she studied Carole Sue's blue eyes.

The volunteer turned her questioning face to the employee sitting at her desk in the office. Before she could speak, Reeves, as her name tag identified her, said, "Go with her, Carole Sue. The investigation is much more important than backup for us in here. I can manage until you're done."

Bobbie made small talk until the door to Duane's office closed. "I'm trying to corroborate where everyone was Tuesday night, Carole Sue. Can you tell me what you did and who you were with late Tuesday, after the visitors left."

"Haven't thought of any more details. Drank coffee. No probably not. Probably drank wine and gabbed with Eddie for an hour or so. Went back to my camper alone, to bed." As before Carole Sue looked very business-like, no hint of dissembling or evading.

"Did you flirt with Eddie?"

Carole Sue's eyes widened for a second. She frowned. "Don't know. Probably. I mean, who wouldn't flirt with a good looking young guy?" Her frown continued as though she was trying to remember details.

Bobbie waited, hoping she'd recall more about the evening. It's amazing how tastes vary. Eddie was pudgy, flabby and so egotistical. He was not fat, but not at all lean and athletic like Chuck. And so self-centered. As the silence grew embarrassing, she spoke. "What about Eddie? Did he flirt with you?"

"Don't recall. Probably. Hope I'm cute enough he would." The frowns, the apparent soul searching, continued. She looked at something through the window behind Bobbie.

Bobbie turned to see what was outside and became aware of the crane's clacking before she saw a few of them flying low toward a field a half-mile south of Nicolson Center. They would probably land in Kearney County, in Al Beasley's jurisdiction, not hers. She turned back toward Carole Sue. "Do you remember what you talked about?"

"Birds. Mostly cranes, pelicans and chickens. Eddie's a serious birder. Takes groups to see prairie chickens and white pelicans and brings them to see both kinds of cranes. He said people are fascinated by all three. Asked if I wanted to go see the whoopers. Thursday we went to see them."

"On Tuesday night *he* invited *you* to go looking for whooping cranes? They're the really rare ones right?"

"Yeah. He invited me. And, yeah, they are very rare. Rainwater Basin is one of the few places where they're easy to see, but only if you know where to look. Eddie always does." The Rainwater Basin is an area of Nebraska south and west of Rowe.

Carole Sue should relax more talking about birds. "How rare are they?"

Carole Sue seemed to brighten. "I think their population was down to under two dozen a half-century ago. Now they're probably something like 750 of them. We don't see them in Rowe itself—they like roosting in lakes instead of rivers. The sandhills are the river roosters."

"When I was in school they talked about using sandhill cranes to teach the whooping cranes where to migrate. Is that how they've increased the population?"

"They tried. Didn't work. Some whooper eggs were put into sandhill nests and joined their flocks. Migrated with them but have stayed with the sandhills for decades. Must not know they're whoopers. Cross-species breeding doesn't work very well. Whoopers were too dumb to realize they weren't sandhills."

"You mean..." Bobbie tried to think of how to ask the question.

Carole Sue finished for her. "At least one whooper migrated with the sandhills for years. Maybe twenty years. If it's still alive, it's probably with them now. Each spring it was reported on the river near Grand Island. Don't know about its love life, but no one's ever reported whoophills or sanders."

"Did you see the whoopers on Thursday?"

"Yeah. Nice trip. Good birding here. Also saw a leucistic sandhill." Carole Sue's eyes became bright and her smile grew.

"What's that?" Bobbie had never heard the word and didn't even try to repeat it.

"Basically that's an albino sandhill crane. Maybe even rarer than a whooper now. Most reports of whoopers near the river are actually the white sandhills, the leucistic ones."

So much about birds that Bobbie didn't know. "Did Eddie seem relaxed?"

"Yeah. Good, voluble Eddie. Always knows where to find birds. He knows them all. Fun drive, as always."

Bobbie gabbed some more with Carole Sue. Nothing she recalled indicated Eddie was under any unusual stress last week. When Bobbie finished her interview she sought out Ruth, whom she found in the classroom, where she watched the cranecam monitor and sat with its control in the lap of her floral print dress. Ruth told a similar story about Tuesday evening. She hadn't gone birding with Eddie. "I did notice he flirted with

Carole Sue. If he flirted with me, I'm too old to notice it. I figured if he was trying to make hay with her and he didn't really want me along anyway."

Bobbie headed back to Kearney and Eddie Stuart's employer. She answered a call from Tom Shirk. "Eddie Stuart left his truck window open so I got some samples of the blood I saw."

"Oh good."

"Yeah. But I don't think it will yield anything—it looks months old. I've sent it off to Lincoln, just in case. Pretty sure it'll only serve to eliminate him."

"Thanks Tom. I'm checking his alibi, sort of. I'll let you know what happens." She knew the lab's attitude, *Police work and then, and only if it looks important for a trial, the CSI stuff.* "Just the fact he gave permission say's he's unlikely to be involved."

At KYH, Principal Lanpow pulled Eddie's teaching schedule up on the screen of his computer and showed it to Bobbie. She looked at it to decipher the meaning. "Oh, he has a free second period? Do you know what he'd do then?"

"I'm pretty sure he's usually in the teachers' lounge." Lanpow's *Nebraska tux,* denim coveralls and a plaid shirt, seemed more appropriate to a farmer than a principal. "He's very conscientious so he would be prepared before class and there's no special paperwork he'd have piled up before him right now."

"Are there other faculty members who might have talked to him at that time? Others with a free second period."

Lanpow paged through schedules. "Let's see. Jim Baker is free then, but he rarely uses the lounge. Ditto Cornwall." His voice trailed off mumbling other names. "Whiting! Whiting is in the lounge whenever she's free. She should have been there at that time."

"Any chance she's still here?" Bobbie looked at her watch.

"Let's check." He leaned over the credenza and looked out his window to the right. "I see her car out there. Maybe we can find her in the lounge." As they walked down the hall Bobbie was transported back to school by the aroma of kids and floor cleaning compound and the sound of a floor polisher. They turned a corner and passed a custodian buffing the hall tiles.

Principal Lanpow introduced Bobbie to Sara Whiting, who taught physics and chemistry. He excused himself and left them alone in the lounge, which smelled of coffee and cheap perfume. Ms. Whiting, who appeared to be about 25, was dressed in a conservative yellow suit. She had the beautiful skin and eyes of a young woman who had not spent much time in the sun damaging them. She smelled of cherry blossoms and something, perhaps from Dial soap.

Bobbie complimented Ms. Whiting on her long brown hair that seemed to match her eyes, then asked, "I'm working on where people were and what they were doing last week. Do you remember if Eddie Stuart came into the lounge during your free second period last Wednesday, a week ago today?"

"My God. Is he a suspect in the murder at Rowe?"

"No. Definitely not," Bobbie lied. "I'm constructing time lines and working on understanding the case."

"I can't remember that day specifically." She stared at Bobbie without focusing her eyes. "If he hadn't been here, I think I would remember." She now made a normal amount of eye contact. "We're always talking about something. I'm sure it would have struck me if I were alone. Eddie's never quiet, you know."

"Yeah." Bobbie nodded and smiled. "Any recollection of anything out of the ordinary that morning?"

"You mean, did Eddie act funny?" She paused, staring without seeing again. "As before all I have to go on is that I don't remember anything. If he did anything weird, I think I would remember that. Sorry, I know lack of evidence is not evidence of lack. It's the best I can do."

Bobbie thanked Sara. She gave the teacher her card. "Please phone me if you recall any specific information." Either Eddie was Joe Cool, a pathological murderer, or not the murderer at all.

Got to be someone else.

Chapter 30

When all probables are eliminated, the improbable must be true

Wednesday, 4:30 P.M.

Bobbie arrived at the Nebraska Institute of Forensic Sciences Regional Center as the autopsy on Mikey was about to begin. She'd never before had two autopsies in a month, let alone a week. She assumed her usual position, near the east wall where she could escape down the hall if she started to feel nauseous. Dr. Fisk Eisenberg had Mikey on the table and his tech, Nancy Lu, prepared for the exam.

Martha Ippolito was not there. Bobbie had described the procedures of the postmortem and must have been too vivid. *Damn it. Hope I did the right thing.*

Both Dr. Eisenberg and Ms. Lu were in white lab coats that covered all their other clothing. Bobbie wondered if the smocks were made out of some material that prevented the smell of death from permeating their clothes. Or maybe they wore no clothes under the medical examiner smocks. Everything she wore would go in the laundry as soon as she was done. And she studiously stayed well away from the corpse, at least five feet away. She had no need for a close look, only to hear and observe.

She paid attention to one diagnosis. Mikey had no defensive wounds, at least nothing visible after the cat and dogs. "No visible injuries on the ulnar side of the right hand," where defensive injuries would show, where he'd have been hit if tried to parry a blow.

Fisk did observe, "Severe lacerations on left shoulder that appear to be inflicted by a large animal, probably a bear or mountain lion."

When the examination completed, Bobbie asked, "Is there any chance he died from exposure before the bear or cat mauling?"

"A heavily clothed and healthy young person should survive for a week, even in our nasty March. It should take a lot more than severe exposure and a lack of will to survive to kill him. We saw some signs of cold or flu, but nothing serious enough. Also, his blood was still flowing when he was mauled. He might have been unconscious, but he wasn't yet dead." Fisk spoke slowly. "If the toxicology tests in Lincoln all come back negative, as I expect, I'll conclude he was killed, probably by a mountain lion."

"Could you tell if Mikey was in a coma when the animals got to him?" Had Frisky said something during the exam? If so, she'd missed it.

"No, no way to tell." No uncertainty in his voice.

"That's even more gruesome than I expected. Ugh. Thank you." Being eaten alive was the worst death Bobbie could imagine.

She returned to Rowe and walked from the Nicolson Center parking lot toward the photo-blind where Paul Capodicasa's life had ended. Maybe retracing the events of that Tuesday evening would shed more light or understanding on what happened. Anyway, the sun and cool air felt nice. She wished she spent more time outside. Except for the feedlot smell, the breeze out of the east felt delightful. She put her hand over her nose. The smell of money to the local farmers. Stink of lucre, to Bobbie. She'd take the moldy, pollen-ridden air of their forests any day.

Eight days ago, at about this time of day, Paul Capodicasa sat in front of the Nicolson Center enjoying the sounds and smells of Buffalo County. What did he think about as he sat on the bench in the rain? He must have been happy to be away from his business interests in New York, in *The City,* as Chuck always referred to it. Could he have had premonitions? If Mikey was off by himself, was Capodicasa irritated that the young man did not talk to him? Or, perhaps they'd talked so much on the trip from New York that he enjoyed the short period of solitude. Perhaps he fretted about being away from his businesses. Just because Bobbie didn't like thinking about business doesn't mean Paul disliked it. Soon he would be taken to the blind for the last time in his life.

Somebody had to have beaten him to death. And if Mikey had been attacked, how'd he get away and across the river with no signs of any defensive injury? Damn.

Mikey was killed by the mountain lion with no detectable bludgeoning injuries. He did have Paul's blood on his clothes. Why would he beat Paul, who had paid for his equipment and trip? Paul had turned Mikey's life around, and Mikey knew it and was grateful by all accounts. He treated Mikey like a son and Mikey revered him like a father. A loved, not hated, father. But Mikey's the only one left. He must have been involved in the murder. Damn.

Eddie said Mikey wouldn't harm anybody, but that he was frightened at being away from everything familiar. Eddie's been working with troubled kids for years. He ought to know. Mikey must have felt alone because so few people even noticed him before they went to the blind. She needed more information about Mikey and especially about his state of mind.

Bobbie looked south across the fields of corn stubble into Kearney County. Dozens of cranes were gleaning corn, getting today's three and half ounce share, and five vultures were working on the carcass of a deer. A tough winter for deer means a good spring for vultures. She stopped and looked at the vultures then turned back toward the visitor center. Vultures could be covered in blood even though they had nothing to do with killing the deer. *Could Mikey have been at the scene after the murder and gotten the blood on his clothes?* Doesn't make sense. Damn. She walked slowly staring at the ground without seeing it.

Bobbie looked up at the woods. She had been relying exclusively on Cousin Eddie's analysis of Mikey Ippolito for the lack of motivation. She needed to find more people who had talked to him. Near the visitor center she decided she'd have to try to talk to everyone who was around last Tuesday afternoon. She walked into Nicolson thinking about the Cow Knee Road incident, when the blind man came to the Nicolson Visitor Center. Everyone was asked to sign in. It would require a bunch of leg work, but she could start with the local visitors. She hoped the registry included guest phone numbers.

After the twentieth call, she tired of identifying herself, asking for the person or persons who had been at Rowe and asking if the visitor remembered seeing Mikey. Usually she had at least one name, but some visitors had not written legibly so all she could do was make a generic request. Three no-answers, eight voice-mail or machine messages, one bad number. Six people said something like "I can't remember seeing any one like that." Two people remembered seeing a kind of creepy guy dressed in black, but they hadn't talked to him.

Creepy? Well, if Mikey were mine, I suppose we wouldn't be talking. He was still at the age when parents are nearly as dumb as logs.

Ruth's description put him outside, at least for a few minutes before they went to the blind. If his entire wait was outside in the drizzle, few people would notice him. Well, maybe calling people who might have talked to him wasn't such a good idea after all. One of the messages could yield something, but it didn't seem likely.

Duh. She hit her forehead with her palm. Wait, there was another prospect. The shrink who had been treating Mikey. Chuck had turned up some information on his therapy and Martha and Anthony have the statements because they were paying. But she didn't want to contact them unless all other resources fail. One way or another she had to find out who the psychoanalyst was. She looked at her watch. It was 5:35 in New York. The shrink might even be in his office. She called Chuck.

"Hello, Chuck. How are you this evening." Bobbie used a sultry voice. Enough come-hither vibes to let him know she still liked him but not so much that he'd be offended. She could see him, in open-neck shirt with two gold chains. That great-looking, athletic body.

"Hey, Bobbie." Businesslike. Not even so much as a *glad you called* or *how's my favorite cop*. Well, if he's forgotten me, I better get over him. Her image faded to a guy in a dark suit.

"Martha said Mikey was seeing a shrink because of what happened in jail. Can you get me the analyst's name and phone number?" She talked like any other conversant.

"Yeah. Hold on." Chuck made various thinking noises and swore at his computer one time then came back with the name, office and home phone numbers and email address. "I shouldn't have given you that home number. Don't call Dr. Covey at home unless nothing else works. I'm pretty sure Mikey was seeing him. I'll check and if I learn anything different, I'll call with the corrected data right away. Okay?"

Bobbie thanked him. She wished Chuck were still in Nebraska. Still his original expensive-aftershave-smelling self. She wondered what scent he wore and guessed it was imported. It was unique.

She dialed Covey's office number as she walked across the Nicolson Center parking lot. "You have reached Dr. Covey's office. We're gone for the day. If this is an emergency, please call nine one one. Otherwise please call back during our normal business hours, between nine and five." Bobbie hung up and returned to her office to update the paperwork on her investigation.

She found a package of almonds, ones she knew she hadn't placed on her credenza. Cyanide smelled like almonds. Could that piece of shoofly pie have had something in it? Better have this package checked. She put on latex gloves, picked up the package by the corner and put it in an envelope. Uncle Mentes Petite had been trying to get her removed from the investigation. Could he be trying to make her sick? She could think of nobody else who could mess with her car, get a piece of Mommom's pie, and drop off something in her office. How can she protect herself?

I should have taken Grayson's watch-my-back advice more seriously. Not for the mob, but for Menty.

Chapter 31

Honey attracts more flies than vinegar

Thursday, 7:25 A.M.

Bobbie was in her office earlier than normal. The office smelled of the industrial cleaners used over-night, not much better than the usual weekend morning aroma of sweaty, unwashed drunks. Something about human aromas makes them permeate everything. Phones were worse than stenches, but they were the only choice for getting any information about Mikey's mental state. She redialed.

"Hello, Dr. Covey's Office." Definite New York City accent.

"Good morning, I am Investigator Bobbie Lee of the Buffalo County, Nebraska, Sheriff's Department." Bobbie pronounced her name slowly and used her most friendly voice.

"Good morning Officer Lee. How may I help you?" The voice had a mature sound that Bobbie interpreted to mean the operator was at least in her forties. She visualized a frumpy receptionist and immediately wondered why that image popped into her head.

"May I speak to Dr. Covey for a few minutes about Mikey Ippolito? It is urgent, but won't take long. Five minutes max."

The receptionist took her number. "I'll relay the message but I don't think Dr. Covey will call back soon. He's a very busy doctor." She sounded more bored than protective. She was probably programmed to tell everyone the same thing.

Bobbie wondered if she could intimidate either the receptionist or the doctor the way the cops so often did on "Law and Order." She decided that polite brevity was the best enticement. "I'm sure he is and I don't want to waste any of his time. But, please be sure the note tells him the call is about the *late* Mikey Ippolito, and that it will be very short."

Twenty minutes later, Dr. Covey called. After he identified himself, Bobbie said, "I am the Buffalo County Nebraska Investigator of Mikey Ippolito's and Paul Capodicasa's deaths."

"Paul Capodicasa's murder was in the papers here, but I had not heard about Michael Ippolito's death."

"He died after Mr. Capodicasa, probably a few days later. The autopsy's preliminary finding is that he died of exposure." Bobbie considered her semi-lie an interrogation technique. "I think he may have witnessed the Capodicasa murder." Bobbie had not really admitted to herself that Mikey had been killed by a mountain lion and she clung to the hope that he had died before the cat found him. She saw the shrink in a red upholstered wing-back chair next to an empty reclining couch.

"Exposure is an unusual cause of death, isn't it? Even out west in Nebraska?"

"Yes and that's a big part of what we're trying to understand. Can you tell me anything about Mikey's state of mind?" She stared at the light on her phone. I wonder if it's hiding any answers.

"Well, as you know, doctor-patient confidentiality prevents me from saying anything about him." He sounded a little like he was trying to convince himself.

"Of course, Doctor," Bobbie said, "I wouldn't want you to violate any principle like that. But Mikey is deceased and we're trying to determine what happened. Nothing more." Bobbie paused and considered whether she should elaborate. She visualized a goateed Dr. Freud looka-like, sitting next to his couch. Someone who could be any of the cartoon psychologists she'd seen.

"Hmm." Dr. Covey seemed to be considering how much he could relate. "Under the circumstances, I guess it is all right for me to tell you I treated him for hyper-anxiety and claustrophobia from the jailhouse rape." He paused. Bobbie could hear no thinking or pause-filling noises.

Bobbie closed her eyes. A hammer smash to the forehead and then the gut. She doubled over and pounded her knees. Straightening, she wrote "Jailhouse Rape!, hyper-anxiety, claustrophobia" in her notebook. She wondered how violent and traumatic rape was for a male. "Were those conditions caused by the rape in jail?" Rape in a jail must be the worst place for anyone. She tried to sound sympathetic and concerned so he wouldn't guess her wrenching from his few words.

She doubted that bullying the psychologist would help and knew that once abuse started, any hope of cooperation would be gone. She wanted him to think she was soft and sweet.

Bobbie waited to "Hmm" a several second pause something mumbled that sounded like "let's see." After another pause Dr. Covey said, "I'm not sure I should have said as much as I did."

"The man is deceased." Bobbie tried to think of the best way to keep him talking. "Patient confidentiality shouldn't be an issue, Doctor." Bobbie looked up at the ceiling, trying to find a way to encourage the psychologist.

"I'm not sure confidentiality stops so soon after death."

"Are you willing to say anything? You know, generic background type info? Something to help us understand the horrible events here. "

"I think I should talk to my lawyer before saying more."

That was a bad sign. "Hmm. Could you talk in general terms?" Bobbie said. "Something only about strictly hypothetical situations?"

"I'm sorry, Detective Lee, my next appointment is here. I have to go." He hung up during the word "go" before Bobbie could say anything. That meant he had his finger on the disconnect button as he spoke. He was well schooled in making rudeness appear pleasant.

Okay, it is almost 9:00 in New York when his next appointment probably begins. He should be free at 9:50. Bobbie called at 9:52 New York time. When the receptionist answered, she said, "Hello. I was talking to Dr. Covey when he had to go to his next appointment. I'm hoping he'll be free for about two minutes?"

"He's a very busy doctor. I'll tell him you called." The voice sounded even more mechanical than before.

"Thank you very much. That would be helpful." She needed to find a connection to the receptionist. Something that would get her past the gate keeper. She googled Dr. Covey and learned his receptionist was Lisl Johnson.

Weird name. She must have been born when "Sound of Music" came out. IMBD.com showed her Ms. Johnson would be about 46, in that case. Sounds right.

When Covey didn't call back, Bobbie planned to try getting through to him at eight minutes before the hour for the next several hours. Four words was all she had. Not much to go on. She was sure she needed more.

Did his remark about a lawyer mean he thought he was guilty of something? Maybe he worried he was liable for some malpractice claim?

Chapter 32

Impasses are invitations missed

Thursday, 9:30 A.M.

Bobbie Lee visualized Quinn and Patrick using TV cop tactics to work on Dr. Covey. She doubted that anyone could apply pressure in a productive way. A court order might open Covey up, but he could well appeal an order, which would tie up any answers so long the info would be useless. No, if sweet talking him didn't work and he talked about needing a lawyer, then she was stuck.

When all else fails, call Al Beasley. Maybe he would talk her into asking Quinn to coerce some answers from Covey. She dialed her mentor's number, talked about the NCAA playoffs and nice spring weather that had finally arrived. When Beasley prompted her, she brought him up to date on the investigation. "My problem is that Dr. Covey won't tell me anything about Mikey. He seemed to be saying that his lawyer will stand between us and him. He even seemed upset with himself for his brief revelation."

"Why is it important that you talk to him?" Retired Sheriff Beasley was never confrontational to her. He was inquisitive and she knew the question meant what it said. He wasn't challenging the need to talk to Covey.

"Well, one possible explanation is that Mikey beat Mr. Capodicasa. I'd like to know if Mikey could harm his benefactor and if so, why." Bobbie put her hand to her throat, to the small indentation where a choker would have held a pendant if she wore one on the job. "I'm not coming up with any plausible explanation, I don't really have a clue to explain what happened Tuesday night."

"Okay, that's a good reason. Why do you think he doesn't want to talk to you? Why would he insist on talking to his lawyer first?" Bobbie visualized Beasley in his Sheriff's uniform, the distinguished elder states-man of local law enforcement.

"Maybe he thinks he did something wrong? Could he think he might have some personal or professional liability?" Bobbie looked vacantly at the ceiling.

"Sounds plausible. So you need to find some other sources to discuss the psychological issues. You have a hint at Dr. Covey's diagno-sis, or so it appears. Now you need to understand what that means in terms of Mikey's reaction, right?"

"Oh that sounds good. Thank you, Al." Bobbie smiled. The last words were spoken enthusiastically.

"So, Al, how's the mud in your little plot? Think you'll be able to plant your veggies on schedule?" Bobbie now saw Beasley in his Nebras-ka farmer's coveralls. The small talk about the mud season and Beasley's puttering in his huge one-acre garden were the real thank you to her mentor. She wondered how he managed to always have a delicious vegetable-garden aroma when he used so much manure.

After she hung up she tried to think who was the best person to explain Dr. Covey's terms. What do hyper-anxiety and claustrophobia really mean and what are their implications for the investigation and her latest theories? Wikipedia or googling might explain Beasley's nice garden aroma, and they could help her understand Covey's description, but probably not enough.

She wished she knew what caused psyche major Chuck to vanish. What'd she do? What should she have done?

No amount of shoulding on herself would answer the questions. Best choice now was to call and ask him directly. See what happens. Don't be pushy. When she selected Chuck's number on her phone she felt pangs. She held her thumb above the hangup key. *No, I've got to at least try.*

Chuck answered, using a pleasant voice. He was even borderline flirtatious. Nothing familiar or amorous in his words, though. Girl talk should be best. "I can't begin to imagine how hard it must be to lose a spouse. How is your mother holding up?"

"She keeps busy watching the conspiracies she sees everywhere. Her convoy is always beset by U-boats. Mostly fantasy subs."

Bobbie visualized Chuck with a glass of wine and the smile she'd go to New York for in a nanosecond. His voice was pleasant. She hoped for some chit-chat. "Do you hear anything about Martha and Anthony Ippolito? They have probably been the most devastated."

"No, haven't heard anything or seen them." His voice tone became serious, the way he'd talk to the maître d' at one of his restaurants, not the tone he'd use to a close friend. No flirting there.

Well, he doesn't seem to want to discuss anything off-topic, so we might as well get down to business. "I spoke to Dr. Covey hoping he could help me understand what might have been going on in Mikey's mind. He said only a couple of words before clamming up completely. I remembered your BA in psyche, and thought you might be able to help me understand the tiny bit of diagnosis I have."

"I can try. What y' got?" The most she'd gotten out of him so far but the tone was clearly business.

"Dr. Covey said Mikey had hyper-anxiety and claustrophobia. Basically those are the only two words I got out of him. He did say they were the result of a jailhouse rape, but nothing more. Can you explain what they might mean for Mikey's behavior?"

"Oh boy. Dredge up the 20 year-old muck. This is like a final exam two decades after cracking a book. I think hyper-anxiety is psychologist geek-speak for PTSD and I've read recently that PTSD and claustrophobia are likely to cause violent reactions." A long pause followed.

Bobbie decided nothing more was forthcoming about Mikey's post traumatic stress disorder so she soldiered on. "So, assuming Dr. Covey's analysis is correct and that I correctly understood him, you think Mikey might have been capable of a violent reaction to being confined in that tiny blind?"

"Yes." Chuck paused. "A rape in jail. That's got to be worse than what happened to Nicola or ..."

Again Bobbie waited several seconds hoping for more information or a more personal response. Nothing. *He couldn't say he considered making it worse than Uncle Menty's raping me. Did I tell him or just worry that I should have told him?* "Please don't talk about this to anyone else. I don't want to upset either your mother or Mikey's with my latest theories and half-assed ideas." She smoothed her hair and tried to sound more girly than cop-y.

"I'm sorry I've forgotten so much and I'm so busy, Bobbie. Do you have any other questions? If not, I have several problems with Dad's businesses that are taking lots of time."

Bobbie ended the call with "thank you," but no "hope to see you soon" that would have been normal for her. She had to put him out of her damn mind.

"Bye. I'll try to research this for you." He disconnected.

Bobbie wondered if she should go see Dr. Covey herself. What was she doing to chase men away? Sometimes she was scared away from them, but Chuck was dumping her and she was clueless.

"Thank you for taking a few minutes for me, Sheriff." Bobbie handed him a sealed envelope. He looked where she'd written yesterday's date, her office address and signature across the sealed flap. "I found that in my office last night. I'm betting the almonds are tainted, perhaps with sub-lethal amount of cyanide."

Grayson dropped the envelope on his desk. "Why would... What makes you think that?"

"When I saw the bag of almonds last night, that's what's in the envelope, I knew I hadn't put it there. Someone who knows I really like almonds is the most likely perp. Last night I realized this might be the third attempt to poison me. Over night, one more occurred to me."

"Are you being melodramatic?" Grayson studied her. "Or maybe paranoid?"

"Maybe or perhaps I'm watching my butt better, as you said I should." She watched Grayson nod.

"What else happened?"

"Okay, the first incident was last Thursday, I think. I went for a walk to cl;ear a headache and discovered both cruisers in the garage right under my office running. They were in a closed room beneath me. That's the one I hadn't connected at first. Then on Sunday, I found a hole in the floorboard of my cruiser and in the muffler. At first I thought it had rusted through, but when I looked at it, I guessed that some perp had jammed his heel through the rusty metal. Whatever caused the hole, it leaked carbon monoxide directly into the car."

"And number three?"

"Yesterday I found some pie left for me. I took one bite and threw it away because it tasted metallic. I figured it had spoiled. I'm pretty sure the pie had been made by my grandmother, but she did not send me a piece. I feel sure that someone took a piece of the pie, put something with a metallic taste in it, perhaps arsenic from rat poison, and left it for me. Mommom said she mentioned at Sunday dinner that I'd asked about her shoofly pie."

"I hope you recovered the pie. We need to test it."

"I wish I had. I put it down the garbage disposer and didn't realize I was possibly destroying evidence until it the disposer had finished its job. Gross stupidity. But that leaves us with the almonds. If my guess is right, there'll be some poison in it."

"Any idea who's doing this?"

"Yes." Bobbie paused. "Uncle Mentes Petite. He used rat poison to make his big sister sick when he was about 12 and sickened his father the same way a few years later, at least that's the family rumor. He was at Mommom's Sunday afternoon when she served pie like the piece left for me. He has access to the garage and my office. He wants me off the Capodicasa case. I think he may be afraid I'll report on the time he raped me."

"He raped you? You better fill me in on what happened." Grayson looked confused and mumbled, "If there'd even been a hint of that, that little twerp would never have been elected."

"When I was in high school and he was in law school I went to the Petite's farm to see a new rifle he had. Incautious of me, but I was young and he was kin. He threw me down and raped me twice. His father killed himself out of shame when I was away in Kansas to hide the pregnancy."

"Crap. Now I see one more reason why I you're so sympathetic to domestic violence victims."

"If you don't mind, sir. It's past and gone. I had suppressed the incident for decades and probably shouldn't have mentioned it now." Bobbie's fists were tightly clenched, but out of Grayson's view. She hoped he couldn't see her abhorrence of the discussion.

"Okay, agreed. But that's still a pretty long string of incidents. And it's all very circumstantial." Grayson frowned and put his hand to his chin.

"Yes. But if anything further happens, I want to be sure you know everything. If he gives me enough poison to cause serious harm, I want you to know where to look."

"Unless the almonds turn up nothing." Grayson pointed at the envelope. "If they don't come up tainted, your whole theory is broke."

"Yes, sir. You're right. Well, maybe not. The almonds might not be part of it. I'll bet there are no fingerprints or DNA or anything like that on the bag in any event. I'll even bet that the amount of poison is sub-lethal. What I really need is for you to help watch my back. You were spot on when you said I need to be more careful. I think we both mis-guessed the most important direction for our attention."

At 9:52 Bobbie was back in her office and put in an unanswered call to Dr. Covey.

Chapter 33

Reconstruction

Thursday, 10:15 A.M.

Bobbie looked around her office. Too early to go out for a glass of wine. She turned to the thought that had helped investigations so often. When all else failed, talk to Al Beasley.

"How's my favorite retired sheriff's time? Got some to talk now?"

"You know retired is an acronym for really tough inserting random extra duties," he said with a glare that was obvious over the phone. She felt sure his eyes twinkled too. Bobbie knew he hid his enjoyment of her call as a special favor to her.

"And a call from me ..." Bobbie tried to rephrase her question. Something so he'd admit he'd be glad to talk to her. Some neat acronym.

"Would be a random extra date." He finished her sentence before she could. "We have to stop meeting like this, Bobbie."

"Random extra? Maybe I should be talking to you about my love life. Or, more accurately, my lack of one."

"Oh, come now, Bobbie." His tone soothed. "A cute girl like you. What could be wrong?"

A *cute girl*? She wouldn't tolerate such a word from any male except Al. "Chuck Capodicasa. He doesn't even have time to talk to me. I did everything I could think of to be nice to him. I felt sure he agreed. I thought we really had something.”

“Oh, sorry. I hit a nerve I didn’t know was frayed. Do you want to talk more about him?” He sounded truly skeptical. “I knew you were close to this case in other areas, but that one never occurred to me.”

“No, no no.” Bobbie’s voice trailed off as she repeated her lying denial. She wanted to talk about Chuck, but with a female. “I didn’t mean to unload on you. That popped out. Please don’t breathe a word of it to Grayson. Okay?” Remember the old saw, *discuss people with women, things with men*. Chuck was not a subject for a male mentor. Not a subject for anything until the case was closed.

“Hmm. Yeah.” He didn’t know about the trouble she was having with Petite. At least she could think of no way he’d have learned all the sordid details.

“No, I mean it, Al. Please promise me you won’t go to Grayson about this. Not a hint to him, promise?”

“Okay.” He spoke his acquiescence like two separate words then paused. “I promise.”

“Thank you. Petite’s trying to get me off the case. I don’t want him to have any more ammunition or Grayson to have another excuse.”

“You’ve sold me,” Beasley said.

“Chuck explained Dr. Covey’s terminology and I wanted to go over what I have on the murder.” Bobbie breathed out in relief.

“Well, that sounds like my department, at least. What ya got?”

“Eddie Stuart has no alibi, but claims he was home in bed at the time of the murder and all his coworkers and friends I’ve talked to say he acted perfectly normally on the two days after the murder.”

“That would seem to rule him out.” Al spoke with deliberation of a judge. “I can’t imagine that some middle aged milquetoast of a guy could suddenly change enough to commit murder and not act weird.”

“Yeah, the blood in his truck had pushed him up on my suspect list. The blood Tom found, did you hear about that, it was old.”

“Old?”

“Tom saw stains on the steering wheel that he was sure were blood. He studied them through an open window and took a few samples. Tom decided it was probably from driving with a cut a long time ago. He said the blood looked old and that it seemed to have two different kinds of dirt on top of it. He felt sure it was unrelated.”

"Okay. He's out."

"Right. So, the only person left on my list is Mikey Ippolito. He obviously can't claim innocence, admit guilt, or offer an alibi. And his motivation should have all been to protect Mr. Capodicasa. He had every reason to like the vic, all reports even said he did like him."

"But?"

"Well, we have Dr. Covey's diagnosis, or at least the first part of it that he shared before shutting his trap. Chuck said he thought an explosive reaction to confinement is possible with Mikey's supposed diagnosis." Bobbie didn't know what else to offer. Al knew about as much as she did. She repeated to herself, "explosive reaction to confinement."

"What's that?"

Bobbie repeated the addendum and thought about it. "Chuck said he was describing PTSD." The news stories of vets committing horrible acts after returning from combat flashed through her mind. "So maybe Mikey exploded because of confinement in the tiny shack, realized what he'd done, and started trying to take the vic back to the visitor center."

"Sounds good to me. How about you?"

"No, it's no good. The perp dragged the body away from Nicolson, not toward it."

"Mikey's a New Yorker, he's a city boy." Al sounded like he was thinking of what might be going on. "What's he know about directions?"

"Oh, I like that," Bobbie spoke pensively. "Wait, still no good. Why'd he go across the river? Even a strong swimmer would worry about being washed miles downstream and the water's so cold it's hard to imagine anyone voluntarily going in. He wore a ton of clothes, you know." Bobbie tried to imagine scenarios that would make him wade north, across the Platte.

After a pause Al asked, "What do you think might make him do it? Let's back up and be Mikey for a few minutes. Let's see if his actions are plausible."

"Okay, so after beating him, he tries to take Capodicasa for help, but goes west by mistake. He realizes the body is too heavy, so he abandons it and starts for help. Two problems, why'd he go north after abandoning the body and how'd he get across the Platte."

"If he has a good memory of where he's been but is turned around, he goes west with the body, thinking it's east, then goes north by himself, thinking it's south toward the path back to the visitor center." Bobbie could see Al nodding, with the sort of thinking smile that makes his mouth into an inverted U, a pronounced upside-down U that couldn't be a frown.

"Yeah, and I forgot the river was not that high at the time of the murder. It had been rising and was still rising all day Wednesday. I think we've got something. Oh, and all those clothes would have made the icy water less of an issue. Thanks, Al. I think you've given me a solution." She jumped up and walked around her office with so light a step she seemed to float.

"Now, if I could only solve your guy problem."

"If only."

At 10:53 and 11:52 Bobbie tried calling Dr. Covey. Again the phone rang ten times with no answer. At least the receptionist hadn't blocked her calls, she just refused to answer. How could Bobbie be friendly with Ms. Lisl Johnson if the woman wouldn't even answer the phone? Unfortunately for Bobbie, caller ID worked equally for both of them.

217

Chapter 34

Post Traumatic Stress Disorder

Thursday, 2:50 P.M.

Bobbie picked up her cell phone and dialed Dr. Covey. The earlier calls had been from the office phone, so this number would look different to Ms. Johnson. Luck. She answered Bobbie's call. It would be late Thursday for her, close to the end of her New York workday. "Oh, you." Her voice added some expletives and something along the lines of "I should have checked the caller-ID and not answered." Only the area code would have been a tip-off that the call was from Bobbie.

"You said you'd tell him I need to talk to him," Bobbie said in the most pleasant tone she could muster. "I want to thank you for that. You're Ms. Johnson, right?"

"Yes."

"I have a question for you, one only you can answer. Do you think there's any chance he'll call me back? I don't want you to jeopardize your job or even waste your time. I only want to know if you think he'll ever call. Are you willing to tell me if you think he is going to keep putting me off forever?"

"Excuse me." Several seconds of silence. "No. I'm only allowed to tell you he's very busy and he'll call back if he can."

"Gotcha. Thanks." *So I'm not getting anything there.* "I don't want to get you in trouble, Ms. Johnson." Maybe honey will attract something.

"I can't afford to risk my job by telling you he doesn't ever intend to call back." Her voice was barely audible.

Bobbie thanked her again and said she wouldn't bother her further. She hung up and made a mental note to send some chocolates or flowers to Ms. Lisl Johnson. Or take them if she ever made it to The City.

So, her only source was Chuck or some other psychologist. Bobbie went back to her notes and worked on the nerve she'd need to call her source. It was never going to get any easier. Might as well be now. She picked up her phone, scrolled down to the Ms, and called. She tilted her head so her hair fell away from her ear and gently slid the phone to her ear. One more postponement before the call to Chuck.

"Hey Quinn, Bobbie Lee here. Got a few minutes?"

"Sure, now's a good time. What was Nevada Barr's first best seller?"

"*Deep South*, set on the Natchez Trace Parkway in Mississippi. Can you tell me what was added at Mos Eisley in the 1997 Special Edition release of Star Wars?"

"They added gobs of background animals putzing around."

"I promised I'd call in a week to keep you up to date, so here it is. I also have some questions for you."

"Okay, let's do it." She visualized a professional wrestler size cop like her SEAL friend Patrick O'Reilley.

She told him she'd found no evidence of mob involvement and that she hoped to have the last loose ends tied up in a few days. "I'd like to find out about Chuck Capodicasa. He came out and seemed helpful. He got us some information about his father and the man who came with him. What do you know about him, about Chuck?" Could Chuck have covered up something, like Mafia involvement? If he hadn't hid a connec-tion, could she rule out the mob-hit possibility?

"I've never heard anyone say anything derogatory about him specifically. All the specific negative info is related to someone else in his family. He has been involved in running his father's businesses." Quinn paused a moment and Bobbie could hear some keyboard clicks. "This is interesting. Not even his ex said anything bad about him. They must get along pretty well. She said they still go to family dinners once a month and often see each other in church." Bobbie saw him working a clunky system like the old one she had, but decided any department that gave rise of fiction like CSI must have better equipment than hers, perhaps he used one of those silver Macs.

"I can understand the church, but I never heard of going out to dinner with your ex."

"Yeah. Must be a pretty brainy guy too. Says here he's got a Harvard MBA. Either he's upstanding or clever enough to outsmart us."

Bobbie laughed and thanked Quinn for the background. After minor flirting and updating on the case, they said their goodbyes. She told herself she shouldn't put off the distasteful call any longer. "Hi, Chuck. I'd like to clarify our discussion yesterday. Got some time?" She tried to sound flirty and seductive.

"Yes, a little time, I have a meeting in half an hour." The image of Chuck changed from the open shirt and gold chains of the Fabio she first met, to a Sicilian Godfather in a pinstripe suit. With a bulge in the left side of his jacket. At least he didn't have any jowls. He was still cliché handsome.

"Thanks."

"And I did check the meanings of Covey's terminology." He used his businessman's tone of voice. "I'd remembered correctly."

"Okay, so if a claustrophobic person with hyper-anxiety is locked in a small hut, how violent and irrational might he become?"

"Well, what you're describing is PTSD, as I said. And you do occasionally hear about vets with PTSD going off the deep end and killing people, so it certainly happens. In those cases, I think there are different triggers, something that reminds the vet of combat, like a backfire, fire-cracker or seeing a red car like the one that blew up near him." The image of Chuck morphed, he was now wearing a tweedy sport jacket with leather patches on the elbows.

"So Covey really was saying he has full-blown PTSD?"

"Yes, I think so," Chuck said. "And for Mikey the photo-blind is so tiny it may have triggered recollections of the jail cell. He may have thought Dad was the guy who raped him, or worse, and another attack was imminent."

"It doesn't take much does it? I recall hearing a vet describe why she had handicap license plates—her PTSD was triggered by walking past a line of cars. She couldn't get the images of exploding cars out of her mind. Basically, she had the wheelchair sticker so she could avoid walking through parking lots."

"Dad could be overbearing at times." she could see Chuck nodding pensively. "I'm pretty sure that would suffice for anyone with severe PTSD. And there's one more thing that occurred to me, something I have not been able to check. If Dad physically resembled the jailhouse rapist, it could be a powerful trigger. And the similarity could be only in Mikey's mind—it doesn't need to be real. Even after several years." Chuck paused for seconds. "I couldn't find any data on the rapist other than his name. Sounded Latino. But if Dad looked the same ..." Paul never finished his thought. "I get sick thinking about it."

"I'd never thought of the last possibility, but the rest of your guesses are what I've been figuring."

"The biggest question in my mind," Chuck said, "and the one only Dr. Covey can answer, is *Was Mikey's condition severe enough to cause such an extreme reaction?*"

"Right. Okay. Got some more time? Want to hear more?"

"Unfortunately, I don't. I'm actually on my way to our attorney's. As I said, I've got a dinner meeting about Dad's businesses in 27 minutes and it'll take me almost half an hour to get there. I'm sorry I'm buried in business problems right now. I'd like to talk and will try to call you when I have a little more time."

"Take care of yourself and your mother. Talk to you soon." She hung up. Why hadn't she told him she wanted to see him? Well, other than being unprofessional and stupid, why hadn't she said it? He had actually thawed a little at the end. She didn't have to be as chilly as him.

Chapter 35

Sugar

Thursday, 8:35 P.M.

Okay. A leisurely meeting with a lawyer can't last more than four hours. Even with dinner and travel, he should be home by now. He deserves a call. Maybe I should try to undo the mess I'm making of my life. She called, forcing herself to visualize the model handsome guy who'd held her hand. His wonderful and unique aroma. No matter what he said or how curt he acted, she had to extend her olive branch.

She smiled, closed her eyes and repeated "I love you" each time the phone rang. In between she said "No, I want you but ..." When he answered, she said, "I owe you the best explanation of what happened to your father." She kept her voice as sultry and inviting as she could. "Even if you don't have time to listen, I think you should tell your mother. She deserves to know what will soon be official."

"Yeah. I'll tell her." Pure business.

"No, it's more than that, Chuck. I want the notice to be as personal as possible. I don't want it to be a phone call and I don't want it to be from a stranger. Or, much worse than that, a query from a reporter."

"Right. I'll do it. I didn't mean to sound sullen." If it wasn't sullen, at best his voice sounded like an attorney explaining divorce laws.

Bobbie told herself she had to continue being pleasant and coquettish, at least on the phone. "How detailed a description do you want? Do you have enough time now?" She worked to see him in the gold chains. The chiseled face, broad shoulders.

"For the first time since Dad's death, I have some time. Give me the long story." He sounded interested. "I'm in the elevator. Nearly home from the lawyer's where I think we have everything related to Dad's estate under control. Finally, I think I'm past my 18 hour days."

Chapter 36

Mikey and Paul

Tuesday, Nine Days Ago, After Midnight

Mikey sweated, so much his clothes were getting wet. Their little photo blind was so cold, they were both chilled, as Paul had said, but Mikey shivered from fear. Being closed in the tiny cell caused both the shivering and sweating. Paul snored softly.

Mikey couldn't bring himself to get into his sleeping bag. He wanted to go out, but the guide had excoriated them once. They weren't even allowed out to pee, they had to use a bottle. With the shutters closed, the blind smelled like pee. Like a jail cell.

He picked up one of the huge lenses and looked at the snoozing man in the darkness. He nodded slightly then looked again. The man who'd attacked him. The man who'd forced him to do all sorts of unspeakable things. He mustn't let the sleeper attack him again. He couldn't recall where the club had come from, but he struck his cell mate.

Thud from his club then a moan. He hit again. He couldn't really hurt the rapist because the cell was too small. He couldn't swing his smooth club more than a couple of feet. He struck again and again. Ten times? Twenty times? Sometimes the crunch of metal told him he had hit the cell bars, not his assailant.

Mikey dropped his metallic club and covered his eyes for a few seconds. He looked around. Oh, Dear God. What happened? What had he done? He'd hit Paul. He had to get him to a hospital. The visitor center would call an ambulance. Mikey pushed open the blind's door and dragged Paul toward help. He struggled, but he was not sure he could not get Paul to the visitor center. Paul was so heavy. Mikey would never make it in time. He must go get help.

Mikey turned and started toward the path. The moonlight reflected from the pavement ahead. He jogged toward it and splashed into a puddle. Crap. How did the puddles get so deep and cold on the macadam? He had to get across the puddles. He slipped and fell. Nearly all his clothes were wet. And cold. Really cold.

He made it across the road with its enormous puddle and kept going. Have to find the path. It's so fucking cold. Where's the path? Got to get warm. He saw a big tree. Maybe it's warmer under there. He crawled in to warm up for a couple of minutes. He shivered and pulled the bushes in around him for warmth. A few seconds to warm up. He slept.

He woke to bright light. All he could think about was attacking Paul. But Paul hadn't attacked him. He recalled the horrible things he'd been forced to do. He closed his eyes, shivered and pictured birds. And that's all he did for days. One night, he was so weak he couldn't move when he heard a deep grumble, like his mom's cat, but deeper. He curled into a tighter ball and felt his back being patted. The man's after me again. He curled tighter and felt a crunch on his left shoulder. Horrible pain, like his arm tearing off, then it subsided and he went to sleep. Deep, peaceful sleep.

Chapter 37

More Sugar

Thursday, 8:45 P.M.

"Thank you for the detailed description." Paul's voice decreased in volume toward the end of the sentence and he mumbled, "I'll tell Mama the whole story."

"There's one more bit of explanation for you only. Don't tell your Mama and be sure that Anthony and Martha Ippolito don't find out." Bobbie paused while she tried to decide how to explain.

"Okay, that should be easy." Chuck sounded curious about the remaining part of Mikey's story. Or was it her story?

"If I'm right, there are four people who share some of the blame. Or probably four things a defense attorney would trot out to convince a jury that Mikey wasn't guilty. Three relating to the murder and one to Mikey's death. First, the rapist who caused Mikey's PTSD. Second, the New York City jail system that didn't protect him from his fellow inmate. Third, Dr. Covey, who didn't warn Mikey, his parents, or anyone else that his condition was so severe, or maybe he didn't even realize the severity himself. And fourth, the Buffalo County Sheriff and me for not finding Mikey more quickly after he hid himself in the woods."

"You can't blame yourself like that." Chuck's voice indicated concern. "The captain of a boat blown off course in a storm has to find himself, but he is not responsible for the storm."

"Thank you. I don't blame myself, but with some luck we might have saved Mikey. If the river hadn't been rising so fast. If they started letting water out of McConaughy a day later. If...if....if... Anyway, your Mama needs to know about her husband and I think she must hear it from you. And get *all* the details from you. Hope to see you soon. Bye"

"Love ya." Chuck said. "Sorry. Got to run."

She hung up, closed her eyes and leaned back in her chair. She rubbed her forehead and wished she were asleep. She thought about *sleep* and tried to analyze her own thoughts. Did she want to be that intimate with Chuck? Would she even ever see him again?

Chapter 38

Sugar and Spice and All Things Nice

Thursday, 9:15 P.M.

Bobbie studied the Cabernet in her glass and wondered if she hadn't made a mistake by not filling it with bourbon. She had a bottle of Heaven Hill Tennessee whiskey, the type her father loved, maybe she should get a tumbler of it. What an exhausting day. No physical exhaustion to mitigate the disasters, just the total-collapse exhaustion that comes from extraordinary emotional involvement in most of the day's events. She hadn't even taken time to get out of uniform, her usual walk-through-the-door task.

Her phone rang. A call from Chuck? He probably wanted more details or explanations.

"Hey, Bobbie. I wanted you to know that I really have been working my butt off day and night. Dad's businesses are a mess and his will is only a little better. I don't know how he managed to file his taxes or even talk coherently to an accountant or lawyer."

"Thank you. I'm glad you called." *Why'd I say that. It's so lame. What should I have said? What should I say?*

"I didn't mean to put you off, I was only doing a clumsy job of trying to get everything settled here. I've had dozens of meetings. At least it feels like that many. I've been buried with accountants, attorneys, tax advisers, family, store managers. You name it. It's all fallen on me. Mama figures I'm the MBA, therefore I understand everything about Dad's businesses, taxes, his will. Everything." Bobbie saw him sitting at a desk with a green eye-shade and an antique lever-operated adding machine, probably a scene out of some old western. "I've been like the old Staten Island Ferry, shuttling back and forth with no time to evaluate the important things in life."

"I still want to thank you for calling. I assumed I must have done something." She tried to make her voice seductive.

"No. No. It's been all my fault. I didn't even realize I was doing it until you signed off after describing the deconstruction of Dad's beating."

"Thank you. I love you." *Oh, my God. I shouldn't have said that out loud. I didn't even know I was thinking it.* She had no idea what to say and all the things that occurred to her sounded too trite to roll out right now. She said no more.

"I love you too. I do." Chuck paused a moment. "I didn't realize what I left when I came back to The City. I've been missing you since I left and did a horrendously bad job of showing it."

Bobbie felt an elation. What a wonderful thing to say. She tried to think of a good reply, but Chuck continued before she said anything.

"Anyway, can you get some time off?" His voice almost pleaded. She visualized Chuck in his understated attire, with two gold chains showing under his flannel shirt. No. In New York he'd be wearing a dress shirt of some light color. Light lavender would look good on him.

She began hoping. Was there a Santa Claus? "Yes, I think I can get away. This case is closed. I only have to get it sealed."

"I got you a ticket to New York. You may already have the notice in your inbox."

Bobbie gasped. Quietly she looked at the wine. Glad she hadn't considered Bourbon any earlier. She went to her computer as she spoke, tucked the phone between her shoulder and ear. "I can probably get away after tomorrow." She logged onto her email. "Uh, oh, Make that I can probably get away tomorrow."

"Wonderful. The sooner, the better. I made you a reservation on the noon flight tomorrow." He sounded seductive. "I can easily change the reservation, if you like."

"I'll make tomorrow's flight. I have United's email. I'll be out of here in time to catch the noon flight you booked."

"I want you to meet my family and you are certainly the best person to answer any detailed questions from Mama."

"I'll be at the Kearney airport in time to fight through all TSA's red tape by flight time." Oh yuck. That's so corny. So trite. She hoped he didn't notice. She looked at the details of the first class reservation. Their relationship wasn't mangled. Bobbie felt a warmth from head to toe.

"But I have one bad-news request."

"Huh?" The warmth faded. She hugged herself.

"I want you to tell Mama about Dad's death. I'll be with you and hold your hand, if you wish, so it'll be coming from both of us."

Hmm. That wasn't so bad. "Deal." As they exchanged good byes, Bear nuzzled her for dinner. She usually fed him earlier than nine o'clock. And he needed a walk. The coziness returned.

She picked up Bear and went to answer a knock on her door. Bear, always protective, growled softly as she imagined Chuck outside her condo. When the door was a half-inch open, it smashed toward her, shattering the door jamb as the security chain tore tore its catch from the wall. Shards of wood flew slowly toward and past her. The door opened in slow motion and slammed into her shoulder. Shock rattled her and Bear went flying. She staggered back, holding onto the knob to keep from falling down. Her chest and shoulder throbbed from the blow.

The small black-covered intruder at the door held a red police baton-size stick in his left hand. A hood covered his entire face, not even any eye slits. She could see nothing but the shape of his body. Even that was probably disguised.

He lowered his left shoulder and ran into her. Very hard. She lost her grip on the door handle and fell backwards. Her police and Marine training came into play even before she landed flat on her back. With him coming down on top of her, she swung her fist at his face and kicked at his groin. Both as hard as she could. He turned sideways and crashed into her too fast. Her fist hit his shoulder. Relatively ineffective. Her knee hit his legs. No deterrence.

His truncheon pushed across her, forcing her back to the floor. The stick mashed into her vest-protected chest. No immediate pain from it. He landed on her full force as her knee was deflected by his left leg. Even though he was not heavy, Bobbie gasped for breath from the crushing of his body on her ribs. The impact of his knee with all his weight on her stomach drove the remaining air from her lungs. She choked, gasping for breath. Her best choice was to go limp. Perhaps she could catch him off guard in a second or two. She relaxed, tried to breathe in and noticed a musky aroma.

He ripped at her uniform shirt. Buttons popped and fabric tore as he pulled it. He grabbed her bullet proof vest at her neck and jerked, but most of the force of his pulling on the vest was absorbed by his own knee. When the vest didn't loosen, he swung his bludgeon at her. Her arm felt broken. She tried to double up from the lack of air, but he held her flat on the floor, aggravating the pain from his knee.

He raised his stick to strike her again. "A no DNA rape." He snarled the words and jammed his knee in her crotch. No recognizable voice. Probably faked. *It must be Mentes. It can't be him—he's never been that physical or maniacal. Has to be him. I don't know when he's been this violent, except when he raped me.* It had to be Mentes.

He had his knee back on her stomach, making breathing difficult. His truncheon made every movement she tried difficult or impossible. She tried. He tore her leather belt open and started to tear her pants with his right hand. With his left he held the club and reared back to swing at her face.

Bobbie hadn't seen Bear since he went flying when the door smashed her. But he was there now, latched onto the assailant's wrist. Growling. Snarling. Bear must have jumped on the guy's left arm when the attacker pulled at her heavy belt. She wished she had a Pit Bull not a Pomeranian. How could Bear hold so tightly? He was just a ball of fluff. A Pit Bull ball of fluff. She clawed at him, hoping some DNA would make it through his covering. Bear and the weapon hit her in the face. Bear's fluffiness softened the blow to almost nothing. No injury. "We have DNA now."

Bear flew across the floor, yelping at his mistreatment. Bobbie was surprised. She knew Bear was much tougher than she. A blow that could fracture her skull, would only bother him. She was okay, or was that the adrenaline helping her and hiding her injuries? The rapist grabbed his wrist and turned for the door.

Bobbie picked up the truncheon and hit his leg as hard as she could. She struggled to stand so she could chase the assailant. He swung his fist at her. When he tried to close the door, it hit Bobbie. She swung her ersatz billy club and hit his arm, knocking his grip from the door handle. He groaned and ran. She started to chase, but her knee collapsed. She held the door jamb and wished she had her pistol. He reached the end of the hallway and started down the stairs.

"If you killed Bear, I'll kill you Menty." If it was someone different, he would think he misunderstood. If it was Mentes, he would know she had him. How many small, left-handed rapists could Kearney have? She bolted the door to her condo and turned to see Bear's condition. She called nine one one.

Chapter 39

Scariest Words to a Cop: "Officer Down"

Thursday, 10:05 P.M.

Tom Shirk, Leon Grayson, and about a dozen Kearney Police officers and Buffalo County Sheriff deputies were there. Bobbie was still dressed in her brown uniform pants and a tee shirt with her Kevlar vest over it. Bobbie held Bear while Tom clipped hair from his muzzle. "Hope some of this blood is the perp's," he said.

"Nothing happened to you?" Sheriff Grayson seemed truly skeptical. The gray stubble on his face showed he'd hurried from home. First time she'd seen an unshaven Grayson.

"No, I'm fine. He did nothing more than knock the wind out of me." Bobbie looked up from her only easy chair. Her bruised arm and leg would heal and her knee couldn't really be that bad because she could still walk on it. "I never thought of this being a chastity belt, but I think it saved me." She tapped her Kevlar vest. "He mashed his knee into my stomach and pinned me with his stick, but nothing serious. Without the vest, I'd be much worse off. I think he hurt Bear more than me."

She held out her hand so Tom could scrape under her nails. "I doubt I was able to get anything. He was completely covered. Maybe you can get some identifiable fibers, though."

"Might get some blood on a bit of fabric." Tom wrote down the details Bobbie could recall of the attack as she put on gloves and examined the billy club. "Looks like a plunger handle." she turned it and handed it to Tom. "I noted a familiar musky scent on him. Probably a men's deodorant."

Grayson turned and talked to the deputies and cops that were standing around. Several of them left. "We probably won't be lucky enough to find anything, but at least we can check all around here." He made a gesture encompassing the area and mimed searching with a magnifying glass. "Any idea who it was?"

Tom was examining her uniform shirt. She turned to the sheriff. "I think it was the same person who was after me before. I smelled that musk last week in your office." She spoke quietly.

Grayson moved so he was between Bobbie and Tom Shirk. "Do you want to be involved in picking him up?"

"Yes, sir. But only with serious backup."

"I'd require that anyway. Both for your protection and to protect My Office."

Bobbie nodded. She took a deep breath and only noticed the smell of male sweat. "And, if I'm wrong, we can't do anything to jeopardize anyone's career." Tom walked away to put her shirt in a paper evidence bag. She glanced around to be sure no one was paying attention. "Can you be my backup?"

"Okay, let's meet downtown in about 15 minutes to plan our next move. We need to do this quickly." Grayson turned to survey the room. Tom had picked up some buttons from Bobbie's shirt and was preparing to clip scraps of carpeting.

"Sounds good." She stood up and set Bear on the chair. He seemed unhurt.

"Tom?" Bobbie spoke loudly. "Can you lock up my condo when you're done? I need to go to the office."

He agreed and took a key so he could lock the deadbolt as he left. The sheriff left. Bobbie went to talk to Tom. "I think the assailant may have been CA Mentes Petite. Grayson and I are going to confront him. As soon as you're done here, can you get a search warrant for his place and meet us there?"

He agreed. She gave him some more details, ones he'd need for a warrant. "Hope that's enough."

* * *

Bobbie drove over the speed limit to the Sheriff's office, but detoured past Mentes Petite's house. Because he lived south of Kearney's city limits, there were no jurisdictional issues with the Kearney PD. The upstairs lights were on and it looked like a light was on in the living room despite the opaque curtains for the ground-floor windows. She continued her rush to Grayson's office.

"At least we can talk privately now." Grayson looked ready. He had put on his Kevlar vest before Bobbie arrived. It barely showed under his uniform.

"Thank you, sir. Menty's house had a bunch of lights on, so we don't have to worry we might awaken him."

"Okay, when we get there, I'll knock on the door. Once we're inside, you take the lead. This is your investigation. But keep weapons holstered. If we shoot someone who helps kids as much as he does and then can't prove his connection to the attack, we're the dead ones."

"Sounds good to me. I can't believe we'll need guns with him. He's generally been more devious than violent."

Grayson looked skeptical. "You don't call attempted rape violent?"

"Well, before tonight. Usually he has preferred poison to confrontation."

At Mentes's house, Grayson knocked on the door while Bobbie stood to the side where she would not be visible when the door first opened. She had her hand on her pistol. Have to be careful. Her arm held the satchel with its evidence collection materials behind her back.

After almost a minute of door knocks and bell rings Mentes came to the solid wood door. "Good evening, Mentes," Sheriff Grayson said. "We'd like to talk. Do you have some time now?"

His voice might be friendly or even cloying, but Mentes shouldn't notice.

CA Mentes Petite frowned. He saw Bobbie moving in from the side. His frown turned into a smile. "Of course, Sheriff. Seems pretty late, but come on in. Must be something official."

They walked into Mentes's foyer. Grayson motioned for Bobbie to step forward. "It is official. Can you tell us where you've been this evening?" The most authoritative voice Bobbie could recall from Leon Grayson.

"I've been here most of the time watching TV." He waved toward the set in the corner. Seemed to be showing some old gangster movie. "I did go over to my apartments on Fourth Avenue for a while. Had some maintenance work." Mentes wore a long sleeve denim shirt and dirty denim coveralls. Typical Nebraska working clothes. His arms were completely covered.

He had a sweaty scent, perhaps from his clothes. Bobbie asked for and received permission to look around the living room. She collected samples, but knew there wouldn't be anything of interest. Menty was too open. There couldn't be anything incriminating in the house. She picked some charred fabric from the fire in the fireplace.

She collected fabric and dander samples from several places. "May I have a DNA sample?" she asked Mentes.

"No. I don't think so. That's going beyond the limits of reasonability." Mentes shook his head and put on an act of disbelief. "I've cooperated with everything else, but that's too much. I won't willingly do that. Why would you want it anyway?"

Good act. Wonder who it's for.

He shrugged his shoulders. "I think you two better leave now. If you want anything else, you'll have to get a search warrant. You know there's nothing here. It'll be a waste of your time and the county's money."

Outside, Bobbie heard the front door bolt click home. He knows Grayson's biases on spending. "I'll bet Mentes has an incinerator at his apartment house. Probably invited us in to buy a few more minutes so the destruction of evidence would be complete." A warrant would get his DNA and force him to show his wrists and arms.

"Can't help that. We have to follow the law." Grayson looked up the road toward Kearney.

"It would be nice to see Mentes in prison with some people he's convicted." Bobbie realized she should not act with such bias. "You worried that I wasn't objective enough. Maybe you were right."

A cruiser drove up in front of the house. Tom got out and handed the sheriff a tri-folded document. Grayson rang the doorbell a second time. After more than 30 seconds the dead bolt clicked and Mentes opened the door. His left hand in his coverall's pocket. Grayson held up the warrant. "We will do a more thorough investigation, now."

Mentes backed into his house and slammed the heavy front door. The storm door prevented Grayson from blocking the door open.

"We need to get more deputies here." Grayson had his pistol out. "Tom go back to the judge and get us a warrant to search Petite's apartments, at least any furnaces, fireplaces or incinerators. Bobbie, watch the back so he can't get out."

Grayson headed toward his Explorer. A shot came from within. Bobbie ran to the front door.

"Careful, Bobbie. You know he's devious. This may be a trap. Wait for backup."

"If he shot himself, we may not have time to wait. Are you ordering me not to go in?"

Madman Leon Grayson shook his head, not to deny her suggestion, but to indicate he despaired and worried someone would be hurt.

Bobbie stood to the side of the door studying him. He may be wild or mad, but he was protective of us. Good boss.

She patted her vest to remind him that she did have some protection.

"Okay. But be careful." He continued shaking his head. "Be careful."

Bobbie opened the storm door and stood as tightly against the door jamb as possible. She turned the handle and swung the door open. Nothing.

She ran into the living room checking behind corners, furniture and doors. Another shot. She jumped. Turned around. "Damn television," she yelled. "Shot came from it." She heard Grayson coming across the front porch. "I'm checking the rest of the house."

She checked the dining room and kitchen, including closets and pantries. Nothing, even the back door was bolted from the inside. Grayson started to go up the stairs. "Come with me, Bobbie. Cover my back." Nothing upstairs. Together they checked the basement. Nothing. No sign of the County Attorney. Double keyed deadbolt on the basement door, so it could have been locked from either side.

"He must have gone out there, sir." Bobbie pointed to the barred window of the basement door. "I'm going after him." She headed back to the kitchen and out the back door. The north shore of the Platte was only a hundred yards south of Menty's house. She saw lights from another cruiser coming up in front. *Hope Menty was dumb enough to go south. He might suffer Mikey's fate. Can't imagine he'd hide in the trees and ambush me, but he did have his hand in his pocket as though he held a gun.*

She limped 75 feet east then headed south into the woods toward Kearney's stretch of the Platte. To the west there was a small pond, so he couldn't go far in that direction. A branch scratched her face. A flashlight would give her away. She heard hundreds of birds take off in front of her soon the air over her was full of birds making guttural squawks. She proceeded as stealthily as she could in the very poor light. Stooped jogging with her hands in front of her face. Every ten feet or so she crouched by a large tree and listened intently. After about 50 feet of that slow progress, she heard a splash. Short distance upriver, but that also meant she was closer to the Platte than she calculated. "Sheriff, sounds like someone's in the river," she radioed. "Due south of Menty's house. Probably need to maintain silence now."

She crept toward the sound, walking about twenty feet between stops. On the second stop, more splashing sound and "Damn, it's cold." Too faint to be sure, but it must be Menty. She did not want show her position so she couldn't call Grayson. At the river bank she was able to see a person heading downstream. "River's awfully high," she called in her best imitation of a male voice. "Need help?"

"No. I'm okay." The reply came from Mentes Petite.

He must be cold and scared not to disguise his voice. He couldn't ambush her from out in the Platte. "Sheriff, Mentes is here in the river," she said into her mike. She turned her flashlight on and shone it in his eyes. "Cold and addled. About 50 feet east of the old Highway 44 cross-ing." She turned off her radio.

"Bet I can shoot your balls off from here, Menty" She took out her pistol. "You've got about two seconds before you're resisting arrest, you little bastard rapist. And if you don't come straight toward me, you're gelded. Why not take your gun out so I can shoot a suspect threatening an officer, you little twit."

"I'm coming. Don't shoot."

"Why not. No DNA justice, right? What could be better?"

Mentes reached the bank and climbed out. Bobbie looked back and saw lights from the deputies, still about 100 feet and lots of willows away. Mentes started toward her, faster than necessary. She swung her metal flashlight as hard as she could, hitting him in the face and knocking him back into the Platte. One of the few times Bobbie thought it would be nice to be strong enough to do real damage left-handed.

Again she aimed the flashlight beam directly in his eyes. "Get out and don't try anything again." His face dripped blood. "Hands where I can see them all the time. And stay on all fours. Keep your hands in the mud." Tom and Scotty came out of the willows. Mentes's hands were on the ground as he clambered up the bank. "Better check him. I think he had a gun in his left pocket earlier."

Sheriff Grayson emerged from the willows. "Which arm did your dog byte?"

"Left wrist, sir." She directed the beam of her flashlight to it.

Scotty held Mentes while Tom Shirk unbuttoned his left sleeve. Slight swelling and a bunch of puncture wounds. "About right for your dog's mouth," Tom said. "What the hell happened to his face?" Tom turned to Mentes. "Did you fall?"

Before any answer came from the attorney, Bobbie answered. "He jumped up out of the Platte and came toward me belligerently. I feared for my safety, so I hit him. He fell back in the water." *Too bad I didn't beat the shit out of him 22 years ago. Might have saved lots of aggravation.*

Chapter 40

Obligations

Saturday, 7:05 P.M.

"Don't worry. You'll be fine." Chuck fastened a heavy gold-plated cross around her neck. Mikey's father had sent it when she arrived in New York. Martha and Anthony would be at the party as well as a few of Chuck's family. "I don't know how anyone can wear something this heavy. You're one tough cookie."

"Thanks. I'll survive and I have to wear it. Martha and Anthony will be grieving for a long time over Mikey's death." And she had to be tough, because Chuck's Mama was one tough mama, and his aunts were probably the same. "The Ippolitos will expect it of me." The card accompanying the cross described how Mikey had acquired it from a favorite priest and they wanted Bobbie to have it now that Mikey had died. It seemed more suitable to hang on the wall, *with a very sturdy nail.*

Chuck held her new coat for her. It still had the smell from the store's moth repellent and plastic bag. The meet-the-family party was at Mama's penthouse. "Mama will want to get to know you and everyone will want to meet you." He had explained earlier that they would go early so she could meet his Mama before others got there.

Bobbie felt about as comfortable as any prisoner going to death sentence hearing. Or before a firing squad. She pushed her fists into her stomach under the beautiful sable Chuck had given her.

Initially Bobbie didn't want such a warm coat and one that was so out of keeping with her Nebraska self-image. Then the reality that 40 degrees in New York felt like 10 in Kearney convinced her the fur wasn't quite so extravagant.

The drop of the elevator aggravated the knots and when it slowed at the basement parking-level floor, the chain around her neck chafed. "I need bigger boobs or something to hold this monster cross. I hope Martha and Anthony appreciate me wearing it."

Mama Capodicasa took the sable. "I think I should thank Chuck. I'd say you're beautiful, Bobbie. They always say we look for people who match our parents, so Chuck's image of me must be beautiful." Mama Capodicasa was beautiful and Bobbie's size. She watched her coat being put on a pretty wood hanger and disappearing into the front hall closet. She wished she could follow it.

Sophie turned to Bobbie. "What a beautiful dress." She eyed her guest. "That shade of lime really works with your blonde hair."

"We came early so Bobbie can tell you herself what happened to Dad." Chuck squeezed her hand to assure her that she had his support.

Bobbie and Chuck sat on the sofa. Chuck held her hand calming some of her angst. She worried that Sophie would think Bobbie was her taking her son, which upset Bobbie more than doing her job of informing a widow. Bobbie related her theory.

When she finished her tale, Sophie nodded in understanding. "Thank you, my dear." she reached to Bobbie from her chair and put a hand on Bobbie's. "Your theory sounds right to me. No one in the family has heard anything about Family action. My first worry was off-base." She stood.

Bobbie and Chuck jumped up. Sophie hugged Bobbie. "It must have been difficult coming into this lions' den. I like strong women." She took Bobbie's hand and started toward the back of the condo. "I was working on some canapés, would you help prepare them?" Mama Capodicasa pointed toward the kitchen.

"Of course, I'd love to." Bobbie felt the cramps return to her stomach.

"Chuck, please go set out some nuts and candy for the men." Mama Capodicasa pointed to a buffet.

"Be nice to her, Mama." Chuck whispered his comment softly. Bobbie was supposed to overhear the request, without Mama knowing.

Bobbie had visions of the rarely pleasant interrogations of dates and fiancées from movies. She tried to recall details of Sicilian family scenes. The scenes that played for her were worse than police interrogations. She smiled at Chuck, fingered the cross and said a small prayer to it. She knew the wobble in her ankles as she walked beside Mama Capodicasa toward the kitchen was from rarely wearing heels. She prayed Mama didn't notice and think she was dying of nerves. She was.

"Don't be afraid of me, dear." Mama Capodicasa said. "Cecilia can be pretty scary, but she's nice. The one to watch our for is Lizzy. Sounds like honey. Habanero honey. Be careful what you say to her."

"Thank you." Bobbie relaxed for the first time since she'd met Sophie Capodicasa. Or was it Mama Capodicasa? Best to avoid that conundrum. At least it sounded like she had one friend and ally, and the one that would trump all the others.

The doorbell chimed and Sophie let a 60-ish couple in and introduced Cecilia and George. The three women started toward the kitchen. The huge kitchen was large enough for five people to work with ease. The counters were wood, marble and granite and the smell was yeast, oregano and Chianti.

"We need some cheese on these." Sophie handed Bobbie two plates, with a pile of crackers and pointed to a small wheel of Brie or Camembert. "If you can put one inch squares on the crackers, Cece can put apple squares on top." The plates were white with two thin gold lines around the edges.

"You're from Nebraska? Have you always lived there?" Cece took an apple and pulled a knife from the counter in front of her. Cece must have spent many hours in the kitchen to know the knives by their handles.

Bobbie nodded. "I spent some time in Iraq during Desert Storm. Been billeted a few places around the country. Went through training at Quantico, but I've always lived in Nebraska."

"Quantico?" Cecelia cocked her head and looked at Bobbie. "You were a marine?"

"Am," Bobbie said. "Once a marine, always a marine." She looked down at the plate where she had arranged a few Trix crackers with cheese. "Is this the way she wants it?"

"Looks perfect. We'll go with it." Cecilia nodded. "Nebraska, huh?"

"Yeah." Bobbie wanted to keep the conversation going, to learn as much as she could. She heard the door chime.

Cecilia held out the plate of hors d'oeuvres as she watched the kitchen door close. "We've never had an agrarian in the family."

Sophie responded to the chime.

She took the plate of crackers and finished each with a wedge of apple. "This is one of Sophie's specialties," she said in a low voice. "Love them or hate them, be sure to pretend to love them," she whispered. "In fact, when Sophie prepares them she cuts the apple in squares to make little pyramids on each cracker. She may not like my wedges, but that'll keep the attention off anything you do that doesn't match the Queen's desires."

Bobbie nodded. Everyone was very helpful. Maybe a little too helpful. "Thank you for the advice and warning," she whispered to Cecilia.

When everything was ready, Lizzy spoke to Sophie. "Do you want Bobbie to take this out now?" She pointed to a plate of steak tartare that Cecilia had finished.

"Yes. Now's good." Sophie nodded as she studied the plate.

"You'll be an instant friend of all the men," Lizzy said. "They all love cannibal balls." She leaned closer to Bobbie and said, "If you don't like the idea of raw meat, at least try to put on a show for Sophie."

Bobbie took one platter of the steak tartare on rye and started for the door. Cece joined her with the apple on cheese canapés. As the door shut behind them Cece asked about Bobbie's never-married status. When Bobbie confirmed it she nodded and said, "Father O'Malley will be glad you were never married *and* he'll like that magnificent crucifix.

Bobbie smiled. "Thank you, Cece." She rubbed her belt, where her holster would be at home, and hoped Chuck would get the messageMaps

Maps

Elm Island Road
Parking Lot
Ian Nicholson Visitor Ctr
Platte River
Jamalee Blind
Stevie Blind
Capodicasa Blind
Map of Rowe Sanctuary

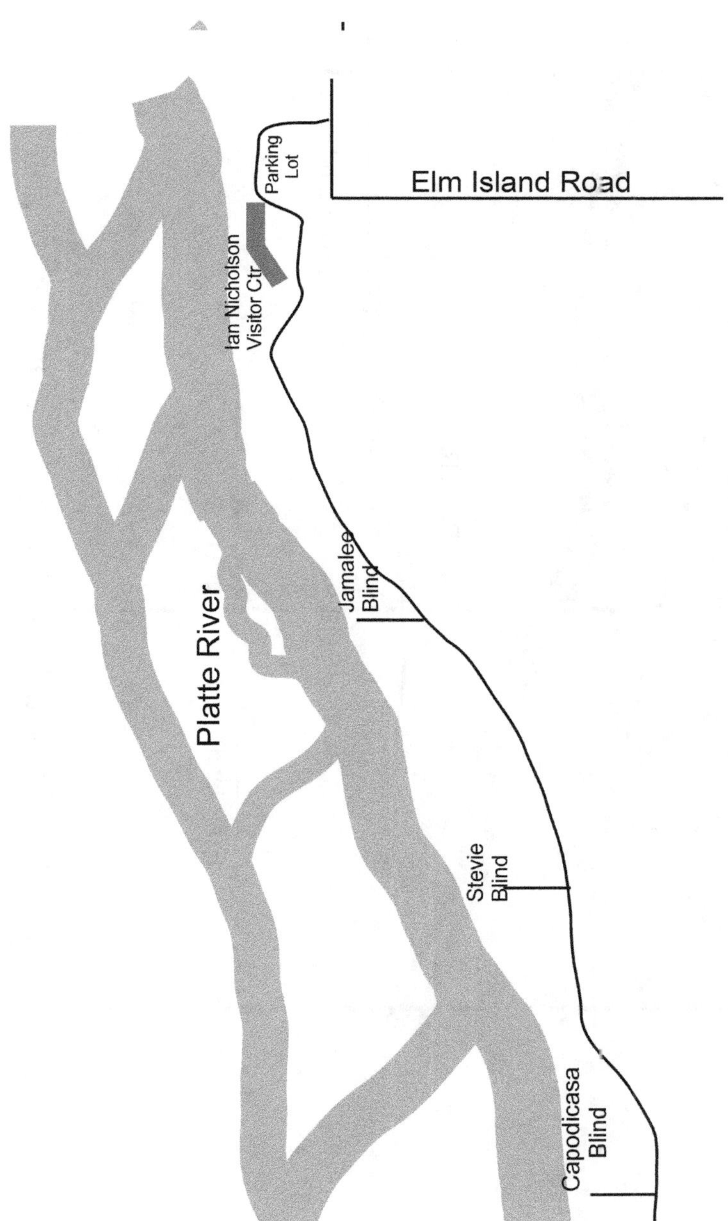

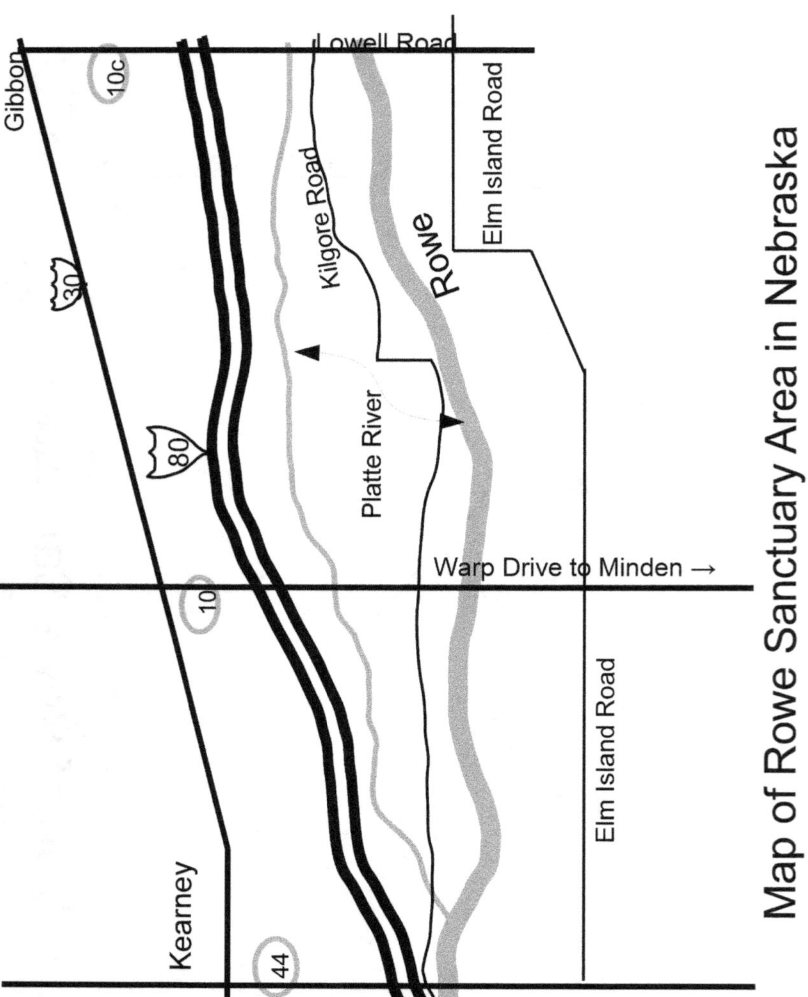

Map of Rowe Sanctuary Area in Nebraska

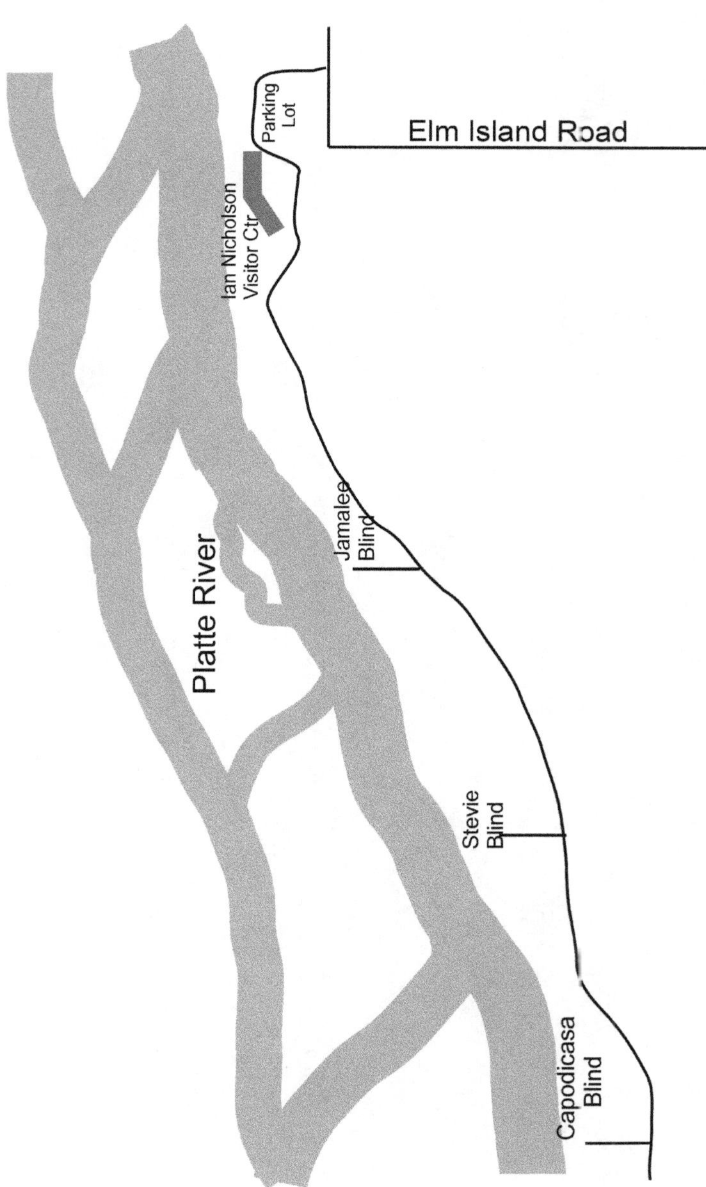

Map of Rowe Sanctuary

9 780692 519608